I0630074

BEHIND THE MASK

CARNIVALESQUE
BOOK 2

TAMARA GIRARDI

WISE WOLF
BOOKS

WISE WOLF BOOKS
An Imprint of Wolfpack Publishing
wisewolfbooks.com
9850 S. Maryland Parkway, Suite A-5 #323, Las Vegas, Nevada 89183

Cover design by Wise Wolf Books

Paperback ISBN 978-1-953944-88-7
Hardcover ISBN 978-1-953944-89-4
eBook ISBN 978-1-953944-87-0

To Josette,
For how much you love animals and for too many other
reasons to count.
xoxo

BEHIND THE MASK

ONE

MY PARENTS' muffled laughter filtered through the ductwork above my head, reminding me I was hiding in my basement to avoid my ex-boyfriend who also happened to be our next-door neighbor. The smell of garlic found its way to me, too, but I ignored the growl in my stomach and brushed a thick coat of white paint across my canvas.

Cinching a plastic bag, I blew air into it until it was full. I dabbed the bag against the white paint, smudging it to reveal the turquoise color I'd already painted underneath.

Too blobby.

I swiped more white paint, covering the mistake.

Trying again, I let a little air out of the bag, like a deflated mylar balloon. A few gentle dabs gave the canvas the floral look I'd envisioned. I dabbed two more spots until the intricate petals of the turquoise bouquet took shape. I wiped my palette knife clean and gently scratched sepals and stems for each flower. A few leaves at varied angles and sizes and...perfect!

I stepped back and admired my first homemade sgraffito painting—Italian for scratch. I'd learned the technique at the

Museum of Art's camp a week earlier and couldn't wait to try it to match the colors I'd painted my bedroom that previous spring. At the end of the project, I'd have my art hanging on the wall—in my bedroom, not a famous museum, but still—my art!

I exhaled and closed my eyes, letting the moment settle over me. Eight months earlier, I'd been on a completely different trajectory—one I hadn't chosen for myself. Nothing made my skin tingle and my stomach flip like conquering a new painting technique or finishing a piece that left me smiling for days. But the one thing about sgraffito was that you couldn't let the paint fully dry before you finished. I'd have to save the moment for another time. When I opened my eyes, one of the leaves caught my attention. Too big, it stood out for the wrong reasons. Careful not to mess up the rest of the painting, I gently nudged the palette knife against the canvas, ready to scratch away a new leaf.

"Whatcha doing?"

I startled and scratched a line across the whole canvas. My body flushed with heat. "Don't you know how to knock?"

"Oops."

Todd Wilkinson's life was filled with one oops after another.

I dipped a fine brush into the white paint and dabbed at the canvas to correct the error. If only every error in life could be wiped away with a swipe of a brush. I huffed while Todd slithered around the room, pretending to honor every piece of my artwork with his deepest appreciation.

"Your mom made you a plate," he offered, attempting to brush his fingertips along my forearm. I moved out of his reach, an action I should not have had to do in my own basement. Todd didn't care about things like boundaries though. If anything, he pushed them every chance he could. Example A: if he'd cared about me eating, he would have brought the plate to me, quietly set it on the table, and walked away.

"How about you keep your paws to yourself?"

"Paws? Seriously, Dinah? Are you insinuating I'm a dog?"

"Dogs are better trained."

He shook his head, that familiar pompous look on his face. "It's only a matter of time until you end this breakup."

"You don't end breakups," I said. "You end relationships. I think you have that confused."

He ignored the lesson. "Come eat with us. I could hear your stomach growling when I came down the stairs."

"That wasn't my stomach."

He flicked one of my canvases and made a fake laughing sound. "Funny."

There's a reason you broke up with him. Many.

I repeated the mantra and dabbed the last dot of paint over the errant scratch, also adjusting the outline for the leaf that had felt too big for its environment, kind of like how Todd acted like he was too big for his.

"Why are you hiding out down here?"

"I'm not hiding," I said, as if I would answer that or any of his questions in any sort of satisfactory way.

"Fine then. Why are you not upstairs?"

I dropped my brush into the water can. "Why are you not anywhere besides my house?"

He perched against the back of the couch we'd watched movies and made out on too many times. "It's what we do. We have a family dinner. My parents are your parents' best friends. You're my best friend."

"Say it all you want, it won't change the fact you are not my best friend. My best friend hates you."

"Is that why you broke up with me?"

I packed my paints, clicking and thumping them every chance I got. "You know why I broke up with you. Don't pretend it has anything to do with Mac."

"It has everything to do with Mac."

"I'm sorry. Did you cheat on me with her?"

He rolled his eyes. "You know that's not what I meant. She never liked me."

"I should have listened to her."

He huffed.

"Todd, this effort—" I fanned my arms. "Whatever you're doing down here isn't going to have the outcome you're hoping for. You should probably leave."

"I miss you, D. There's no one like you."

We paused at the sound of footsteps on the stairs. Mac's feet, then her face appeared. She held two plates overflowing with pasta and had tucked water bottles between her forearm and stomach.

She smiled at Todd. "That your big swing? 'There's no one like you'?"

He gritted his teeth like an epic villain in a post-apocalyptic movie. "This conversation doesn't involve you."

Mac set the plates and drinks on the table and pulled up a chair. "No. This evening doesn't involve *you*. It's me and my best friend, and I'm pretty sure I heard her ask you to leave."

"Thanks, Mac," I said, swirling my fork through the angel hair and watching the steam rise from the pasta. "I got this though. Todd?"

He stepped closer to me, hope in his eyes. I could have felt badly for him. I could have let his hope soften the shell his many mistakes had crystalized around me.

"Leave," I said. "Or so help me, God, I will go up those

stairs and tell your parents what their precious son did to me and the real reason we broke up."

Todd sucked in a slow breath and shook his head as if I were making the biggest mistake of my life. Too late. I'd done that all the months I'd spent as his fool of a girlfriend. He stomped up the first few steps, but lightened his footing closer to the top of the stairs, eager to uphold his all-American boy persona with our parents, no doubt.

Mac swirled her pasta onto her fork against a slice of my mom's homemade garlic bread. We ate in silence for a few minutes.

"You're dying to say something," I said.

She pointed upstairs. "Not about he-who-shall-not-be-named. I'm curious about your art. How's it going?"

I blew a raspberry.

"It can't be that bad."

"No," I admitted. "I love what I'm doing, but I feel like I have so much to learn."

Mac tried to console me. "We all do."

"The kids I went to camp with…" I shook my head. "They've gone for years. They knew different techniques and experimented with all these forms."

"Dinah, you only got into art a few months ago. Give yourself time."

I twirled and twirled my pasta. "I know, and I don't expect to win a big art show spot or a fancy scholarship. I just want to be able to see like an artist. You know?"

"See how?"

I dropped my fork to use both of my hands to punctuate the emotion of what I was about to say. "Artists see the world, like, better or different or deeper than everyone else. It's up to them—us—me to reveal the world to a greater depth so that people can experience the beauty of it in ways they didn't even realize they had been missing."

"I get it. Like when some people hear something interesting, they give it a thought and move on. When I hear it, my mind starts working out how to turn it into a news story."

"Exactly," I said.

Mac was an award-winning journalist with her plans for the future as solid as the table we ate on—editor-in-chief position for our high school newspaper, *The Muse,* undergrad degree at Northwestern, and then either the perfect job offer or an impossible-to-score master's program. A year earlier, I'd mistakenly thought I was on the same path and once you're on a path, it can be hard to step off of it.

"You have a journalist's brain," I tried to explain. "What if I don't have an artist's brain? Yeah, I like art, but what if I can't see things in a way that helps me make art from them —art that makes people *feel* something? And if I can't make people feel something, how can I call myself an artist?"

"Sounds kind of heavy."

"It got heavier when Todd showed up. He's like the ultimate destroyer of my creativity."

"I'm sorry, D."

"Forget him," I said, wishing my parents would find new best friends and literally let me forget my ex, although there was the added complication of him living next door and his bedroom window facing mine. "In better news, I have a present for you." I dug behind my piles of half-painted canvases to reach the gift bag I'd set aside for her.

"It's not my birthday or anything," she said, but she took the present anyway, a silly little grin on her lips.

I laughed. "It's just because. Open it."

Mac whipped the tissue paper out of the bag, tossing it to the ceiling and letting it trickle down around her. Her wide eyes couldn't touch the massive smile on her face when she lifted the glittery painting from the bag. Knowing how important Carnivalesque was to her, I'd spent an after-noon of free time at art camp painting a carnival mask in her favorite color—emerald green. Everyone in my group had glitter stuck to the bottom of their shoes for the rest of the day.

"It's gorgeous," Mac said. "Thank you."

"My pleasure." I squeezed all the best friend love I could into a hug for her. "So…how are things going with Kierk?"

Mac's eyes glazed over with a filter of hearts. After meeting him in the carnival in the winter and then breaking up with him, they'd reconnected over the summer when she was away at a journalism camp and he had been on campus taking summer classes. I'd been at art camp getting tidbits by text and video chat but still hadn't met the boy she'd fallen so completely for.

"That amazing, huh?"

"It's perfect. Truly perfect. Like we should be characters in a movie or something. We completely fell for each other wearing Mardi Gras masks, Now, being out in the city, going on dates, seeing each other's faces…it's like we fell again but in an entirely different way. And—oh my gosh, I realize how corny I sound."

"You do. No doubt."

She twirled her spoon, securing a thick helping of noodles. "I don't even care."

"I'm happy for you, Mac." I glanced toward the stairs, wondering if Todd had finally given up and left to do who knows what, or if he was still upstairs trying to woo my parents toward his cause of us getting back together. "I hate that I wasted so much time on Todd."

"Don't think of it as a waste but, instead, a learning experience."

"To avoid cheaters and losers? I definitely got that."

"I'm sorry, D."

"I'll get through it. In fact, I have an idea."

"Uh oh."

Mac has spent months going to Carnivalesque on the weekends. Todd had gone, too. As a member of the committee that planned the exhibits and events in the carnival, he'd been there all the time. With other girls, of course. I shook thoughts of Todd away and refocused on my best friend and the night we were about to have together— finally. "My parents read your article, and they trust your opinion on the carnival. If it's an indoor amusement park, then it can't be that bad."

Mac practically bounced off her chair. "Are you saying what I think you're saying?"

I couldn't blame her for her surprise. I'd never been allowed to go with her before. I finished my last bite of pasta. "Don't you think it's time for your best friend to meet your dreamy boyfriend?"

TWO

MAC, who I had to call Sparx in the carnival since everyone claimed new names for privacy's sake, led us through the back door of the carnival.

"We're skipping that massive line out front," I observed.

She held up a VIP pass. "Kierk gave it to me."

Of course, he had.

Even entering through the back door was culture shock. Everyone wore Mardi Gras masks. So many colors, sparkles, feathers, and sequins. A lot of them wore cute dresses or even outlandish costumes. One guy wore dress pants with suspenders—no shirt. His torso was covered with tattoos that glittered.

"People really commit to the vibe," I told Mac—ugh, Sparx.

"You have no idea. One time, Kierk and I saw someone wearing full knight's armor."

"Interesting."

We weaved through hallways with twinkle lights and into an elevator.

"He's usually in the Milkshake Ballroom," she said.

"Sounds like your kind of place."

Nobody made milkshakes like Mac.

"Kierk told me they're serving my butterscotch banana recipe."

We pushed through the crowds in the ballroom too fast for me to appreciate the elegance of the decor. Mac stopped next to an empty table where someone with dark hair and a red and black mask cleared glasses. Mac whispered something to him while his palm grazed her lower back. He kissed her without abandon—so different from the way Todd had kissed me when we were together. Kierk treated kissing my best friend more like a privilege than a right.

Mac introduced us, and the last eight months of my best friend's life made sense. Kierk managed an edgy, smirky persona that coincided with a warm friendliness like a double whammy of attraction—the good kind and the potentially dangerous kind.

"Yep," I said. "I see why you've swept her off her feet."

"Speaking of that," Mac said. "We need your expert services."

I shook my head at the opulence of the room while I tailed behind them to the bar. Whoever had built this factory and office building that housed Carnivalesque had come from old money and had equally aged style. To walk from the parking lot and the grey hallways into the Milkshake Ballroom felt similar to what it might be like to step out of my living room and suddenly be looking at the grand staircase of the Titanic.

A live band played cover songs. People danced and drank milkshakes. Mac had told me more times than I could count about the odd sensation of not seeing anyone around you because of the masks. It had been impossible to fathom. Like the girl smiling at me with the red mask—did she know me? And the guy with the green and black mask wearing jeans and an 80s band tee—was he hitting on me with that grin?

Would Todd be there among the masked faces?

I adjusted my mask, hoping that if he was, he'd never recognize me, and refocused on Mac convincing Kierk I needed to meet someone new. I tried to protest, but she shook her head. In the car, she'd insisted. Ever since I'd broken up with Todd, he'd been running a full-court press. He showed up in the afternoons to swim in the pool with me. He dropped off cupcakes from my favorite bakery. He helped my dad with projects around the house.

No matter how many times I insisted otherwise, Mac feared I'd wander into trouble with him all over again. I didn't blame her fear. I'd forgiven Todd too many times. I'd said before, "Never again." And then I'd get back together with him, and Mac would have to bite her tongue about how he didn't deserve me.

About six weeks had passed since the night my parents had gotten musical tickets for the three of us. Hours before the show, I'd gotten so sick I'd thrown up until I couldn't breathe. My parents wanted to sell their tickets and stay with me, but I had expelled the culprit from my stomach along with all of my energy.

"I just need to rest," I'd said. "Go without me."

"Dinah, no," Mom had said.

"Seriously, I'm going to turn all the lights out and collapse in my bed. Don't let the tickets go to waste."

My mom had packed a mini cooler with Gatorade and set it next to my bed with a trash can, a bucket, and a charged cell phone.

"The Wilkinsons are out tonight, too, so call if you need anything. I'll leave my phone on."

"I'll be fine," I'd promised and had promptly fallen asleep.

No light peeked through the blinds when I'd woken up to the sound of laughing outside. A tiny hammer had pounded in my skull, so I'd downed a Gatorade and lay back against the pillow. More laughing. Who was being so loud?

I'd rubbed my temples and made a trip to the bathroom, which happened to overlook our backyard. Intuition had nudged me to pull back the blind and look down into our swimming pool. It hadn't been empty.

Two people had been night swimming—a guy pinning a girl against the wall of the pool with her legs wrapped around him. I'd had no idea who the girl was, but I'd have known the guy anywhere.

Todd was cheating on me.

In *my* swimming pool.

He'd even lit the tiki torches.

Lucky for me I'd been sick. Otherwise, I might have kept my head buried in the sand forever. My best friend had nothing to worry about with Todd. His charms had lost their magic.

Before I could correct my best friend's incredibly flawed thinking, someone hugged her from behind. Taller than Kierk, this someone wore a bright blue mask that contrasted his brown skin. The sleeves of his t-shirt were purposely short and tight across his biceps. The white cotton didn't leave much room in his chest area, either.

Unlike Kierk, this guy exuded *only* the edgy kind of attraction—and lots of it.

"Good to see you again, Sparx," he said. "I knew you'd be back eventually. This guy over here was too smitten."

Kierk punched this new guy in the arm, and they laughed off his teasing. That's when he directed his grin at me. His gaze fell to my heels and then climbed my body with patience, taking in my dress. He puckered his lips and tilted his head. "Hello, beautiful! Wanna dance?"

There were many reasons not to: The potential of Todd watching from the gold-kissed balcony. Mac and Kierk insisting it was a bad idea. My urge to avoid human males for the next decade—at least.

The fact he was clearly trouble.

My mystery man's intentions were made clear by the tightness of his muscles, and the smoothness of every other part of him. Honesty about his intentions, even if they weren't entirely honest themselves, refreshed me. Todd had worn polos and khakis, went to church on Sundays, blushed when elderly women gushed over his good looks, and slept with other girls behind my back—or right in front of my face.

This guy wore his intentions in his crooked grin and the few inches of space he left between his face and mine.

I tipped my head to the side in a way that hopefully challenged him. "I'd love to."

He lifted my hand above my head and spun me twice on the way to the dance floor. The music switched from a slow song to one with a fast beat.

"What's your name?" I asked.

"Harvey. You?"

"Diamond."

"Diamond?" he repeated. "Go big or go home, huh?"

"It was Mac—uh, Sparx's idea."

Harvey jumped to the refrain of the song, holding both of my hands, and nodding for me to join him. My feet pressed into the ground as if it were a trampoline. Each jump took me higher. My hair swooped around my face, finding its own rhythm, and my body warmed from the exercise and the closeness of everyone on the dance floor. Someone bumped me while I was in the air. I reached for

Harvey's shoulders. His hands gripped my waist and steadied me.

"You good?" he yelled over the music.

I pulled him closer and swayed my hips against his. His arms slid around me, and I responded by intertwining my fingers against the back of his neck. When the carnival had first opened ten months earlier, Todd spent time with me on the weekdays and disappeared in Carnivalesque's exhibits on the weekends. Since phones weren't allowed, I never knew what he was up to inside. My parents didn't trust the place, but that didn't matter to Todd. He'd go without me. Sometimes I wondered if he had fueled my parents' suspicions so they'd keep me home.

Dancing with Harvey made me wonder if that had been what it was like for Todd all those weekends here. Had he asked a girl he didn't know to dance, one who'd given him a name she'd made up on a whim, and then ran his hands along the curves of her body? Had he given a thought about me and paused for even a second?

I shook the thoughts away, closed my eyes, and combed my fingers through my hair, lifting it from my sweating neck. The beat thumped in my ears and my core. I leaned so far backward that I barely held myself up. Harvey's strong arms around my hips did that for me.

The song ended, and a ballad poured from the speakers.

He leaned close, his mouth smelling of peppermint. "Do I get another dance, or are we stopping at one?"

A few more notes played, and I recognized the song as one of my favorites. "I like this song."

He held out a hand, and I took it. He spun me again, this time making me laugh, and led me to the edge of the dance floor where the ceiling fans had a hope of cooling us off. Away from the center of the crowd, the temperature dropped about fifteen degrees.

"I like how you dance," Harvey said.

"Thanks." The painting on the ceiling caught my eye, and I gasped.

"Pretty cool, huh?"

"Who did that?"

"Art students from around the city."

"They did amazing work."

"Do you paint?"

I shrugged. "I try."

"Why haven't I seen you here before with Sparx?"

"My parents didn't think it was suitable."

Harvey pressed his lips against my ear. "I wonder what they don't find suitable? Maybe rubbing your hips on some guy you just met on a sweaty dance floor?"

I bit my lip to hide my smile. "I'm sure that's part of it."

"Only part? What other horrors did they expect?"

Before I could answer, someone tapped my shoulder. I turned to find a girl about Harvey's height thanks to her heels, wearing a tight, black cocktail dress and a flaming red mask outlined in black.

"Excuse me," she said as if her voice was melted chocolate. "Mind if I cut in?"

She didn't give me a chance to reply. Instead, she gently nudged me aside before an explosion of milkshake rained down on Harvey—vanilla, chocolate, even some chunks of butterscotch from Mac's signature butterscotch banana shake that had become the most popular selection at the bar.

I tried to push past the girls, but they tugged me back. "Oh my gosh. Are you okay?"

He closed his eyes and spat droplets of milkshake.

A circle of girls surrounded him. They all wore heels, short dresses that hugged every movement of their bodies, and identical red masks. They posed with their hands on their hips identically, too.

"Who are you?" Or maybe the more interesting question: what had Harvey done to set off their wrath?

"Apparently, we're his carnival conquests. You should join the pack since he's clearly picked you as his latest."

"I'm not—"

"You thought we'd never figure it out with everyone being masked?" the blonde girl in the front asked, pushing her finger into Harvey's chest. "Guess what, we've seen behind your mask, and it's not much to look at."

"Seen a few other things that weren't much to look at, too," one of the girls said, followed by lots of laughter.

"You thought you could ignore all of us tonight and hook up with this new girl?"

"It's not like that," he said, slipping his fingers under his mask to wipe chocolate from his eyes.

One of the girls handed him a napkin. "We want to make sure you see who did this to you."

When his eyes lacked milkshake residue, he opened them and smiled at each of the girls.

"Hello, ladies."

"Is this all necessary?" I asked.

A brunette with an empty milkshake glass in her hand answered, "We're doing you a favor. Harvey likes to collect girls at the carnival. Same MO." She lowered her voice and imitated him, "'Hello, beautiful! Wanna dance?'"

Those *had* been his exact words.

"After you dance," she went on. "There's a special little spot in the carnival he wants to show you."

"Only you," another girl contributed.

"But a week later, you see him dancing with another girl and taking her to that special spot that was *only* for you."

Harvey had the decency to bow his head.

"Sound familiar?" another one asked.

"Only the dancing," I said, "but I didn't plan to marry him."

"Good thing because he didn't plan to marry you," she answered.

One of the girls pushed her way into Harvey's face. "You honestly thought we'd never find out?"

"I hoped not," he replied with a cool smile.

A security guard grabbed my arm and another girl's, too. Within seconds, masked security surrounded us, tugging everyone away from Harvey.

I tried to push the guard's hand away but his grip held on. "I didn't do anything. Stop. Harvey?"

"Not her," Harvey said, pointing to me.

The guard let me go and I scuttled out of the pack. Harvey and I stood side-by-side, watching security move the girls through the ballroom, making a scene the whole way. A few minutes later, the room had settled back into dancing and laughing and the staff had cleaned up the milkshake mess on the floor leaving me and Harvey to stare at each other.

"Exciting night," I said.

"Yeah. I was trying to cut back on carbs. This is a travesty."

Not for the first time, I tried to hide my smile at his witty reply. "You should get cleaned up."

He squinted through the holes of his mask at me. "You just watched eight girls assault me with milkshakes and accusations that weren't unfounded. Why are you not running away from me right now?"

"I wasn't lying. I didn't plan to marry you and I had you pegged you for trouble the second I saw you."

"Oh, thanks."

"It comes from experience." Too much experience. I should have learned the lesson a lot earlier. "Although it would feel good to pour a milkshake over my ex's head, I kind of feel bad for you."

"I can get on board with compassion." He grinned flirtatiously. Those girls had been as right as my intuition.

"If I help you clean up, can you find Kierk and Sparx for me?"

He threw a towel the security staff had given him over his shoulder. "So you can leave me forever?"

"Do you really want me to answer that?"

THREE

HARVEY MOVED through the crowd keeping as much space as possible between him and everyone else—a good plan considering he was dripping milkshake. We slipped through a door marked "Employees Only" into a small room with shelves of black clothes, a small sink, and a bathroom stall.

"Before we do this, we're violating some rules here."

I pointed to him and then back at myself. "*We* are not doing anything."

"Not like that, and that's not against the rules, by the way."

I rolled my eyes as dramatically as I could manage, and he laughed.

"You don't strike me as a rules guy."

"You don't strike me as a rule-breaker," he answered.

"I said I would help. What do you need?"

He pressed his hand against his forearm, and it stuck.

"Gross," I said.

"As many wet paper towels as you can manage." He locked himself in the stall. After a few seconds, he gasped.

"Are you okay?"

"The water's cold."

"Serves you right," I teased.

"So much for your compassion." He gasped again, and I couldn't stop my grin at the thought of him squirming from the cold water running from the tap.

I wet a stack of paper towels and wrung out the excess water. "What rules are we breaking?"

"You're not supposed to de-mask in the carnival," Harvey answered.

"Our masks are on," I said.

"Mine isn't."

"But I can't see you."

He grunted.

"You okay in there?"

"I can't reach the trail down my back."

"Come out here," I said with a sigh. The stall lock clicked. I expected a maskless Harvey, but by the looks of it, he'd rinsed, dried, and repositioned his mask. His short, black hair glistened with water, not milkshake.

His chest, though, was bare. I gulped and reached for my stack of paper towels. "Turn around." He did, but it didn't help much. His shoulders and back were as toned as his front. I took a deep breath and pressed a wet paper towel against his skin, forgetting how cold it was. He sucked in a breath and tucked his body away from me. "Sorry."

"It's okay."

I wiped every droplet of sugar from his skin, but it still smelled delicious. A memory of the girls joking that Harvey hadn't been much to look at sounded loudly in my mind as the bravado it had been.

"Thanks," he said. "That would have driven me wild all night."

"You're welcome."

He dug through the shirts on the shelf and found a black

tee with the Carnivalesque logo. He slipped it over his head, but it caught on his mask. He squatted to my height, so I could gently maneuver the edges of the shirt over the mask's corners without tugging it and revealing his face. He thanked me again—all charm, manners, and trouble.

The shirt didn't hug his body with quite the same appeal as his white tee had, but I didn't believe any article of clothing could manage to diminish every ounce of his physical appeal. He crossed his arms and smiled at me.

"So you believe the milkshake girls? About me?"

"Shouldn't I?"

He tilted his head from one side to the other.

"Basically, yes," I said.

"I may have made some reckless decisions," he admitted. "But what about you?"

"What about me?"

He tapped his index finger playfully against the tip of my nose. "You said you pegged me for trouble the second you met me, but you danced with me anyway." He pressed his lips together and shook his head. "And the way you danced…"

I crossed my arms. "I came here to have fun."

He stepped closer and slid his hand around my waist. "How much fun?"

I created distance between us. "Not that much."

He rubbed the back of his neck.

"So? Kierk and Sparx?" I said, reminding him now that his body was as free from sticky sugar as possible, it was my turn.

"Right." He threw the mess of paper towels in the trash and straightened the pile of shirts. "Let's go."

We didn't get far. Outside the bathroom, which was in the back corner of the Milkshake Ballroom, a wave of people rushed by so fast that Harvey had to pull me back to avoid getting trampled. I lost my balance and had to lean against him to steady myself.

"Thank you," I said.

He rested his chin on my shoulder and whispered in my ear, "You're welcome."

Someone from the wave stopped in front of us and stared. I didn't place him until he spoke. "What the hell?"

My freaking luck.

"Let's go," I pulled Harvey by the hand and tried to walk around Todd, but he dug his fingers into my forearm, tugging me toward him.

I swung my other arm into his shoulder. "Get your hands off me."

Harvey wrapped a very large hand around Todd's arm. "Maybe you should listen to her."

"Dinah," Todd whispered. "Is that you?"

"It's Diamond," Harvey said, knocking Todd's hand away and then taking a closer look at Todd. "Wilkes?"

Wilkes? For Wilkinson? Original.

Todd didn't give Harvey a moment of attention. He reserved it all for me. "You're here with him? Really? Do you have any idea of his reputation?"

As if a director with a sense of humor had orchestrated this entire scene, a beautiful girl looped her arm in Todd's.

I laughed in his face. "*His* reputation? Are you serious? Hours ago, you cried to me about how much you missed me, and now you're here with her?"

"I did not cry," he said.

"That whole time, you had plans to come here and hook up with whoever this is."

"I'm Fox," the girl said with a friendly smile.

"Nice to meet you, Fox," I said with manners that would make my mother proud, wrapped up in the kind of snark that would impress my best friend. "But it doesn't matter."

"Weren't we going?" Harvey asked. "To that, uh, special place I wanted to show you?"

I couldn't help but smile, which was probably what Harvey wanted.

"You're not going anywhere with him," Todd said.

"Oh, great. The macho, misogynist approach. Are you going to take my hand and lead me out of here like a child? Take me home and tell my parents the carnival is a big, bad place, and they should never let me come back?"

"I might."

"While you're at it, why don't you tell them why we broke up?"

Harvey offered me his hand, and I took it. Before we could escape Todd's hypocrisy, my ex-boyfriend stepped in Harvey's face. "To think I came looking for you because I heard about the milkshake bath and wanted to make sure you were good."

Harvey winked at me. "I am."

"You two know each other?" I asked.

"We work together on the committee," Harvey whispered, honoring the privacy of the carnival, or at least trying. In the ten months since it had opened, many of its original secrets had been revealed.

"Wilkes, let's go," Fox said.

"In a minute!" He paced a few times and ran his fingers through his hair.

"You should listen to Fox," I said and pulled Harvey through the crowd.

"D! Wait," Todd called, but I had no intention of waiting for him ever again. I didn't stop walking until we'd climbed the grand staircase and escaped into the hallway, my chest heaving.

"You okay?" Harvey asked.

I shook my head. "Can we get some air?"

He punched the up button for the elevator, and a few seconds later, the doors opened to a small rooftop.

"Is this your 'spot'?"

He bowed his head.

"That predictable, huh?"

"Apparently," he said.

I leaned against the railing beneath a faux ceiling of twinkle lights and a clear sky of stars and breathed until I had pushed thoughts of Todd as far from my mind as possible.

"What a night," I said. "Definitely more than some first date reveals, not that this is a first date."

"As far as first dates go, this one might be more memorable."

Couldn't disagree with that.

"So, Wilkes?" Harvey went on. "That was interesting. He's your ex?"

"I always think people use the word 'interesting' when they don't want to say what they really think."

He inhaled and nodded. "Yeah. That was messed up."

"Yeah."

"He like that with you all the time?"

"Mostly."

"I only know him from the carnival. Haven't seen that side of him before."

I wrapped my arms around myself and shivered.

"Come here," Harvey said in a soothing voice. "You look like you need a hug."

He wasn't wrong. I rested my head on his shoulder. He smoothed my hair, letting me drink up his consoling as long as I needed. Which was way too long considering we'd just met.

"Thanks," I said, pushing myself back to my personal space.

"Any time," he said with a nod.

Under the stars, I replayed Todd's accusations and arrogance in my mind until all of Harvey's consoling had been undone by the heat of rage expanding from my core.

"Why is it any of his business?" I snapped.

"Excuse me?" Harvey said with wide eyes.

"He hooks up with multiple—*multiple*—girls while we're dating, lies about it, and then when he gets caught because he does it in my pool—"

"Wait. Wait. Stop."

"What?"

"What did he do in your pool?"

"A brunette," I said, trying not to picture it.

"Wow."

"Before I saw it with my own eyes from my bathroom window, I stupidly gave him chance after chance, ignoring my best friend when she saw him here with two different girls. Two! And those are only the ones we know about." I squeezed my temples. "I mean what an idiot am I? Because even after all those chances, what did he do?"

"Did it again?" Harvey guessed.

I raised my arms in victory. "Ding! Ding! Ding! He did it again! And then, he sees me with you and has the audacity —the freaking audacity to call me out? Like *I* did something wrong?"

I paced under the net of twinkle lights between us. "And the worst part is I have to listen to my parents gush about how wonderful he is. He's like a son to them. We're so meant for each other. It's every song and book and romantic movie and—ugh, suck it."

Harvey stood as still as a person could with eyes wide enough to fill the holes in his mask.

"I haven't even told my mother what he did. I don't know why. It's certainly not to protect him. Maybe I'm protecting myself because part of me wonders if she'll even believe me. Her own daughter."

I sighed. And followed it with deep breathing.

After my heart rate managed to decelerate to a normal rhythm, another group of girls launched water balloons out of nowhere at Harvey. Within seconds, he was soaked, and they were gone.

"Wow," I said. "That happens to you a lot."

We locked eyes and crumbled into a fit of laughter so intense he pulled me away from the edge of the roof for our safety. Against the wall of the stairwell, I leaned into him until our giggles settled into sighs and eventually silence.

"Aren't we a pair?" he said.

"I'm sorry that I unloaded all of my Todd—excuse me, *Wilkes* drama on you like that. Life's too short to spend it on people who don't deserve you."

"Better to have drama unloaded on you than fifty bucks worth of milkshakes or fifty water balloons."

I scoffed. "I bet."

"I like talking to you," Harvey said. "When I spend time with girls in the carnival, we don't do a lot of talking."

"That shocks me to my core."

He pressed his lips together in that adorable way of his and nodded acceptance of my jab. "I just mean you're cool, Dinah."

"Scandalous! Are you real-naming me?"

"I guess I am." He held out his hand.

"What are you doing?"

"I told you I'd take you to Sparx and Kierk. I think it's about time we abandon this disaster of a night. Don't you?"

I slid my hand into his, wishing I hadn't noticed the softness of his palm or the strength of his grip. And the way my whole body drifted into him as if there wasn't any other place it would rather be.

FOUR

SUNDAY MORNING WAS God's morning in my house. A piece of fruit for breakfast, a sweet summer dress, and a drive with my parents to St. Joseph's, the Catholic church in my hometown where my parents had been married, and their parents, and so on.

The church sat on a hill, its red brick facade climbing to the sky like the temples in the Bible. The closer the building was to God, the closer its people could find themselves, too. My seventeen years visiting the building hadn't convinced me of that, but every time I stepped out of the car and looked up at the stained glass rose window and the intricate architecture, the artist in me felt a mix of awe, admiration, and apprehension—mostly that I'd never be able to create something so beautiful.

Inside the vestibule, my parents stopped to chat with another parishioner, so I found us seats in a row that would only fit three people. My mother raised an eyebrow at me when she slid into the pew, knowing exactly what I'd been up to.

No room for the Wilkinson family.

I lowered the kneeler and bowed my head, asking for the patience to deal with Todd and for God to convince him to leave me alone. Best to cover my bases. Hymnal music played in hushed tones. People who'd known me my whole life offered whispered greetings on the way to their seats. My eyes closed. I thanked God for welcoming me back.

When I finished my prayer and slid back into the pew for the start of mass, someone across the church caught my eye, mostly because he had no shame in all out staring at me. He gave me a nod. My brain registered some familiarity, but I couldn't place him. The whole time the priest processed into the church and through the first readings and hymns, the mystery man snuck glances at me.

During the Gospel reading, he curved his fingers around his eyes to form a makeshift mask, and I gasped.

Harvey!

My mother patted my forearm and raised an eyebrow. I waited for her to shift her attention back to the priest and side-eyed Harvey, finding him grinning.

"What are you doing here?" I mouthed.

He pointed to the priest who stepped into the aisle for the homily. I tried to pay attention, but memories of Friday night in the carnival tempted me. When I thought of something Harvey had said or the expression on his face when he'd been pelted with water balloons, I'd have to stifle my laughter. Remembering our quieter moments had me shaking my head at the fact I'd allowed myself to be so attracted to him so quickly, but there was something about his personality and his laugh—and his gorgeousness, who am I kidding—that was magnetic. Even from across the church, I could feel it.

My mom had her own superpowers, like her ability to recognize when I wasn't paying attention. She elbowed me lightly, and I redirected my attention to the altar where our priest talked about the importance of faith. When I checked to see how Harvey was taking Father's message, I couldn't find him. Maybe he'd moved to sit somewhere else, although no idea why he would. I searched the pews behind and in front of us.

Mistake.

My eyes connected with Todd's. I looked away instantly and finished the mass without looking in his direction again. During the final hymn, my phone buzzed. I slipped it out of the side pocket of my cross-body purse and peeked. A text message from an unknown number read, *Meet you outside the main entrance. -H*

For all her, "Stay away from Harvey," messaging, my best friend had clearly given the boy my number and my Sunday morning location.

My curiosity gave me no choice but to find him and ask why.

———

"Stalker much?" I teased when I found Harvey lounging on a cement bench near the statue of the Virgin Mary.

"I come here every week." His face didn't show any signs of humor, but he had to be joking. I could not have seriously gone to church in the same building as Harvey for years and been completely clueless about his identity in the carnival.

Although that was the whole point of the carnival, wasn't it?

No.

"You're lying."

He laughed. "I'm lying."

"So what are you doing here?"

Harvey jumped up and pasted a friendly expression on

his too-cute-to-look-too-long face. "Good morning, Mr. and Mrs. Zimmerman."

My parents had snuck up behind us.

"Good morning," Dad said.

"I'm Darius Moore, a friend of Dinah's."

I made a mental note of Harvey's real name. I'd known some Moores, but his full name didn't ring any church bells for me.

My dad extended his hand. "Darius, good to meet you."

"Nice to meet you too, sir. Wonderful homily today."

I side-eyed him. He'd left at the beginning of the homily.

My mom smiled. "I was saying that exact thing to Dinah's father. I loved the connection to our everyday lives."

"Those are the ones that always speak to me, too," Darius said.

"I haven't seen you here before," Dad said.

I crossed my arms and raised an eyebrow at Darius. He fought off a smile.

"No, sir. I live on the other side of town, so I don't usually come to this church. Dinah recommended it."

His ease with lying rivaled that of a politician.

"I know you probably have brunch to get to," Darius said. Mac had clearly filled him in on my Sunday routine. "But that park next door has been calling my name since I saw it this morning. Would you mind if Dinah and I went for a walk to catch up? I'll bring her home myself."

My parents looked sideways at each other. Darius gave me a nod, setting off my curiosity even more.

"Just a few minutes," I added. "It usually takes that long to get the food ready anyway."

"Sure," my mother said. "It's a beautiful day for a walk."

We said our goodbyes and waved to my parents as they pulled out of the now nearly empty parking lot.

Once they were gone, I glared at Darius. "What exactly is happening? Am I in an alternate universe? What is this church boy routine? And why are you here?"

"Can I answer one question at a time?"

"No," I said.

He scoffed. "Let's walk and talk."

We crossed the parking lot and started down a sidewalk shaded by a row of massive oak trees.

"Spill."

"Mac gave me some intel. I told her I wanted to see you again, and she said I could find you here."

"She told me to avoid you."

He smiled. "I can be very persuasive."

I looked away, not doubting the truth of that statement for a second. "Do you normally go to church?"

"Yes. Just not this one."

"Okay," I said. "Next."

"I had another rough night."

An image of the mob of girls surrounding him Friday flashed in my mind. "Still raining milkshakes at old Carnivalesque?"

He rubbed the back of his neck. "Not exactly. My clothes kind of went missing?"

I stopped walking and stared at him. "Your clothes?"

"Yeah."

I waved Harvey—or Darius, whatever—on, eager for the full version of the story. "How exactly did they get your clothes *off*?"

He cringed. "There might have been a beautiful girl who suggested we spend some time together."

I groaned. "You fell for that?"

"It's not unheard of for a girl to want to spend time with me."

"Right after you were publicly milkshaked by a horde of girls?"

"There may have been some bad judgment there."

To put it lightly. "Go on."

"When we were...spending time together...my clothes disappeared. Then she disappeared."

I covered my mouth and laughed. And then laughed harder.

"Stop. Please."

I raised my hands in an attempt to surrender, but the laughter didn't stop coming. An image of Harvey running through the carnival, wearing only a mask and covering his nether regions with his hands had me doubling over.

"Dinah. Oh my gosh. You are brutal."

I shook the laughter away. "Sorry. So sorry. I, um..." Deep breath. "Sorry. Where did this happen?"

"The roof. In the rain."

"The *cold* rain?"

He glared, and I laughed even harder.

"I consider myself a black Adonis, but I admit searching the carnival for stitches of clothing humbled me."

I slapped Harvey on the shoulder. "Don't get me wrong. I appreciate you sharing that story. It made my day. Truly."

"I see that."

I laughed again. "But that doesn't explain why you're here."

He pointed to a bench further along the trail, and we sat.

"There's also a social media campaign. The milkshake girls figured out my real identity and have me on blast. They're sharing stories about...my ways. It's everywhere. They've used my videos and pics online against me with some wicked duets and memes."

I scratched my head at this boy sitting in front of me, kind of getting what he deserved, but also maybe earning a little sympathy from me. I refused to psychoanalyze whether forgiving Todd so much over the years had primed me for this exact reaction to Darius' current predicament.

Still, the way his leg bounced and he couldn't stop looking over his shoulder tugged at me.

"Can I ask you something?"

He nodded.

"Friday night, you didn't seem bothered by the accusations. I might even argue you enjoy being the kind of guy you are. Why do you care if people call you out on a part of yourself you seem proud of? Does it ruin your game or something?"

"If I answer that truthfully, you'll laugh at me."

"I've already laughed at you more than once, and if you don't tell me the truth, then whatever you came here to ask me for is a definite no."

Darius looked anywhere but at me.

"I have brunch to get to," I said, standing.

"Fine."

Glad my bluff worked, I sat back down.

"I decided I didn't exactly want to be that guy anymore. It was fun for a while, but the reason that I did it—"

"Why did you do it?" I interrupted. I'd heard the whole *I turned over a new leaf* speech before. What I hadn't heard was why the new leaf was necessary in the first place.

"Why does a guy do anything stupid?"

"I have too many answers for that question."

He sighed. "There was a girl. *The* girl—at least I thought she was at the time. Except she didn't want to be my girl. She wanted something from me, and when she got it, that was it."

"So you thought you'd do the same thing to unsuspecting girls who weren't *that* girl and didn't deserve it."

He scrunched his face into a pained expression. "Which is why I wanted to stop doing it."

"And you got over the girl?" I offered.

"That and I saw Kierk and Mac being all lovey. It was kind of nice. Maybe I want that with someone who wants it with me."

"And none of the random hookups wanted that with you? Or you didn't with them?"

He looked away. "There was one."

One. But he'd messed it up.

"Was the one in the milkshake group?"

He gave a slight nod.

"Okay, I get everything you said, but, last night, you still ended up naked with a random girl in the carnival. How is that turning over a new leaf exactly?"

He lowered his head. "I don't have a defense other than to say it was a moment of weakness. I need to do better. I *want* to do better."

I tried to piece together everything he'd said to find some logical explanation for why he'd found me in church on a Sunday morning, introduced himself to my parents, and led me on this confessional walk in the park.

"Darius?"

"Yes?"

"Why are you here?"

He took a deep breath as if he were about to jump out of an airplane. "The thing is my reputation is so trashed right now that I don't have any hope of someone trusting me."

"Give it time," I said.

"Last night, girls put up signs at the milkshake bar to avoid me at all costs."

"Change your mask. Change your name."

"I still work in the same places, and not many people on the committee look like me. Not to mention the tattoo on my wrist. I'm kind of memorable."

I scoffed.

"Hey!"

"Fine," I said. "You're memorable. What do you expect me to do about all of this?"

"Glad you asked. I have an idea."

I took an exaggerated look at my watch. "Are we finally getting to the big reveal after the saga of the century?"

He covered my wrist. "You're respectable."

My heart stopped. Was he suggesting that he and I start something? After the worst first date ever that wasn't even a date? "I'm not sure I like where you're going with this."

"Hear me out."

"I'm not interested in a relationship."

"That's not what I meant—not that I wouldn't want to date you. You're hot." He shook his head. "I'm getting away from the point."

"Which is?"

"I want to *fake* date you."

FIVE

I WATCHED Darius for any sign that he was joking, letting the words play in my mind over and over. I'd heard them right, and the intensity in his dark brown eyes told me he'd meant it.

"Fake date me?"

"Yeah."

"How does that work exactly?"

"You know like in the movies and books. We pretend to date for our mutual benefit. In this case, being with a respectable girl and not hooking up with other girls shows people I've changed, and rebuilds my reputation."

"I think you're thinking too much. Next week, this will blow over."

"The internet is forever. My only hope is replacing the bad chatter with good."

"Not that I'm not a charitable person," I said, gesturing toward my church, "but how do I benefit from this?"

He puffed out his chest. "I'm your buffer."

"My buffer?"

"Yep. Your parents can't encourage you to give Todd

another chance when you have a new boyfriend, and Todd won't challenge me. I can promise you that. He'll leave you alone, so you can paint or do whatever you want."

"Todd doesn't leave me alone."

"Have you ever dated anyone else?"

I ran through my paltry list of previous boyfriends. Didn't take long since there were none. "No. I dreamed of dating Todd, dated Todd, and then regretted dating Todd."

He shrugged. "See."

"I don't know. It seems extra."

"I think it's brilliant. Look. I'll throw in some other benefits."

I scowled at him.

"Not those kinds of benefits, although I wouldn't completely take them off the table."

"Focus!"

"We have some projects at the carnival. Painting, design, stuff like that," Darius continued. "I could bring you onto the committee. There might just be a special project only you can pull off."

"You're bribing me with art?"

"I'd bribe you with anything I could. When you see the posts, you'll understand."

The opulence of the Milkshake Ballroom, the map murals throughout the carnival, and the parade float I'd gotten a glimpse of when Mac and I had passed them in the parking lot had me groaning inside for the opportunity to collaborate with the artists responsible. If summer camp had taught me anything, it was that when it came to my artistic voice, I was severely lacking.

"You've sweetened the deal," I admitted. "But there's one problem: I don't lie to my parents."

He tilted his head to the side. "So don't lie. Minimize the truth."

My phone buzzed with a text from Todd.

Todd: *Where are you? Your mom's burning the bacon.*

I leaned my head back, letting the sun shine on my face, and took a deep breath.

"How often does he text you?" Darius asked.

I swiped Todd's name on the screen and tapped the "block" icon. "Not at all anymore."

Darius crossed his arms. "If that's all it took to get rid of him, wouldn't you have done it weeks ago?"

My phone rang. It was Todd's mom's number.

Darius did a poor job of hiding his smirk.

"Fine."

He pumped his fist.

"Come to brunch today. If you can buffer me—" That didn't sound right. "If you can *buffer*," I corrected, "like you think you can, I'll consider it."

He kissed my cheek. "Done."

"What's with the kissing?"

"I can't kiss my girlfriend?"

I tapped the tip of his nose. "Not yet."

"Hands off. I promise."

Harvey—*Darius*—promised. No reason I shouldn't trust that.

Ugh. This was such a bad idea.

———

While Darius drove us to my house, I replayed every movie I'd ever seen with fake dating. Most of them avoided spending time with family—the people who knew them best in the world, considering they'd probably pick up on the fact they were, you know, faking!

"This your driveway?"

I nodded, and Darius parked. I glanced at my front door

and imagined my parents behind it, preparing Sunday brunch the same as they did every week with no idea I was about to walk in with a new "boyfriend." My chest tightened, causing me to take deep breaths.

"It's cool, Dinah. We're having brunch. That's all. I'm a friend you invited. Let Todd fill in the blanks, okay?"

I nodded.

"No lying to your parents. I promise."

I nodded again. After a few deep breaths, I calmed myself enough to realize Darius was holding my hand, his thumb rolling calming circles over my palm.

"You ready?" he asked.

I shook my head, and he laughed. "Come on."

Maybe because he had more time to prepare or he was naturally suited to it—I didn't know him well enough to say—but Darius exuded the kind of charm the characters had in those fake dating movies: all laughter and smiles and jokes. He talked football with my dad, asked questions about the photos on the mantle, and helped my mother in the kitchen. I even caught my mom looping her arm in his and kissing him on the cheek.

"I am crushing this," he whispered in the garage when we went to grab more juice.

Todd had noticed, too. The ever-polite mask he wore for our parents' benefit faltered when Darius took my hand at the table to pray. We weren't the hand-holding type during prayers, but the way Todd glared across the table encouraged me to take on a new tradition.

My mom ushered us away during clean-up. "Darius helped cook. Why don't you show him your art?"

Darius tucked his hands into the pockets of his shorts. "I'd love to see it."

Standing in my kitchen with my family and Todd swirling around us, scooping dishes, drinks, and condiments off the table, I felt to the core of my soul that Darius meant the words. He *did* want to see my work. The butterflies closing up my throat and soaring through my stomach told me I wanted to show him, but a slow sadness crept over me.

If I agreed to fake date Darius, how often would I wonder if what he said to me around other people was for show or for real?

"Dinah?" Mom nudged me.

"Right. It's downstairs."

Darius slipped his fingers into mine and squeezed. I squeezed him back, a gesture that wouldn't be lost on Todd no matter where he was in the room. I closed the basement door behind us and at the bottom of the stairs collapsed into the couch.

"That was exhausting," I muttered.

"Your family is great," he said, sitting next to me. "And no lying. Just a little hand holding and they can fill in the blanks for themselves."

"And it probably pissed off Todd."

"Gotta love a bonus."

I laughed. "So what's the next step?"

"You agree, or you don't."

"What are the rules?"

He scratched his head. "The rules?"

"All the rom-coms have rules."

"Whatever you want them to be, I guess."

"I have to come up with them by myself? On the spot?" I exaggerated crossing my arms and huffing. "What kind of relationship is this?"

He followed my lead, emphasizing an eye roll. "Fine, girlfriend. Shall we brainstorm?"

"Yes, please," I said and waited through the silence.

"Not going well." He pointed to my art corner. "Maybe we should check out the art instead."

"This is important," I insisted. "Let's start somewhere. What about physical relationship stuff?"

His face turned serious. "I get it. Boundaries would be good. Maybe up to kissing in public, for show?"

"Up to?"

"Like hand holding, hugging, stuff less than kissing, up to kissing. You good with that?"

My gaze fell onto Darius' lips, the possibility of kissing them any time I wanted inciting the butterflies in my stomach.

"Okaaaay."

"Your enthusiasm is very encouraging," he said, completely misinterpreting my apprehension. "But I'll try to ignore that for now. Your turn."

"My turn? I'm the one who suggested the last rule."

"But I'm the one who defined the terms of the rule," he said. "See? Teamwork."

"We're already fighting like we're together."

He rested his arm across the back of the couch behind me. "This is going to work."

Maybe. If we could get the rules right. I mentally reviewed what I'd read and watched, and one theme became apparent. Secrecy. "We don't tell anyone it's a ruse, not even Kierk and Mac."

His eyes widened. "You can lie to her like that?"

"Not easily. She usually knows when I'm lying, so telling her about us will be our first test."

"I don't lie to Kierk."

"If we tell one and not the other, we're forcing them to lie to each other."

Darius shook his head. "That wouldn't end well."

"Exactly."

He weighed the options and nodded. "Secrecy. Agreed."

"We spend as much time together as possible to pull off

the lie," I said. Potential rules and situations were flowing for me now. "But if we need some time alone, we can tell each other without taking offense."

"I like company," Darius said. "If you want time to yourself, take it, but I can promise being around you will never get on my nerves."

An interesting challenge.

"And most importantly," I said, taking a deep breath. "If at any moment—like ever—this becomes real for either of us, we have to say so. Right away."

He scoffed and did that thing where he licked and then bit his lip, that thing that tempted me to use the couch pillow to fan myself.

"What's the face for?" I asked.

"I have to pretend because a girl like you would never fall for a guy like me."

My mind fluttered in search of a witty response until footsteps sounded on the stairs. Darius raised an eyebrow, asking a silent question. I nodded a second before Todd appeared in the stairwell.

He stopped at the bottom of the stairs and crossed his arms.

"How's it going, man?" Darius asked, standing to extend a hand that Todd didn't shake.

"I thought you were looking at your art," Todd said.

"I thought you were cleaning up the kitchen," I answered.

Todd opened his mouth to say something else that I probably didn't want to hear, but Darius stopped him.

"Listen, we all have to get along, right?"

"Wrong," Todd answered.

"Wilkes, I know you and D have a past and all, but no hard feelings."

Todd's cheeks reddened. "A past?"

"Yeah." Darius showed off his acting skills, drawing out the word. "A past."

Todd side-eyed me. "We have more than that."

"I'm not here to cause any trouble," Darius said. "Dinah, do you want me to go?"

Todd looked back and forth between us. I pushed myself up from the soft cushions and looped my arm in Darius'.

"Is this a joke?"

Maybe I had been wrong in assuming Mac would be the difficult one to convince.

"I make one mistake, and you refuse to forgive me," Todd said.

"*One* mistake? One!"

He continued to talk over me. "This guy hooks up with half the carnival, and you think, 'Oh yeah. This is the guy for me.'?"

The rest of the world faded into a blur of color. It was just me and Todd, toe-to-toe, and the heat of anger surging through every part of me. "You made way more than one mistake."

"I said I was sorry!"

"Everything okay down there?" my mom called from the top of the stairs. Her voice was like a sprinkler system, suppressing the growing fire from overhead. When the blur of anger cleared, I realized Darius had positioned himself between me and Todd without me even realizing it.

"We're fine, Mom," I called.

The three of us stared at each other, not moving.

"Forget this," Todd finally said, shaking his head.

I held my breath until he made his way up the stairs and closed the door.

"That went well," Darius said, still holding my arm.

I shook out my arms and took deep breaths to rid myself

of Todd and the negative energy that overtook me every time he was around.

"You okay?"

"Getting there," I said with a sigh.

Darius pulled me into a hug. "You shouldn't need a buffer. It should be enough for a girl to say leave me alone for a guy to do exactly that."

I had no intention of arguing the point, but, given Todd's behavior only two days earlier in that very basement, Darius had proven himself the ultimate buffer and earned himself the esteemed position of my fake boyfriend.

"You good?" Darius asked, rubbing my shoulders.

"He's always the perfect gentleman in front of our parents. He's a kind, God-fearing, loving guy. Which is why they can't understand why I don't want to marry him right at this moment." I raised my hands to surrender some of my snark. "I exaggerate, but still."

"It has to be exhausting to pretend like that all the time."

I gave him a stare-down.

"I didn't mean us. This," he pointed back and forth between us, "is going to be fun."

SIX

THE FIRST CHALLENGE of our fake relationship was successfully lying to our best friends. Darius was scheduled to work at the carnival on some project with Kierk, and Mac and I had a climbing date planned. My new "boyfriend" and I had agreed to tell our besties first. If we couldn't pull that off, then we couldn't pull the fake dating thing off at all.

My only saving grace was the proposed location.

Mac loved The Climb, an indoor rock climbing gym. She went with her dad most days, but I still ended up there too often. I don't climb. Not purposely anyway. Mac, on the other hand, climbed anywhere and everywhere. She didn't care if she had safety equipment. She had no concern for how large or soft the mats beneath her were because she didn't fall. She scooted around climbing walls demonstrating impressive arm strength, swaying her hips, and at times, even swinging her legs to curl her toes around a hold. People watched Mac climb and felt instantly inadequate. It was because of her epic climbing skills that she even met Darius and scored an invitation to the carnival in the first place. That seemed forever ago now.

"Do you want to start on the low wall?" Mac asked while she chalked up her hands.

I pulled a sketchbook and pencils from my bag. "I'm good here."

She rolled her eyes. "Dinah, how exactly is this friend time if I'm up there climbing, and you're down here sketching?"

"We're both doing what we love?" I suggested.

"Is there anything I can do to change your mind? Any route? Any amount of safety equipment?"

I shook my head.

"Strap you on my shoulders like a backpack?" she continued with a grin.

"The fact you could probably do that is kind of embarrassing." I opened my notebook to a blank page. "Seriously, I'm good here."

With a sigh, Mac grabbed the notebook from my hands and flipped the pages. "What has the artist been sketching lately?"

I didn't plan it—at all, but the pages being filled with attempts to capture Darius's likeness was as good a starting point as any to convince my best friend the new relationship was legit.

Mac's eyes widened, her body stilling as she took in the sketches. "Darius?" she whispered.

I took the notebook back. "Glad my sketches are getting close to the mark."

"Dinah?"

"I've been working on it, but I can't get that spark in his eye quite right. Or the way his cheeks puff up when he's smirking, but that smirk..." I took a deep breath, thinking of what it did to my insides. That part was *not* a lie.

"Dinah!"

"Yes?"

"You and Darius?"

"We're spending some time together," I said, doing my best to avoid lying.

"Darius, like Harvey—Darius?"

"No matter how many times you say his name, or both of his names, the answer isn't going to change."

"I…" Mac's mouth hung open. I felt the need to rescue her before a bug flew by and took up refuge.

"You're the one who told him where to find me Sunday."

"First of all, I didn't think he would go through with showing up at your church and your house for brunch, which is exactly why I told him that's where to find you."

"You underestimated him."

"Not sure about that. Second of all, if he did show up, I had no expectation, like none on the planet, that you would go out with him."

I'd expected Mac's reaction, but now that I was witnessing it firsthand, I had no doubt that Darius had been right—he needed something like this to rebuild his reputation. He'd become a dating pariah. Drastic measures were necessary, but that didn't mean I had to be part of those measures. I'd agreed to it, probably more out of wanting revenge against Todd than needing Darius. Still, I appreciated Darius as my ally.

"Maybe you underestimated me," I told my best friend.

"Or overestimated."

"Mac, be nice."

"I'm sorry, D, but I don't want you to get hurt—*again*."

"Who says Darius is going to hurt me?"

"The internet. The girls who dumped milkshakes all over him. The ones who threw water balloons at him, and let's not forget the ones who stole his clothes."

I took a deep breath. She wasn't wrong. All of Darius's

red flags would have turned me far away from him. They had. But Darius and I weren't really dating, making the whole arrangement logical to me, but not to my best friend.

"We're spending time together. We're having fun, and I am working on art projects and restoration in the carnival."

Mac squinted at me. "You don't need him to get on some committee. I could get Kierk to do that."

"Why don't you call him Soren?" I asked.

"Don't change the subject."

"I mean it. I thought it was carnival names in the carnival, and real names outside of it."

"Kierk will always be Kierk no matter where we are. He mostly calls me Sparx, too. As long as we don't use real names in the carnival, we're following the rules. Now will you answer my question?"

"Your question about me using Darius to get better at art?"

"That's the one," she said.

"Thanks for the vote of confidence," I said, hurt. "You think I'd use someone like that? Someone who's already been used and is pretty wrecked about it?"

Mac lowered her gaze. "No. Sorry."

I settled into the cushiony floor, ready to end this conversation and get back to sketching. "Darius is fun and charming, and having him around keeps Todd away."

Mac resumed stretching. "*That* I can absolutely get on board with."

"See. So do I have your blessing?"

"This is not the Middle Ages. You don't need anyone's blessing. Make your own decisions. Whatever. Just be careful."

"Done."

Mac shook her head, but I could tell she'd already given in. I held my breath, afraid that if I let out the sigh I wanted to release, a giggle would escape, too. I'd convinced Mac more easily than I'd expected. Maybe this whole fake dating thing would go well after all.

"One more thing?"

Uh oh. Maybe I spoke too soon. "Yeah?"

"Kennywood day's coming up. This year, we're taking dates!"

Not waiting for confirmation from me that I wanted to take Darius on our annual amusement park adventure, Mac started her climb, leaving me too distracted by the prospect of Kennywood to sketch anything. Every August for years, Mac and I had gone to the park the day our school band performed in their annual summer parades. The whole school went, along with other schools who were performing that day. That meant for years, we'd waited in lines for roller coasters while couples snuggled against each other, flirting and stealing kisses. As little girls, we'd laughed about it, but as we got older, I'd secretly and naively wished one of those girls could be me.

The year before, I'd watched Todd with one of his many former girlfriends. He must have noticed because he caught my eye more than usual and even smiled a couple of times. When we shuffled around the group for a ride, he'd announced that we were riding together. Since we had been family friends forever, his girlfriend of the day thought nothing of it. When the coaster hit the turn that launched the smaller riders into their partners, Todd had rested his arm on the back of the seat, but by the time the cars pulled back into the station, he'd wrapped it around my waist, pulling me to him without the need of any centrifugal force.

"That was fun," he'd whispered in my ear, his lips brushing my cheek.

My throat nearly closed at the memory. Todd had known about my crush on him and exactly what he was doing on that ride. Within a couple of tumultuous weeks, he'd asked me to be his girlfriend. After years of family vacations, brunches, game nights, and pool parties, I'd known Todd Wilkinson and I were meant for each other. I'd been so sure that I'd completely ignored the fact he'd had a girlfriend the day we'd ridden the coaster together. Or the reality that he never dated one person for long. Three months—Mac always said.

I'm not sure we even got three months into our relationship before he helped himself to benefits with who knows how many other girls.

There I was a year later, planning another Kennywood trip. It wouldn't just be me and my best friend. We'd have boyfriends.

Only mine would be fake.

————

I came away from my best friend date at The Climb with a few new sketches and a very weak calorie burn, especially compared to Mac, who had dripped with sweat. My consolation had been the revelation that convincing her Darius and I were together had been easier than expected.

That was the thing about easy street, it gave the illusion of being a long road. Within hours, Todd's name appeared on my phone, reminding me of its many potholes and the fact I should not have unblocked him.

Todd: *Just wanted you to know what you were getting into.*

Todd sent the text with an array of screenshots showing the latest social media posts targeting Darius. Anger bubbled inside me, and I tapped my fingers against the screen.

Me: *Too bad nobody was here to warn me about you.*

Todd: *Endless bubbles. No actual text.*

Good. Maybe that would shut him up for a while.

Scowling at my phone, or more accurately, at a virtual Todd on the other end of the connection, I opened the text again and enlarged the images. One showed a popular meme of a famous actor laughing with the caption, "Darius Moore —now a one-woman man."

Clever.

Although it succeeded in dragging me into the social media rabbit hole. Deep. I read the accusations, cringing at the worst parts. Anger sizzled in me for the girls my *supposed* boyfriend had wronged.

But he'd been wronged too. I searched for the article his ex-girlfriend had written about the carnival. Mac had told me months earlier about Darius. He'd been wrecked by his girlfriend, literally and figuratively. Painful breakups led people to do stupid things. I sat up in my chair. Had my breakup with Todd led me to do something stupid, like fake dating a guy the internet hated for instance?

I guess time would tell on that one.

I scrolled a little more, vowing to stop after three more minutes. Five tops.

My finger screeched to a stop on one post.

"And now he's set his sights on a new girl. Poor soul."

Don't read the comments. Don't read the comments.

I read the comments.

"Does she know what she's getting into?"

"How could she not with all these posts?"

"Maybe she thinks she's better than the rest of us."

"Good luck with that."

"She's eating up whatever lines he's feeding her."

And on it went. I threw the phone on my couch and ripped one of my sketches of Darius from my notebook. After I clipped it onto my easel, I dug through my art drawers collecting watercolor paints and supplies. Yes, Darius had messed up, but he was my fake boyfriend. If he had my back with Todd, I had to have his back with these online bullies. As my painting of Darius came into shape in front of me, I considered posting it online, but that would only redirect their wrath to my fledgling artistry.

I had to do something, though.

I dipped the brushes back into the water, retrieved my phone from the couch, and scrolled through my photos until I found a silly one he'd sent me of us at the park. It would be our first shot as boyfriend and girlfriend, he'd said. I'd told him, "Not so fast," but we both knew I was a goner. I could even see it in the amused look on my face when he kissed my cheek at the exact moment he took the pic.

Deep breath. I tapped the icon for my social app, uploaded the photo, captioned it with a series of hearts, tagged Darius, and hovered over the bright green button that would send my declaration out to the world.

Deep breath again.

I closed one eye and squinted at the screen. If I did this, there'd be no turning back.

None.

Ever.

My finger hit the green button at the same moment a text popped up from Darius. *Just a heads up, don't go scrolling through my online hate mail today.*

Too late.

And if you do, definitely don't read the comments, he texted.

Too late again.

"*For her sake, I hope she knows what she's doing,*" the last comment on his hate thread had read.

Me too.

Satisfied with my "declaration of love" post, I lost

myself practicing the watercolor techniques I'd learned at camp. Making sure the paper was always wet, I layered the paint, darkening the facial features on my sketch until they matched Darius'. His hair and clothes followed. Finally ready to lay down my paintbrush, I grabbed my phone to compare the watercolor to a photo of Darius and found more notifications on the home screen than I'd ever had before.

I'd gone viral—at least locally—and not for the right reasons. I took a deep breath and silenced my notifications.

.

SEVEN

DARIUS KNOCKED at my door the next morning after breakfast with the biggest smile on his face. "I can't believe we're doing this."

"Me either," I said.

"But you changed your profile."

"I did."

"And you posted our first picture as man and wife."

I rolled my eyes.

His grin was delicious. "No turning back now."

"Darius?" my mother called from behind me. "Is that you?"

I groaned.

"I got this," Darius whispered before answering my mom in a tone that dripped with honey. "Mrs. Zimmerman! So good to see you again."

"And so soon," Mom said, glancing at me as if her passive aggressiveness had gone unnoticed.

"Yes, ma'am. And I hope to be spending even more time with Dinah if that's all right with you."

Mom raised an eyebrow at me, and I smiled. "As long as

you treat her with nothing but the respect she deserves, I suppose that can be arranged."

"Without question." Darius charmed my mother with an intensity that had her blushing and pressing her manicured fingers to her chest.

"Moms love me," he said a few minutes later when we were alone in my garage.

"You were very crafty," I said. "Very careful with your words."

"I promised you I wouldn't lie to your parents. I'll never break a promise to you, Dinah."

I swallowed, hoping it might minimize the tightness in my chest. "Thank you."

"You're welcome," he said. "Now where's the stuff the big, macho man has to carry for his darling fake girlfriend?"

I playfully slapped his arm and pointed out the boxes of paints and brushes I'd packed for our work at the carnival. He kissed me on the cheek and carried the boxes to his car. Very chivalrous. Committed to my social medial posts now, I snapped a few pics, including one of him reaching into the trunk, his arm muscles flexing at the box's weight. I zoomed in on the image, not sure if it would have a positive or negative effect on my audience. Eh. Better wait it out and decide later.

Darius rested his chin on my shoulder, sneaking a glance at my phone. "What's that?"

"Some pics for my public relations campaign."

"Ah." He rubbed the back of his neck. "You read the posts, didn't you?"

"Me? No."

He opened the passenger door. "You're right. You're a terrible liar."

"I did silence notifications to my account."

He closed one eye and scrunched up his face like a child

who had stolen one too many cookies. "Probably for the best."

Oh gosh. How bad could all the responses be?

After he walked around the car and slid behind the wheel, I picked up the conversation. "There's so many of them, Darius."

"Yours or mine?"

"Yours," I said. "I told you I didn't read mine."

"I know. I know it's bad." He puffed out a sigh. "I don't have a defense. Definitely young and stupid. Now I'm paying for it."

"You mean by pretending to date me?"

"Doesn't sound like much of a punishment, does it?"

"I sure hope not," I joked.

I watched Darius merge through traffic, meticulous in his turns and attention to the road. He worked hard at the carnival. Kierk trusted him as his number-two guy in everything. He'd shown nothing but politeness to my family. Weirdly, he was more responsible than just about any guy I knew, yet he was being trashed online as if he'd been one of the worst.

"Tell me about the one you liked."

He scratched the back of his head.

"What?"

"It's weird talking to you about the other girls."

"We're not actually dating, though, so it's okay."

He shrugged. "Doesn't feel okay."

"If I'm going to help you through this, I need to know everything. We're a team. I'm not another one of your girls."

"Don't say it like that."

"Answer my question," I pressed.

"Fine. Yes. I tried to cover the fact that I liked her by... spending time with...the other girls."

"You were afraid to like her."

"I wouldn't use the word afraid."

"Would you use the word scared?"

He scowled. "Very funny."

"I get it. You got hurt. Your heart was tender, and you tried to protect it by pretending you didn't care."

"True."

I wanted to ask Darius which girl he had liked and what had happened with her, but that felt like pushing my luck. If he'd wanted to talk about her, he would have offered more information. Instead, he'd avoided my questions and my gaze.

He guided the car along the winding back roads of the carnival property until we stopped behind the factory building that housed the parade route.

"Can I ask a favor?" I asked.

"Sure."

"Can we enter the carnival like regular people do? Mac took me through this back entrance and straight to the Milkshake Ballroom last time. I sort of feel like I'm missing out."

He nodded, pensively. "It's not the same vibe with everything closed down. We can do that this weekend if you want."

My hopes deflated. By then, I'd have so much backstage experience that I'd never be able to recreate that instant magic Mac had described her first days at the carnival.

Darius squeezed my hand. "I promise you will not miss out."

"Thanks."

"In fact, I kind of have a surprise for you. Nobody has seen this yet."

That sounded magical.

"Leave your supplies here for now," Darius said, pulling

me across the empty parking lot at a run. "You're going to love this."

The factory sat dark and silent except for our feet hitting the floor. Darius didn't break the run except to slip his key in a door and unlock one of the rooms that branched off of the main parade route. He flicked the light switch and stepped to the side. "Ta-da!"

The room, massive in its own right, housed a motionless carousel, one like I'd never seen. Every inch of it lacked color.

"What is this?"

"An old carnival company had some equipment as part of an estate sale. We were able to get this for a good price. We worked out the mechanical issues last week."

"You mean it runs?"

"It does." Darius rubbed his hands together. "The company had been in the process of restoring it, which is why all the horses are sanded and primed, but not painted. That is where you come in."

I ran my fingers along the personality-less horses, waiting to be restored and brought back to action.

"You want me to paint a whole carousel?" I mentally urged him to say yes.

Lucky for me, he did.

A project like this one could be epic. Huge for my portfolio. Put me on the map as a budding artist—at least the carnival map. As quickly as my excitement soared, it also plummeted. That was the thing about imposter syndrome.

"I've never done preservation work," I said.

"Is that what this is?" Darius shrugged. "Makes sense I guess, but wouldn't that be a great resume builder?"

"I'd think so if I could pull it off."

"I have no doubt you can pull it off. You have great

style. It's technically strong, and the internet has the answer to everything."

"You really think I can do it?"

"Dinah, listen. This is an important project for me. Epic. Huge. Once in a lifetime."

"I get it," I said.

"I wouldn't have asked if I didn't think you could do it."

I blew a raspberry.

"Please, D." Darius climbed onto one of the horses and leaned his adorable face against the pole. "I might as well come clean since you'll learn this soon enough, but I'm a nerd. I love the carousel. It's my favorite."

I had a hard time believing it. "Isn't the carousel kind of a kid's ride?"

"Shh." He covered the ears of the horse he sat on. "The horses will hear you."

I shook my head and climbed onto my own horse a few spots ahead of his, having no doubt that I'd given him the best possible view of my butt. To his credit, he didn't react.

I imagined the cheerful music brightening the quiet space and swore I could feel the horses move. They would rise and fall while the carousel spun on its axis. Sounds of laughter even trickled into my mind.

"Can I tell you a secret?" Darius whispered.

"You're my boyfriend. It's kind of the rule."

"When I was a kid, my grandparents took me to Kenny-wood every summer while my parents worked. It was mostly for me. They didn't ride much, but they knew I loved the roller coasters. The double dip on the Jack Rabbit got me every time. My Grams rode it with me and some other ones, too, but my Pops would only ride one thing."

"The carousel?"

He pointed at me. "Yep. It was the first and the last ride of the day every time. He passed a couple of years ago, but every time I'm on a carousel, it's like I can feel him on the horse next to me."

I imagined young, sweet Darius looking up to his grandfather, waiting until the end of a day of roller coaster riding to sit on a painted horse that slid up and down without much fanfare. The story was too cute.

"I took my carnival name because of my grandfather. It was his first name."

"Your grandfather's name was Harvey?"

Tears glistened in his eyes, and his voice cracked when he answered, "He was the best."

"Oh my gosh," I said, wiping a tear from my cheek. "I'll do it."

"Don't cry." He threw his long leg over the side of his horse and took a couple of steps to stand next to me. "Oh my gosh. I did not tell you that to make you cry."

But I couldn't stop. The entire exhibit was a tribute to Darius's grandfather, and he wanted my help to pull it off? Sob city! "I will watch as many videos online as I need to, and I will restore every inch of this for you."

He rubbed my back. "Dinah, don't cry."

I slid off the horse, falling forward into Darius's chest. "That was intense."

He slipped his fingers through mine. "Sorry."

"Stop apologizing."

He pulled me closer. "Thank you."

I took a breath and looked into his deep brown eyes. For a few seconds, or minutes, or who knows how long, I was lost there.

"You're welcome," I managed.

Darius brushed a tear off my cheek. At his touch, our rules stumbled through my memory. We'd agreed to "everything up to kissing" when we were in public, but this wasn't public. This was him and me in a room alone in the carnival.

This was very, very private.

But his hand wrapped around my back, and his body pressed against me. And his eyes were doing this thing where they devoured me and uplifted me and told me all the things he was thinking.

I remembered our other rule, too. If this ever became real, we'd have to tell each other. At that moment, I wouldn't jump directly to real, but the flutters in my chest weren't fake either.

I smiled like I always did with the older ladies at my church and stepped back from him. "I have two requests."

He tucked his hands behind his back. "Whatever you need."

"First, I need a helper that at least knows how to paint."

"Okay. And the second?"

"This is non-negotiable," I said.

"Hit me with it.

I crossed my arms and gave him my most intimidating expression. "You have to promise me you won't come back in here until it's completely done."

He grinned. "Promise."

EIGHT

WHILE DARIUS FOUND another artist on the committee to help me paint the carousel horses, he had another project lined up for me—paint touchups for the bumper cars. He carted my painting supplies from his car to the bumper cars exhibit and left me to work while he did whatever people like him and Kierk did in the carnival. Sitting on a stool in the silent room, dabbing paint from my brush onto a particularly beat-up car, I couldn't help but laugh out loud at how much my life had changed in a week.

The week before, I'd rotated hours by the pool and in my basement studio with this contradictory feeling of not wanting summer to end yet wanting to move forward with my art to a future where I at least felt some confidence in it.

Okay, so the bumper car wasn't going to end up in the Louvre or anything, but it was real. Practical. Relevant. It mattered more than the experimental pieces nobody would ever see in the boxes of my basement. It wasn't where I ultimately wanted to be, but for the first time, I felt like I was at least on a road that led there.

"How's my artist?" Darius asked from the doorway.

I spun on the stool with a smile on my face.

"You look happy."

"I'm having a lot of fun. This might be my first practical art project."

"Practical?"

"Yeah, like people are going to see it. The cars are part of something bigger."

He climbed over the barrier separating the bumping zone from the rest of the room and inspected the cars I'd already finished. "They look like new."

"Thank you."

"Have time for a break?"

"Does it involve a snack?" I teased.

"At the carnival?" Darius said. "Always."

That's when I noticed the greasy paper bag he'd left on a shelf by the door. I cleaned my work area, closing the lids on the paints to preserve them and returning the brushes to the water. Darius handed me a square donut wrapped in a napkin.

"Are these the beignets Mac raves about?"

Darius grinned. "Could be."

I bit into the sugary treat. "Oh. My. Gosh."

"Yep."

We ate in silence, honoring the beignets as they were meant to be honored. So much of the carnival deserved that kind of deference. My heart thumped when I wondered what my next art project at the carnival could be—after the carousel.

"Thank you," I said.

He lifted his own beignet and nodded. "You're welcome."

"Not for the beignets," I said. "I mean, thanks for those, too, but I meant for bringing me here to work on the exhibits."

"Are you kidding? You restored two bumper cars already. I'm not doing you any favors. It's the other way around."

Except I was also getting paid as an official committee member, so it wasn't quite a favor. My first job as an actual artist! The carnival gave everyone on the committee the chance to earn money to do something they loved like the ultimate internship experience.

"You do realize how incredible this place is, right?" I said, thinking about the facade everyone who attended the carnival on the weekends experienced and the behind-the-scenes opportunities for the committee. "It's like an architectural and artistic miracle."

Darius smiled with sugar on his cheeks. "It was cool to be here at the beginning. People thought we were out of our minds. They said nobody would come, it was a waste of money, too far off the beaten path, all that stuff. Not to mention, getting people to pay to come somewhere and wear a mask?"

"At least it's a fun mask."

"Kierk brought me on right at the beginning. I was just glad for a job."

"What did you do before that?"

Darius cleared his throat and pressed two fingers to his ear. "Hello. My name is Darius. Thank you for visiting our drive-thru today. What can I get started for you?"

"I think I ordered a triple stacker from you once," I teased.

He laughed. "Everyone did. I was there forever. Started college and had no idea what to do with my life. I'm one of those general education majors." He gestured to the mound of paints in my work area. "Unlike you, I didn't have my whole life figured out."

"Not my whole life. Just the part that involves art. It

took me a while. I was in journalism with Mac, but it felt...
colorless to me."

Darius perked his eyebrows. "Colorless?"

"Yes," I said cautiously, and he nodded with an evil grin.
"What's going on?"

Darius dusted off his fingers and searched the paints.

"What are you looking for?"

"A color you're not going to need today."

"Why would you do that?" I asked, my heart rate
increasing.

Darius selected a tube of hunter-green paint and twisted
the cap.

I backed away. "What are you doing with that?"

"Just giving you a little color."

"Darius," I warned.

He grinned, and I ran, swiping my own tube of paint on
the way out the door. I didn't stop until I soared past the
other committee members munching on beignets in the
Starlight Cafe, still running all the way to the massive
factory parade route. When I turned to catch my breath, I
was alone. Light crept through the windows, but the best it
could do was elevate the factory from dark to dim. I spun in
the center of the room like a character in a horror movie,
waiting for the villain to appear. None of the doors opened.

Darius had longer legs than mine, and he was athletic.
There had to be a reason he didn't catch me. A plan. I'd
need one too, but nothing spectacular came to mind. After a
minute or two, the soft vibration of footsteps sounded from
the same hallway I'd used. I hid next to the door, twisted off
the cap, and readied the paint. The anticipation of seeing
pink paint splattered across Darius's face made me suppress
a giggle.

The footsteps sounded louder.

Louder.

Louder.

I took a deep breath. The moment I saw movement through the door, I squirted. The paint landed in the long blonde hair of someone that was so not Darius Moore.

"Oh my gosh. I'm so sorry," I said.

"What just happened?"

"I thought you were someone else?"

"Me?" Darius whispered from behind me and smeared paint across my cheek.

I ran my pink fingers across his short hair, leaving a series of stripes. We chased each other until we'd wiped every trace of paint from our hands.

We laughed and breathed heavily, which is when I remembered the blonde I'd painted pink. She stood in the doorway with her arms crossed, looking furious through the eye holes of her mask.

"Of course, it would be you, Harvey. Have you taken her to the roof yet?"

Harvey sighed. "Didn't recognize you without your short skirt, Barbie."

"My carnival name isn't Barbie."

"Who's mistake was that?" Harvey pushed.

I watched them spar. Barbie's jabs landed hard, too hard, which meant only one thing. She was the one who'd gotten away.

"Care to introduce me," I whispered.

"Oh, we've met," the girl who wasn't Barbie said. "At the milkshake baptism."

"That's what you and your crew call it?" Darius asked.

She tipped her head to the side and smiled. "Isn't that what it was? You're born new, right? A one-woman kind of guy?"

I found a roll of paper towels on a shelf in the corner and handed them to our new friend. "I'm Diamond."

"Of course, you are," she laughed. "You found your diamond in the rough, Harvey?"

"Lay off her," Harvey said, stepping between us. "Hate me all you want, but leave her out of it."

She smiled sweetly at me. "I'm Em. I'm on the committee."

"More like bought your way onto the committee."

"I make contributions in many ways." She waved. "Thanks for the new hairstyle. I was thinking of going pink."

She headed for the exit that led to the garage of parade floats.

Darius didn't move. Instead, he watched her walk away.

———

We cleaned up in separate bathrooms. I got the sense Darius didn't want to talk, so I made my way back to the exhibit and touched up the paint on more bumper cars, my emotions as varied as the colors in my paint collection. Em had to be the one. The way Darius had watched her walk away confirmed what I'd assumed when they'd argued seconds earlier. The whole incident showed that he still cared about her, and maybe under all of her anger, she felt the same way about him. Yet another reminder not to let myself like Darius. But if she was on the committee, she would be around all the time, and I'd have to watch them together.

After an hour or so of me fighting off feelings of jealousy, Harvey appeared at the door, watching me.

"You need something?" I asked.

"Just checking to see how it's going?"

"You mean with the painting or the fact I attacked your ex with paint?"

He shrugged.

"She the one?" I asked, trying to sound nonchalant.

His gaze snapped to mine, his eyes wide.

"So she *is* the one."

"You're clever, aren't you?"

My turn to shrug, but I couldn't stop the grin on my face. I was uncovering his secrets.

"Yeah," he said. "She was the one and probably a mistake."

"That's a bit harsh isn't it?"

"I don't mean it like that. Like I said before, she's the kind of girl you date, not hook up with. I don't blame her for being hot about it. She told me she didn't want a stupid hookup, and I ignored it."

"That's…"

"The kind of thing that leads to a milkshake baptism." He tested the cars I'd finished to make sure they were fully dry and pushed them back to their starting spots. "I guess you sometimes…I don't know. It probably won't make sense to you."

"Why?"

"You're a nice person."

"Why doesn't something make sense because I'm nice?"

Darius sat on the hood of one of the cars waiting to be painted and crossed his arms. "You probably never looked at yourself in the mirror and didn't like the person you saw. Someone like you doesn't have that experience."

Feeling his heaviness from across the room, I left my brush in the water bucket, closed the paint, and joined him on the bumper cars. "I don't know. After I let Todd treat me the way he did for so long, I couldn't look at myself in the mirror either. We all judge ourselves for different reasons."

"I'm not the only one judging. The internet is loving all the stories about me. I wish I could say they weren't true."

"Now Em is on the committee? Are they trying to take over every aspect of your life?"

"Her dad wants to franchise the carnival."

"Franchise? I didn't even know you could do that with a carnival."

"This would be the first. I wasn't lying. He has a ton of money, so in that way, she did buy her way onto the committee. She's studying hospitality management, and she wants to spend next summer opening another carnival location. She's here to learn every inner workings of the carnival."

"In her article, Mac talked about how packed the carnival always is. It makes sense that it's lucrative."

"It is, but you have to have the buy-in. We had so many connections locally that led to the development of the exhibits—different high school and college programs and art students. Pittsburgh has so many colleges and universities and tech programs. I don't know if it would work in any other city."

I nudged his shoulder. "You sure you don't want to work on the franchise team? You seem to know how it works."

"Nah," he said. "I've been here since the beginning, but Pittsburgh's my place. Besides, the internet follows you everywhere."

"Harvey?"

He rested his head on my shoulder. "You can call me Darius when it's just us."

"Okay, Darius?"

"Yeah?"

"Have you thought about just apologizing?"

"Apologizing?"

"Yeah. Telling the girls you wronged that you're sorry?"

"I don't even know if it would matter if I apologized. It's not going to mean anything to them."

"I get it." Maybe it had been naive of me to suggest it. They'd lost trust in Darius, and an apology now would look like he was only giving it to silence his haters online. "When someone is sorry, it's hard to trust that. You have to show it."

"Right. Like being faithful and dating someone who is girlfriend material."

"Yes, but definitely making sure nobody ever finds out that it's for show. That will not work out in your favor."

"I told you this isn't for show. I like you and like spending time with you. Of course, *you* like me because who couldn't? It's real in that way."

I guess it was.

NINE

FRIDAY WAS my first day off from the carnival that week. I floated in the pool all morning, the early August sun beating against my skin. When my fingers and toes wrinkled from the moisture, I dried off and headed to the basement. I hadn't worked on my watercolor techniques since earlier in the week, and my portrait of Darius sat unfinished. I mixed up a few skin tone paint options and wet the paper before dabbing the brush to his face and neck, pulling darker for the shaded areas and lighter for those I wanted to catch the light.

I lost myself in the rhythm of mixing the paint, wetting the paper, and brushing until the color blended perfectly until my mother came down the stairs with bags of groceries to store in the basement freezer.

"Let me help you," I said, taking a bag that looked to be slipping from her fingers.

"Thanks, honey," she said.

We loaded waffles, pasta, and ice cream until the freezer was packed. She tossed the bags in our recycling bin and asked, "Mind if I take a look at what you're working on?"

"Sure. I've been practicing watercolors. I love the way the color spreads through the water, but it's also tough to get the shades just right."

With one hand pensively resting against her chin, Mom stood in front of my easel, examining the painting. "I see what you mean. The colors on the face are great, but the neck ..."

I gestured with the brush. "It needs to be lighter here, but I'm afraid I already messed it up with the darker shades."

"Sounds like a good learning experience," Mom said and raised an eyebrow at me. "You want to talk about the subject of the painting?"

"Smooth segue, Mom."

She waited for an answer.

"What do you want to know about Darius?"

"How are things going?"

"Great," I said, and it wasn't a lie. As fake relationships went, mine was great. Darius and I were having fun. I had my art projects at the carnival and Todd hadn't bothered me all week.

"You spent a lot of time together in the last week."

"I finished paint touch-ups on the bumper cars. Did I tell you all of the cars have Mardi Gras masks painted on the front? It's kind of cool."

Darius and I had taken beignet breaks together every day that week, and we had the good fortune not to run into Em again.

"Sounds like a big project."

"I took pics for my portfolio." I swiped through my phone to show her, and she raved about the designs. "I didn't design the cars, but I will be designing the horses for the carousel."

Mom squeezed me into a hug. "It all sounds very exciting."

"It is," I said, apprehension about designing twelve horses mingling with excitement.

"What is it?"

"Paint touch-ups are easier than choosing all the colors and bringing the horses to life. What if I mess up?"

She shrugged. "Then you paint over it."

I laughed at how simple she made it sound.

My phone buzzed with a message from Darius. He was coming to pick me up in about an hour to go to the carnival.

"Is that Darius?"

"Yep. We're going to the carnival tonight."

Mom pursed her lips. I braced myself.

"Dinah, why did you and Todd break up?"

I sucked in a breath. My mom had never asked me such a direct question about boys before. Her approach was usually the passive-aggressive, beating-around-the-bush type.

"I know it had to be something serious because you're so angry at him, but I also get the sense that you don't want us to know."

"You're best friends with his parents."

"But I'm *your* mother."

I couldn't break her heart by admitting I'd wondered if that would be enough. After a few seconds, she smiled at me and headed for the door. "If you ever want to tell me, I'm ready to listen."

———

My mom gave no hint of our earlier conversation when Darius knocked on the door to pick me up. Instead, she offered him dinner, and he politely ate a plate before we left, raving about her cooking.

"You didn't have to do that."

"Eat food? Not exactly a hardship. You excited for the carnival?"

I was, I guess. Maybe excited for everyone to see the newly painted bumper cars. Some of the touch-ups had been so minor, I doubt anyone would even notice. But I did add some of my own flare to a few cars. Darius entertained me with stories of behind-the-scenes fails that week at the carnival while he drove.

"At the beginning of the summer, everyone asked us if we would be open daily since school was out." He shook his head. "People don't get how hard it is to be ready for Friday night."

Thousands of masked patrons packed the carnival each Friday and Saturday. I doubted it would hold the same appeal if people could go every night.

"But the carnival's ready for tonight?"

"Oh yeah. Be prepared for the carnival experience of your life."

We turned off the main road onto the carnival property, but we didn't take the usual route.

"Where are we going?"

Darius smiled.

"What are you up to?"

His response was a laugh.

After a few more turns on dirt roads, he parked in the woods next to a string of other cars and handed me my mask. "Better put this on."

I positioned the mask under half of my hair like Mac had taught me, and walked hand in hand with Darius through the trees. When we got closer to a few people wearing Carniva-lesque shirts, he pulled his wallet from his pocket.

"You're paying to get inside?"

"You wanted a true carnival experience, right?"

Memories of Mac telling me about her first night at the carnival trickled into my mind. She'd parked in the woods and played games at a smaller outdoor carnival before getting to the main building where she met Kierk.

Sure enough, twinkle lights peeked through the trees, and carnival music sounded in the distance.

Darius extended his hand, fingers wide, and I grabbed it. "You excited?" he asked.

"Like a dorky child," I said. "Please don't tell anyone."

Oh, that smile. It tortured my heart.

We followed the path to a small village of carnival booths, all painted black with gold embellishments and masks. Twinkle lights lined each one. Darius shelled out bills for us to play all the traditional games. We threw darts at posters of masks and stocked up on a few options to mix and match. We tossed ping pong balls into fish bowls, and I won an adorable stuffed fish I named Harvey. We even scooped up rubber ducks, winning free beignets.

It didn't take long to feel the carnival magic.

"I don't think I've played games like this for ten years."

"Sometimes I think that's why they're so popular. You get to be a kid again," Darius said.

"But win big girl prizes."

"Big girl prizes? Like that stuffed fish?"

"Don't hate on Harvey."

He shook his head, but despite his attempt to protest, he couldn't suppress his smile.

"It resembles you," I added, enjoying his laughter.

"You ready to go inside?"

"Do we have to solve a riddle?" I asked.

"Eh. I kind of gave us VIP passes. I'm sorry if that's not authentic enough for you."

I looped my arm in his and kissed his masked cheek. "It's perfect."

———

Perfect proved an interesting sentiment as we made our way inside the carnival. Calm before the storm may have been a better descriptor. In the Milkshake Ballroom, we danced a Scottish reel that had me spinning like an infinity decoration on an office desk. Sparking our competitive sides, we rode the bumper cars—with me destroying him—and played hide and seek in the maze—victory to him since he knew the carnival so well.

All perfection.

Until…

"We have a new-ish exhibit I haven't gotten to yet," he said.

"How is that possible?"

"I spend most of my time mixing shakes in the ballroom or helping Kierk with random things."

"Wow." I tsked at him.

"What?"

"I gave you an opportunity. Tossed the ball right up there. You could have hit it out of the park."

"I don't follow."

I exaggerated a sigh. "I asked about why you haven't been to this exhibit. You could have said something charming like, 'I never had anyone to share it with until now.'"

His shoulders slumped. "You're right. Wasted opportunity."

"Yet another thing for you to learn," I teased.

He gave me a smoldering gaze that could have rivaled

even the best rom-com hotties. "You think I need lessons on how to be charming?"

Um, not when he looked at me like that.

"I'll take that as a 'no'," he said. "So about that exhibit?"

"Lead the way."

Clusters of masked people pushed through the doors to a small, makeshift auditorium. We found two seats together in the front row.

"What's the show tonight?"

"A comedian, I think."

"That's cool. Someone local?"

The masked comedian stepped onto the stage and waved before tripping over a stool and falling. Darius and I winced.

She recovered and stood, her mask crooked.

"Anyone else think it's hard to see in these things?" she asked, and the crowd laughed. She launched into a bit about mask jokes that kept us laughing. "And let's be real. For all the carnival exhibits they offer, they are missing two of the ones we want the most. But before I tell you more, I'm going to need two volunteers."

"Go ahead, D," Harvey suggested.

"No. Not even a little. Just no."

"How about someone from the front row," the comedian said. "That way people don't die when you try to walk to the stage in these death trap masks. You two on the end." She pointed to me and Darius.

Oh no.

TEN

HE TOOK my hand and pulled me to the stage while the crowd cheered. The comedian asked for our carnival names while her stage crew rolled something behind a curtain onto the stage.

"You were so kind to volunteer," she said.

"We didn't," I reminded her, and everyone laughed.

"I hope you brought a change of clothes!" She tugged at the curtain. It fell, revealing a dunk tank and a spinning wheel with wrist and ankle straps.

"No." The word was like a reflex. My next reflex was to run from the theater, but the comedian was already taking my hand and leading me to the dunk tank.

"Probably want to avoid spinning you upside down in that dress. That's not the kind of show we're going for."

Some of the guys in the audience booed. Behind the dunk tank, someone from the stage crew gave me shorts to slip under my dress and helped me kick off my shoes to climb onto the tank.

"I'm not so sure about this," I told them.

"We have some cool bonuses for helping us out," the

comedian said and then whispered, "besides, I promise you won't get wet."

Tough promise to keep to someone sitting on the bench of a dunk tank.

The crowd chanted, "Climb the ladder! Climb the ladder!"

Who knew peer pressure could be so annoying? Across the stage, Darius chanted, too. I climbed the first step and reached for the bench seat, which was solidly in place. Secretly, I'd always wanted to try a dunk tank, although maybe in a more private way. I climbed the rest of the way to the seat and gingerly sat across it. The room cheered.

From my spot on high, I had the perfect view of the stage crew strapping Darius to the wheel. They pulled the waist strap tight around him and secured it to the back of the wheel.

"Should we give him a spin to make sure he's not going anywhere?"

Anyone could guess how the crowd responded. Darius spun like the wheel on The Price is Right. I covered my face and laughed. What had we gotten ourselves into?

More volunteers lined up in the aisles of the audience. The comedian gave my line tomatoes and Darius's line knives. The audience gasped.

"Just joking!"

My heart resumed beating when she tucked the knives back into her bag and instead waited for the stage crew to bring her pie pans filled with white cream.

"Here's how this is going to work," she called, gesturing for the crowd to quiet down. "Our dunk tank line will throw tomatoes at the target. Our spinner line will throw pie pans. The first to hit the mark is the winner. Let's go!"

The stage crew spun Darius, and people from my line wound up and launched their tomatoes—miss after miss after miss. Pie pans landed on the stage, far from Darius. Just when I thought neither of us would ever get hit, the population of the lines shifted in an obvious way.

They were all girls wearing short skirts and red masks.

Uh oh.

The tomatoes meant for the dunk tank smacked against the spinning board, splattering red juice on Darius. One hit him in the chest, and he grunted.

"Hey," the comedian shouted. "That's not the game."

But the girls didn't stop there. The first egg splattered against Darius's chest. The second hit the wood next to his head and dripped into his hair. Within seconds, people were launching eggs at him from all directions.

It was the milkshake baptism and the water balloon attack all over again, except Darius was strapped to a board unable to protect himself. I swung my legs to the side to climb out of the tank to help him, but someone finally hit the target, dropping the bench, so I fell into the water.

The chill cut into my skin, shocking my nervous system.

By the time I righted myself and climbed out, security was evacuating the theater. The stage crew navigated the pieces of tomato and egg on the stage to release Darius who was so messy that a dunk in the tank could have done him good.

———

"It has to be Em," Darius told Kierk an hour later in the residential suite after he'd showered and changed into a carnival uniform.

"After the last incident, I told her if she did anything like this at the carnival again, she'd be done," Kierk said. He glanced at me in a way that felt unfriendly. Did he think I was helping the girls terrorize Darius? "I don't think she would have risked her entire future to be involved."

"She was talking about the comedian exhibit at the committee meeting. Loud enough for me to overhear."

So that's why he'd wanted to go? To run into Em? Between Darius's admission and Kierk's unfriendly glances, I found myself pressing my fingertips against my temples.

"I'll talk to her," he said.

Mac handed us both hot chocolate.

"It's August, Sparx."

"It will make you feel better," she insisted. "Drink."

Kierk's walkie-talkie sounded, and he stepped into the other room. We sipped our drinks in silence—Harvey likely in anger and me, I guess, the same. After all, he'd planned our carnival date around chasing an ex to an exhibit.

Kierk leaned against the doorway.

"What?" Darius asked.

"Someone told the comedian to pick you two as volunteers. Of course, she doesn't know who because they were masked. She wasn't blonde, I know that much. Looks like they took advantage of a situation. They stole the eggs from the bakery." He scratched his head. "I'll talk to Em."

Our friends left, and Darius opened his arms to me. I fell into them, pulling at him in the tightest hug I could manage.

"Are you okay?" I asked.

"Furious. They're taking it too far."

"I can't believe they egged you like that."

"Someone knocked you into the water, too."

"That was part of the show, though."

"No," he said. "It wasn't. The target is calibrated so high that nothing would have triggered it. That's the only reason I let you climb onto that bench. The joke is that the biggest, strongest, most macho guys in the audience could hit the target right on, and you wouldn't budge."

"Oh," I said. That's why the stage crew guy had promised me I wouldn't get wet. But then how had I fallen into the water?

Darius pulled his phone from his pocket and sat on the living room couch.

"What are you doing?"

"I have to figure out a way to show them," he said.

"Show them what?"

"That I've changed. That they should direct their wrath someplace else."

I sat next to him and looked over his shoulder at the screen. "Isn't that what we're doing?"

"That was the plan, but I might be making it worse. They see me being decent to you and wonder what's wrong with them that I treated them the way I did."

"We'll figure it out. In the meantime, I have your back."

"Thanks. You, Kierk, Mac, and that's it."

He scrolled and scrolled, his eyes intense. I caught the time in the upper corner of the screen.

"It's almost my curfew," I said.

He tucked the phone into his pocket. "Let's get you home."

"Before we go, how did Kierk react when you told him about us?"

"Eh."

I stilled. "What is eh?"

"He doesn't get it, but I told him he didn't need to. He knew I wanted to stop messing around before the milkshake situation happened, but he doesn't get why you are giving me a chance."

So he was as disbelieving as Todd. I stood, surprised my best friend took it the best. Maybe because she was a female who could see Darius's appeal. "He doesn't see how attractive you are," I told Darius on our way out of the room.

He ate up the compliment complete with a lick of his lips. "You know how to cheer a guy up."

"Oh don't pretend you need a self-esteem boost where your looks are concerned," I said, and he laughed.

"I'm sorry your magical carnival experience ended this way. We may have to spend time together outside the carnival. At least until this all cools off."

"I was hoping that you would be my date for an epic tradition."

"Are you inviting me to a wedding?"

"No," I laughed. "I'm inviting you to mine and Mac's annual Kennywood day."

ELEVEN

ON THE WAY to the amusement park Monday morning, Kierk and Darius regaled us with stories of their Kenny-wood tradition—running through the park from one coaster to another to see who vomited first.

"We won't be doing that," Mac said.

"Hey," Kierk teased. "You can't just dismantle our traditions."

Mac parked her car, and we headed for the entrance. "Okay. How about when Dinah and I grab lunch like civilized humans, you two can make yourselves vomit."

The guys looked at each other and shrugged.

"Sounds good to me," Darius said.

Mac slapped Kierk's shoulder, and he responded by sliding his arms around her waist and pulling her to him. Darius gave me a sideways look and whispered in my ear, "Is that what we should be doing?"

Peppermint mixed with his rugged cologne, and I bit my lip. Why did my fake boyfriend have to be so attractive?

Kierk had spent the weekend investigating the comedy show incident, but all he could prove was that Em had not been involved. Darius and I had texted each other a promise to let it go and focus on having a fun day at Kennywood. Darius had also promised Kierk that he'd stick to behind-the-scenes work at the carnival until tempers from his former women scorned cooled down.

"We are in public," I managed the courage to whisper back, my boldness awarded with Darius's delicious grin.

The line to enter the park moved a few steps, and Darius intertwined his fingers with mine. "This is going to be fun."

"Riding so many roller coasters that you vomit?"

He hip-checked me. "No. Going to Kennywood with my girlfriend."

"It's a new experience for me," I said after we walked through the metal detectors and our hands reconnected.

"You mean the other one never brought you to the amusement park?"

I laughed at his refusal to say Todd's name. "The other one and I rode the Thunderbolt together last summer. While he had a different girlfriend, and he didn't behave appropriately for having a girlfriend. Let's leave it at that."

Darius's eyebrows shot up.

"I know. I still went out with him after that major red flag. Turns out ignoring red flags is my signature move."

He thumped his hands over his heart and pretended to be injured before straightening and nodding, ever so serious. "It's true, though."

We made our way through the entrance tunnel, a simple work of engineering that set off all sorts of emotions. Walking through the tunnel in the morning set off butterflies and bouncing on your toes at the thought of the rides that would swing you this way or that, take you to heights and drop you so fast you gasped for breath. The tunnel was your initiation into the magic of the day. Darius squeezed my hand and pulled me closer, an act that caught Kierk's eye.

I smiled at my best friend's boyfriend, who was also my boyfriend's best friend, but he didn't smile back. He turned away, leaving me to wonder if something else was going on that day besides roller coasters, smothered fries, and cotton candy.

"First ride?" Mac asked and then answered. "Jack Rabbit."

The guys shook their heads. "You ride the biggest roller coaster first. The morning is when the line is the shortest."

"Right," Mac argued. "But if you ride Jack Rabbit and Racers on the way, then you get two rides done with no wait, and then you maybe only wait ten minutes more for the big ride. Everyone who rides that will move to the smaller coasters immediately after, leaving you to wait behind those same people all morning."

And on the theorizing went. I mostly ignored them and instead took in the design changes in the park. They'd hired someone to paint murals on the sides of the buildings and in the entrance/exit tunnel. The change was a simple one, but it added so much flavor and nostalgia to the park.

"You look deep in thought," Darius said. "What's up?"

I pointed to the mural I'd been studying on the wall next to the Jack Rabbit line. "I want to paint a mural."

Darius studied the brick wall and nodded. "Sure. You could do that."

"At the carnival?" Kierk asked.

I thought about it, but murals already decorated the carnival's brick walls. "I don't think so. There are already some good ones there."

"Always room for one more," Darius suggested.

The line moved forward, forcing us to leave the mural behind.

"It doesn't have to be now or soon or whatever." I shrugged. "It's something I want to do someday. That's all."

Planning my future was a relatively new experience for me. For so long, Mac had our future in journalism planned, not because she was overly controlling but because I didn't know what I wanted and sort of went along. My parents had my future with Todd planned, another thing I'd gone along with and had since completely changed my mind.

Now, I knew my future included art. I wasn't sure exactly how, but I didn't need to know now.

That would come in time.

I hoped.

———

By the time we'd worked our way halfway through the park, I'd forgotten about the odd look Kierk had given me that morning until he suggested we ride together. Mac looped her arm in Darius's without a second thought, but Kierk stood stiffly next to me.

Neither of us spoke until we'd settled next to each other on the spinning, spider ride.

"Is everything okay?" I asked.

"I prefer coasters to rides that spin, but other than that."

I could have let it go. Maybe I should have, but the vibe lingered.

"I feel like you gave me a look earlier."

"A look?"

I nodded.

"I just don't know you that well," Kierk said.

"I feel like I know you. Mac has been talking about you since the first time she came to the carnival. I think she fell for you long before she even realized it."

He smiled. "That's something we have in common. But what about you and Darius?"

"What about us?"

He looked away and sighed as if debating the biggest decision of his life. "I don't get it."

"Get what?"

"The two of you."

"I'm not good enough for your friend. Is that what you mean?"

"You show up in his life when all this shit is happening online. You watch girls basically assault him, and you know he has a reputation. But you jump from one relationship where a guy wasn't right to you into another one with a guy —who is my best friend and is a solid guy, no doubt—but has made some mistakes lately."

"I guess that's one way to look at it," I said, my throat dry. "We like spending time together."

He rolled his eyes.

"What was that about?" I wanted the ride to end, but people were still boarding, and it hadn't even started.

"What's in it for you?"

"Excuse me?" I said.

"Why are you with him?"

"Do you have such little faith in your friend?"

"It's not him I don't have faith in."

Wow. Okay. "So it's not that you think I'm not good enough. You think I want something from him."

"Well, do you?"

I shook my head, wishing I could be anywhere other than strapped into this ride. In a way, Kierk was on the right track. Being with Darius benefited me, but it was a mutual benefit that we had agreed to, and I couldn't defend myself without telling him the secret Darius and I had agreed to keep.

"Have you talked to Darius about this?"

"You didn't answer my question."

"Look, Kierk. What you think doesn't matter. This is between Darius and me."

"Still didn't answer it."

The spider legs lifted and spun, twisting us around in silence. Despite the wind, I got hotter and hotter until anger flamed through my body by the time the ride ended. I fumbled with the unlocking mechanism to escape as quickly as possible. The crowd had swallowed Darius and Mac, so I pushed through, away from Kierk until the people thinned, and I found the two of them, laughing. Clearly, their ride had gone better than ours.

I forced a smile and pressed myself into Darius's side, but as usual, my best friend picked up on everything.

"Dinah, what's wrong? Are you sick?"

"I'm fine."

Kierk caught up with us, and I refused to make eye contact with him, afraid I'd tell Mac everything she needed to know with a look.

"Babe, what is it?" Darius whispered before looking back and forth between Kierk and me. After a few seconds, his body tensed. "Tell me you didn't."

"Didn't what?" Mac asked.

Darius pulled me behind him and stepped up to Kierk. "What did you say to her?"

"Nothing," I said. "It's fine."

"No. It's not," Darius insisted. "Kierk?"

"I said what you think I said."

"Which is?" Mac asked. "Will someone clue me in here?"

"Kierk thinks Dinah is using me to get a position on the committee, to paint projects inside the carnival and build her portfolio."

Mac's eyes could have fallen out of her beautiful face. "Excuse me?"

Kierk crossed his arms in response.

"Did you seriously just ask to ride with my best friend, so you could accuse her of being manipulative and dishonest?"

"I didn't use those words," Kierk said.

Mac threw her hands up and stepped backward. "I can't believe this."

"I'm looking out for my friend."

"I don't need you to look out for me," Darius said. "I need you to treat my girlfriend with respect. What the hell, man."

"She didn't deny it."

"She shouldn't have to," Mac said.

"Mac's right," Darius said. "Dinah doesn't have to deny it."

Kierk opened his mouth to say something, but Mac stopped him. "Maybe we should split up for the next ride. To cool off," she said and glared at Kierk. "And to have a little chat."

They left Darius and me standing in silence.

"You okay?" he asked after a minute.

"Questioning myself as a person."

"Don't. Not because of Kierk. He doesn't know, you know."

"Yeah, but nobody knows me better than Mac, and she asked me something similar when I told her about us."

"This not the epic Kennywood date day you imagined?"

I huffed. "Not even close."

"Nothing fixes bad moods like Potato Patch friends," he said, nudging my shoulder.

I hoped he was right.

TWELVE

"THAT WAS A NIGHTMARE," I said thinking back on the way Kierk had scowled at me while I dipped my fries in ketchup.

Darius squeezed my hand. "I'm sorry about him."

"He's not entirely wrong."

He leaned back. "You wanna explain?"

"You *did* offer me work in the carnival to sweeten the deal, remember?"

"He still shouldn't talk to you like that."

Maybe, but Darius had a lot of people coming at him with negativity and accusations. At least Kierk cared. "I'm glad you have someone looking out for you. You need that."

He pressed his lips to my ear and whispered. "I have you."

I smiled at his ability to flirt even at a time like this. "I just wish he didn't have to hate me because I kind of like him."

Darius gave me the side eye. "Like him how?"

"Oh my gosh. Are you accusing me of going after my best friend's guy? This is already a rough day for me."

He raised his hands in surrender. "My bad. Just have to know you're not into my boy."

"Would you be jealous?" I teased.

"Hell yeah."

We laughed, losing ourselves in each other's eyes slowly until the laughter settled and left behind still breaths and a swelling desire in my chest.

Darius rubbed the back of his neck and looked away. We ended the conversation by stuffing our faces. When we'd finished, Darius said, "I'm sorry about Kierk. Wanna do something that will cheer you up?"

"Obviously. I am at Kennywood," I said. "What did you have in mind?"

He took my hand. "Let's go."

Darius and I twisted and turned through the crowds, never letting each other go, until we stood in front of the carousel.

"I thought this was for the last ride of the day," I said.

"Or any time in between. You can't ride a wooden horse in a circle to loud music and not smile."

"Sounds like a refined science."

"No doubt."

"What about after eating a massive pile of French fries?" I asked.

"There is potential for disaster there," he answered, but held in place in line. I guess we were gonna chance it.

We moved through the short line quickly, scoring two horses side by side on the second ride. Darius studied the horses around us.

"What is it?"

"I think they might have painted over my favorite."

"You have a favorite?" Oh my gosh. Cute alert.

He covered his eyes for a second. I hadn't thought Darius was the type to embarrass easily.

I peeled his hands back from his face. "Tell me about your favorite."

"It was the one I always rode with my grandfather. I know it sounds stupid, but it was black. The only black horse, and, honestly, it made me feel seen."

The image of a young Darius waiting in line, desperate to ride his favorite horse tugged at the most nostalgic parts of me.

"What if someone was already on it?"

"My grandfather would tell the operator we wanted to wait for that horse, and they usually let me sneak ahead of the crowd on the next ride to get settled before someone else took it. This one guy even stopped the carousel, so the horse was right at the entrance."

"That's sweet."

"It's that little kid magic, right? People love doing special things for little kids."

I sighed. "But we're big kids now."

"Don't think about Kierk."

"Who said I was?"

"Your face," he said with a laugh.

The bell rang, and the carousel shifted into motion. I tilted my head back and watched the mechanism above the horses lift them up and lower them again and again. The children around us laughed, and a few looked a little green. A light breeze greeted me as the music enveloped the ride.

Darius was right. It was impossible to ride a wooden horse in a circle to loud music with children and not smile. He caught my eye, and we laughed. When I looked back at him, though, neither of us looked away. The world behind him blurred.

It was me and Darius.

His gaze was like a rush of air, filling my chest until I felt so overwhelmed I couldn't breathe. When the horses slowed and the ride finally stopped, I looked away to climb down. My foot caught in the leather strap hanging from my horse. Darius held me by the waist while I freed myself.

"This is embarrassing," I joked. "I almost fell off this ride like a little kid."

My feet touched the ground, but Darius didn't let me go. His fingertips grazed the bare skin around my waist. When I lifted my head to look at him, his eyes locked on mine. I tried to think of something clever or silly to say to break the tension, but no words came. He leaned closer and licked his lips. My lungs stopped working.

The tips of our noses brushed. Darius tilted his head and pressed his lips against mine.

It was like the carousel exploded to life again. Blaring music. The essence of spinning. All of the good feelings life could offer. All wrapped up in that kiss.

He pulled away and asked, "Is this okay?" In response, I ran my thumb over his bottom lip and kissed him again.

The carousel bell rang, and we jumped apart. Everyone had exited the ride but us. The worker watched wide-eyed, and a few parents in line had covered their children's eyes.

Oops.

I buried my face in Darius's chest. "So embarrassing."

"We should go," he said with a laugh.

Hand in hand, we ran off the ride, laughing the whole way.

"Maybe that whole rule about public should come with nuance," I said.

"Smart," Darius nodded.

Mac waited for us at the exit. She stood, arms crossed, wearing an amused expression. "You do know you're not wearing masks here, right? People can see you."

"Very funny."

She hugged me. "I'm sorry about Kierk."

"Don't be too mad at him. He's looking out for Darius."

"Oh, I'm furious. He will not question my best friend like that. He's ready to apologize." Mac pointed toward the pizza shop. "He's over there on a bench."

"He doesn't have to—"

"D," she interrupted me and pointed to the bench more emphatically.

"Okay." I let Darius's fingers slip through mine. Going to talk to Kierk meant leaving him behind. Since Mac thought we were really dating, she hadn't realized that had been our first kiss—the first time his beautiful lips had touched mine. I glanced over my shoulder to see Mac chatting animatedly with Darius, but his eyes were on me. I turned away again before he could see my satisfied smile.

————

I found Kierk waiting exactly where Mac had said he'd be. I was a few feet away before he noticed me. I held out the ice cream cone I'd picked up for him. "Peace offering."

"I'm good."

"I can't eat two."

He sighed and took the cone. "Thanks."

"I know it's not a milkshake, but it was the best I could do."

"I do like milkshakes," he said and licked the cone. "I think that was why the universe put me and Mac together."

"She makes a mean milkshake. Have you had her strawberry cheesecake one yet?"

He turned his head sideways to lick the base of the ice cream. "I haven't. Every time I go to her house for dinner with her and her dad, she makes a new flavor. We have a whole list we're working through."

We licked our respective cones in silence for a minute.

"Look," we both said at the same time, and then laughed.

"I'm sorry for what I said," Kierk said. "Both Mac and Darius have made it painfully clear I was out of line."

"You care about your friend. I'm glad because honestly, he needs people looking out for him right now. Would you believe me if I said I'm looking out for him?"

He squinted at me. "That's an odd way to describe a relationship."

I didn't respond, mostly because he was right, and maybe I had wanted to give him a hint that he could turn over in that philosophical brain of his.

"You asked about my work at the carnival. Honestly, when Darius and I first met, he offered me the opportunity to work on some art projects there, and I'm excited about them."

"At least you're honest."

"I try to be."

"You're not out to hurt him?"

"I can assure you that I will not be hurting Darius."

He bit into his cone with a crunch. "Nobody can promise that. In relationships, people get hurt."

I knew that from experience. Unfortunately. "It won't be intentional."

"I guess that has to be good enough," Kierk said and polished off his cone.

"You mean it?"

He shrugged. That might have been as good as I was gonna get.

"I'm glad you feel that way because I need a favor."

Kierk raised an eyebrow at me.

"I get it. Our—" I pointed back and forth between us because I wasn't sure exactly what to call us. Maybe friends? "Is a bit tenuous, but this is for Darius."

"Go on."

"Could you talk to his mom for me? I'd love a picture of him from when he was little. Or a couple of pictures even."

"A picture of Darius as a kid? Why?"

I glanced at the carousel across the water, spinning on its axis, the horses smoothly galloping up and down. "I need a picture of him riding the carousel with his grandfather. I want to recreate his favorite horse in the Carnivalesque carousel."

Kierk studied me, a slow grin spreading across his face. "You'd do that for him?"

I blushed, and Kierk laughed.

"You could have led with that hours ago, and it would have prevented this whole thing."

"Glad I won you over," I said, finishing the last bite of my cone.

"That guy is a giggling child for a carousel ride. You should have seen him convincing the board we had to buy it."

"I would have loved that. So, can you get the picture?"

He looped his arm around my shoulders while we walked to the bridge over the pond where we'd agreed to meet Mac and Darius. "I got you."

When Darius came into view, he was grinning at us—his best friend and fake girlfriend finally getting along. And that grin—deep breath. I was going to paint the hell out of that horse until it was absolute perfection, and I couldn't wait to see the look on his face when he saw it.

THIRTEEN

AS THE SUN SET, the bright lights of the park painted the scenery, twinkling over the edges of the rides and buildings, creating the ultimate view from the tops of the coasters. The crowd had thinned after the families left the park to put their kids to bed. With the shorter lines, Kierk and Darius convinced us to explore the park their way.

Coaster after coaster after coaster.

"Fine," Mac said. "But I'm not puking."

"Where's the fun in that?" Darius teased.

Darius hadn't kissed me since the carousel, so I selfishly hoped that nobody would be puking. Not exactly the kind of thing that elicited desire.

"Thunderbolt first," Darius declared and then whispered to me, "we're going to ride it again and again until you forget ever riding it with the other one."

Part of me wanted to reply that if he kissed me in line for the Thunderbolt the way he'd kissed me on the carousel, forgetting Todd would *not* be a challenge. We'd been in public all day and that had meant—according to our rules—his hands were always holding mine, grazing my waist, pulling me close to him, or rubbing my shoulders. I blamed the nonstop touching for the flutters in my stomach.

The four of us played rock, paper, scissors in the short line and boarded in about five minutes.

"The line's so short," Kierk said. "This is going to be like two years ago."

"No," Darius insisted.

"What happened two years ago?" Mac asked.

Kierk raised his arms into the air as the coaster rolled out of the station. "You're about to find out."

We thudded around the wooden track. The bends whipped us around so fast that I slid across the seat and into Darius's side. He didn't even flinch.

"Don't worry," he said. "You're a lot smaller than Kierk. He always makes me sit on the outside."

When the ride halted, my hair tangled around my face in a massive knot. Mac's strawberry blonde curls were wilder than ever. The guys pulled us out of the cars and we ran back to the line, demanding answers about what had happened two years earlier. Kierk smirked at Darius who threatened him to be quiet or else.

Our attention was so focused on learning the details that we didn't notice Todd in line a few people in front of us.

"He-who-shall-not-be-named," Mac whispered.

Todd caught my eye and nodded. I looked away and leaned into Darius.

"You okay?" he whispered.

"Yep," I lied. I'd woken up that morning expecting to see Todd. I'd known it was coming but something about seeing Todd in line for the ride that we'd ridden together a year earlier—deep breath. I mean, could it have been fate? My parents and his parents and even Todd argued that we were meant to be together. I had believed it for years. Was us standing near each other in this line some hint from the universe?

Oh my gosh. What was the tradition of the Kennywood doing to me?

I shook any thoughts of reconciling with Todd out of my head. It was all his game. He'd shown up here with another girl just to mess with me.

I laughed at the irony. A year earlier, I'd watched him with another girl, wishing he was my boyfriend. Now, he was watching me with another guy, probably wishing the same thing.

"Is he with Em?" Kierk muttered.

I clenched my fist and urged my body not to turn in his direction for visual confirmation that he and Em were together.

Darius rubbed the back of his neck. "You're right. This might be like two years ago after all."

"Okay, now you have to tell us," Mac insisted.

But we'd gotten to the front of the line. The last four riders to slip through, our seat options were limited. Todd and Em had taken the back seat and the only open space was right in front of them.

"God has the popcorn out tonight," Darius joked.

As the smaller rider, I climbed into the seat first. Darius tapped his toes and fidgeted, his energy completely different than it had been on our last ride.

"You okay?" I whispered.

"Great."

Clearly not true but I couldn't ask questions with them right behind us. Maybe we should have said we wanted the front seat and waited for the next ride, except I'd already given Todd too much control over my life. I'd ride the roller coaster on my own terms.

"Darius," I whispered again, and he leaned closer to me. "Kiss me."

His eyes widened, but I didn't have to tell him a second time. He kissed me with as much passion as he had on the carousel, not stopping until the car jerked into motion.

As the car soared down the first hill, he said, "You know how to distract a guy."

He knew how to make a girl forget everyone else.

————

I floated in our pool Tuesday morning trying, and failing, not to replay and analyze every moment of the day before. After the Thunderbolt ride of horror, Todd had glared at Darius before stomping away.

"Nobody's puked yet," Kierk had said to lighten the mood. "Again!"

We'd boarded with a little less enthusiasm, but once the car had left the station, our laughter had returned. We'd ridden coasters until our heads spun and then finished the night off with the carousel to honor Darius's family tradition.

When we'd walked through the tunnel, hand-in-hand, holding boxes of fudge and cotton candy to take home, I hadn't wanted to leave.

Like usual, the daylight shown on a reality I'd done my best to ignore the night before. My Kennywood day—and my Kennywood kiss—had been with my *fake* boyfriend. Maybe I could tell my mom the truth, and she would break ties with the Wilkinsons until Todd and I graduated. Then, I could "break up" with Darius and find someone to have *real* experiences with.

I dipped my hand in the water and spun my float around. Breaking up with Darius would set off more social media harassment for both of us. Everyone would speculate why I'd done it, landing on the inevitable conclusion that he'd cheated, especially since he was away the next three days visiting family in Erie. And I would be confirmed as the idiot who shouldn't have given him a chance.

I couldn't do that to him. Or me for that matter.

Movement on the second-floor balcony of Todd's house caught my attention. Her morning coffee in hand, Mrs. Wilkinson waved and called out a greeting. I waved back. Todd appeared next to her, but he didn't wave. He telepathically yelled at me for kissing Darius right in front of him the day before—or something like that. I spun my float again until I couldn't see his house.

The clock above the pool read 9:15 a.m. Slowest. Day. Ever. When Mac had first started going to the carnival around Christmas time the year before, she'd told me that sometimes the week felt like a waiting game, like she wasn't living until the weekend came around and she could go to the carnival again. The weekdays were the desert; the weekend, a cold glass of milkshake.

Darius hadn't found me a helper for the carousel project yet. Everyone was already committed to other projects for the week, and I hadn't had time to finalize my plans since the week before had been designated for the bumper cars touchups. I splashed out of the pool and dried off enough to click around on my laptop on the poolside table. I sketched some of my favorite horse designs, embellishing to honor the carnival's style and adding masks to honor the ultimate rule of Carnivalesque.

By noon, I had three horses sketched, a rumble of hunger in my stomach, and no new notifications from Darius. He probably just arrived in Erie and had a lot of family to greet.

But he hadn't messaged me the whole ride when he'd been in the car with nothing to do.

Maybe he drove. Yes. He wouldn't make his mom drive. He would offer. And he wouldn't be able to drive and text. I wouldn't want him to.

My stomach rumbled again.

Dry from sitting in the heat for hours sketching, I headed for the kitchen sans towel to find Todd sitting at the table with my father. My mom made them sandwiches at the kitchen island. I stared at her.

"You know what, honey," she said to my father. "Maybe you can work with Todd in the office, and I'll bring your sandwiches as soon as they're ready."

"Hello, Dinah," Todd said.

Why was he always there? I grabbed an apple and banana from the counter. "I'll eat by the pool. I'm working on some sketches." I hoped that would give everyone the message I didn't want to be bothered, especially by Todd.

I ate, sketched, and checked my phone more than I should have. I shouldn't miss my fake boyfriend. One of our rules had been if we needed space, we could ask for it, but the last thing I'd wanted was to be away from him.

From images online and pictures I'd taken of Kennywood's carousel, I designed ten of the carnival's twelve horses. I'd give myself a day before looking at them with fresh eyes to make any changes.

The last two horses would be side by side, with special tribute designs. One after Darius's favorite horse as a kid and the other after my favorite horse—the one I'd been leaning against when we had our first kiss.

FOURTEEN

DARIUS RETURNED from Erie late Thursday night. I'd spent the day at Kennywood, sketching "my" horse and mastering the colors so we could replicate it for the carnival carousel. I'd also ridden the carousel way too many times and sketched the coloring and designs for some of my other favorite horses. I expected—no, hoped—to see Darius that night, but he said he was tired from the drive.

The next morning, he was tired, too.

That afternoon, he had to handle something at the carnival.

That's why he's your fake boyfriend, I told myself. He didn't *have* to come and see me.

With all of my sketches complete until Kierk got me the childhood pics I'd asked for, I reverted to my watercolor portraits. Of Darius. Not because I was thinking about him too much or anything. I'd sketched him so many times that my notebook was filled with Darius sketches, perfect for practicing watercolors.

I'd worked my way to my third sketch when footsteps on the basement stairs shook me from my artist zone.

"Knock, knock," Darius said.

I couldn't stop blinking. "You're here?"

He laughed. "Did you miss me?"

"Shut up."

He bit his lip. "I missed you."

"Dinah?" my mom called from the top of the stairs.

"Yeah, mom?"

"Do you two need anything to eat?"

I glanced at Darius. He shook his head.

"We're good. Thanks, Mom."

I draped a cover over the watercolor portrait of him and sealed my paints. "Everything good at the carnival?"

"I was working on a new exhibit, and I thought you could be the first to see it."

"Sounds fun," I said. "Let me change."

Darius stepped in front of me, blocking my path to the stairs. "Is everything okay?"

Okay? Sure. If okay means kissing you at Kennywood leaving me confused and thinking this might be real for a minute—not that I would say that.

I took a deep breath, reminding myself what this was—a mutually beneficial, fake dating situation. Darius was fun and attractive, and that should be enough for now—until he got his reputation sorted, and I managed to expel Todd from my kitchen on weekday lunch breaks.

"Sorry," I said. "I was kind of lost in my painting."

"Can I see it?"

"It's not ready." I squeezed his hand. "But I'll let you know when it is."

The car ride to the carnival was like a reset button. By the time we parked—in the parade lot this time—the earlier awkwardness had faded.

"You ready, *Diamond*?" he asked.

I groaned.

"What?"

"I hate my carnival name. It's so pretentious. Mac—excuse me, Sparx suggested it, and if I would have known how much time I'd be spending here, I would have thought about it a lot more."

"You can change it," he suggested.

"It's not just that. It's hard to call Mac Sparx and you Harvey, and Kierk, nobody ever calls him Soren."

"Yeah," Darius said. "His carnival name kind of stuck. Tell you what, if we're alone in the carnival, call me Darius or Harvey or whatever. And I'll call you D or Dinah. Deal?"

It sounded like a plan, at least until I could decide on a different name.

"Deal."

Walking to the building, Darius spun me and pulled me to him. "I can't wait to show you this surprise."

"Did you make a milkshake dumping exhibit to get revenge?"

His eyes widened behind his mask. "I like the way you think, but no." Hand in hand, we weaved through the back hallways of the carnival. "As you know from experience, the carnival is massive. There are rooms everywhere, and when someone on the committee has an idea for an exhibit, especially one that doesn't cost much money or take a lot of prep work, usually we can make it happen pretty easily. The bonus is that people on the committee can kind of suggest exhibits that might impress someone they know or like."

Like a fake girlfriend.

Kierk had done that for Mac once. When she'd told

Kierk she loved climbing, he'd installed an intense climbing wall far above the parade floor with twinkle lights and glow-in-the-dark climbing suits. All to impress my best friend. I asked Darius if this was like that.

"Oh no," he said, scanning his band to open a door otherwise closed to carnival goers. "Not like that at all. That cost a fortune, but Kierk held the purse strings and was smitten but too afraid to admit it."

"It worked," I said remembering how Mac had kissed Kierk the first time that night.

Darius pressed his lips against my ear. "I hope it works again."

Tingles trickled down my back. I closed my eyes. *So your fake boyfriend is crazy hot. Enjoy it. Don't overthink it.*

"We have to hurry though," Darius said. "First stop is the shop, so you can pick out whatever you want."

"Ooh! I want blue hair. Mac always does blue hair."

"Done. Anything else?"

"I want to try a yellow mask."

"Blue hair and yellow mask coming up." He glanced at his watch. "The exhibit opens to the rest of the carnival in forty minutes. We have just enough time to get in and out before that."

"You mean we get a sneak peek?"

"Girl," Darius said. "It's your exhibit."

I kissed his cheek. "Let's run then."

Hand in hand, we ran through the carnival to the shop. He grabbed the blue hairpiece and yellow mask, calling to the staff to put the purchases on his account.

"You do not have an account," I teased.

"You're right. Occasional accessories are part of my perks."

We stopped by a Welcome Room, and he helped me work the hairpiece into my ponytail. I weaved the blue around my own hair color until all you could see was the new look. We secured the mask under the ponytail and set off again.

Darius tugged me to a stop in front of a door that had paint splattered all over it. "We're here."

"Interesting paint job," I said.

"Gets better inside." He swiped his band once more and the door opened to a room where the floor, ceiling, and walls had all been painted black. Three Carnivalesque staff members in the uniform of black shirts and masks greeted us with ponchos.

"You ready?"

"Are we painting a mural on this black wall?"

"Not a mural." His smile couldn't be contained as he handed me a plastic tray of the most random items ever.

"Water balloons, water guns, and paintbrushes?"

He lifted one of the water guns and pulled the trigger. Bright orange paint splattered the walls.

"The water balloons are filled with paint?" I asked.

In response, he tossed one at the wall, and bright blue paint exploded. Oh my gosh.

"You wanna try?"

So much yes. I took a pink balloon and squealed as I released it and let it splatter. "That felt amazing."

"Right! That's the brilliant part about the exhibit. We can repaint it black as many times as we want."

"Did you design this?"

"I hung the walls and painted everything. Installed the hooks for the canvases too."

"You're so crafty. Are you sure you don't want to own your own construction company or something? You could specialize in unique playrooms or something. For adults and kids."

He slowly smiled and nodded. "I like that. You might be on to something."

"You're welcome," I said. "What are the brushes for?"

"We have tubs of paint people can buy and use the brushes to splatter on the canvases, too," one of the staffers said.

"But you, my dear," Darius said, "can choose any paint you want for free."

I kissed his cheek. "Pays to be connected."

He mock gasped. "Don't say that in front of Kierk."

I glared at him.

"Too soon?"

I pointed my paint gun at his chest, and he raised his arms in surrender.

"Point taken."

"We have about fifteen minutes, Harvey."

"Better get to it then." He pointed out a canvas for me.

"We just shoot it?"

"Sure." He sprayed his canvas with a mix of red, orange, and yellow.

"But what if I don't get the paint where I want it?" I stood as close as I could and pulled the trigger. Purple paint splattered in bright dots across the black canvas.

"It's not supposed to be a meticulous landscape," Darius said. "It's more of a try and see approach."

Try and see, huh? He swapped the guns around, spraying way too much paint until it became a brownish mix, dripping in massive globs onto the floor. The resulting art looked worse than finger paintings my parents had saved from my preschool days, but the smile on his face while his paint splattered—that I could respect.

He caught me staring. "You're not painting."

Properly scolded, I turned my attention back to my own canvas. "I don't know what to paint yet."

Darius raised the gun in his left hand and sprayed my canvas.

I gasped. "What are you doing? This is mine."

"Then paint it."

"Fine."

His teal paint had mixed beautifully with the purple. I took the gun from his hand. Double fisting my little plastic painting tools, I sprayed both at the same time. I didn't want so much paint that it would drip. A few drips, sure, but not the waterfall that was Darius's painting.

Darius reached for one of my guns, but I playfully slapped his hand. "Stop rushing me. I'm trying to decide."

"Decide what?"

"If I have enough paint in the upper left corner or if it needs another spray."

Without shifting his gaze from mine, he reached for one of the water balloons in his tray.

"You wouldn't!"

He grinned and launched the balloon. It soared wide of my canvas, but a few bright blue splatters found their way to my painting. I turned my gun on him and fired.

Darius gasped and raised his hands to protect his face. "I missed on purpose. I surrender."

I didn't.

I swept all of the guns off our trays and pointed as many as I could at him, spraying a mix of red, yellow, and blue onto his poncho, but the plastic couldn't fully protect him.

"That's it," he said, reaching for the last water balloon.

"No!" I looked around for cover, but there was none. The carnival staffers had rushed out of the room when they saw the writing on the wall—pun intended—and slammed the door. That left me and Darius alone in the once pristine space with nothing but paint and a thirst for vengeance. "Harvey, stop!"

"Wish I could, but I have paint in my eye."

"Let me get you a paper towel," I offered.

"Get yourself one." He tackled me.

I tried to squirm free and swat the balloon out of his hand, but it popped and rained blue paint. All over my face.

"Stop!" I laughed and spit out a mouthful of blue. Fortunately, my eyes had been spared.

"Stay still. I can scoop most of the paint off your poncho." He scuffled around the room, retrieving wet wipes. A few seconds later, we were relatively clean, our ponchos were in the trash, and the room was back in action with the first splatter painters, other than us, paying for their supplies and claiming their spots.

"Your painting is epic," Darius said, pulling it loose from the hooks and moving it to the drying shelves.

"It's boring," I said. "It has two colors, but I had no idea of what to paint or how."

"We can come back any time."

Not sure it would matter.

"Can I tell you a secret?"

"I expect you to tell me all of your secrets," I teased.

"I like being in public with you."

I liked being in public with him, too. In public, I could run my fingers along his forearms, kiss his cheek, and openly flirt with him. When we were alone, all of those actions, not to mention the long gazes, became complicated. Were they happening because we'd gotten in the habit of them? Or because of simple attraction?

Or was it something more? Something that could derail this whole thing? What is it that I'd told him before this all started? *If at any moment this becomes real for either of us, we have to say so. Right away.*

The good news was Darius liked being in public with

me, hopefully for the same reasons I liked being in public with him. Only one way to know for sure.

I caught his eye and tilted my head to the side as flirtatiously as I could manage. "Why's that?"

He rewarded me with a grin, but didn't stop there. He stepped closer and lifted his paint-splattered hand to my cheek. I closed my eyes and leaned into his touch. The tip of his nose brushed mine, our masks catching slightly.

"We haven't done this before," he whispered.

"Was it so bad that you've forgotten?"

"No," he said emphatically. "I meant in the carnival. Where people know us and are watching us. Kind of ironic that we're masked here but more on display than being the center of attention at Kennywood."

"Harvey?"

"Yeah?"

"Will you please shut up and kiss me?"

"So demanding."

I grabbed the front of his paint-splattered shirt and pulled him to me, our lips crashing against each other. He gripped my hips, steadying us both, so that his soft mouth could do its work. And oh my gosh could it work.

The room erupted in applause so loud, we both startled.

"When did all these people get here?" he joked.

I pressed my mouth against his ear, so he could hear me over the crowd. "No idea. I was a little distracted."

More people flooded through the doors until the staff stopped them because the room was at capacity.

"We should go," Darius suggested, and at a perfect time since a few seconds later, someone shouted, "Is that Harvey with a new girl?"

"Definitely," I said.

He took my hand and pulled me through the crowd to our next carnival adventure—or mishap.

FIFTEEN

AT THE STARLIGHT CAFE, we got in line for burgers and fries and drew the attention of everyone around us because of the smears of paint across our skin. Darius told anyone who asked about the splatter paint exhibit. By their reactions, I expected it to be busy all night.

"Thank you for the exhibit," I said.

"You're welcome. It was a sacrifice."

"Getting splattered with paint?"

"No. Coming here last night and this morning to work on it instead of spending time with you." He stepped up to the counter to order leaving me to turn his words over in my head. He did that a lot.

Once we were settled in at a table under the stars, he asked about my carousel progress.

"Can I see the sketches?"

"Absolutely not," I said.

He groaned. "You're playing."

"I'm not. Did you find me a helper so I can start Monday?"

"Tuesday," he said. "The head of the art department has

it under control. He insisted. No pressure or anything, but I can't wait to see it."

I pointed at him with a french fry. "If you want it finished, you'll keep your promise."

He crossed his heart. We people watched for a few minutes. Nobody launched themselves, milkshakes, or water balloons at Darius.

"Things have been relatively quiet on social media, don't you think?" I asked.

"Positive thinking or calm before the storm?"

I shrugged. "I guess time will tell. I'll work on the carousel exhibit next week, and we can decide after that."

"Decide?"

"Yeah," I said, dipping a fry in ketchup. "Whether we need to keep, you know, or what."

"Has Todd left you alone?"

"Not exactly."

Darius looked around and then leaned close. "So we agree. At least one more week of fake dating."

"Agreed."

He smiled. A lot. In fact, I'd guess he even went to sleep that night with a smile on his face. I know I did.

———

I did not wake up with a smile, though. I woke up to Todd leaning over me.

I pulled the covers around every part of me, which luckily had already been covered. "What are you doing here?"

Without answering, he set his phone on the bed next to me.

"Seriously, Todd, just because your family has a key to

my house doesn't mean you're invited to use it. You need to leave."

"Look at the phone."

I pressed my fingertips to the bridge of my nose.

"Please, D."

"Fine." I picked up the phone and oriented myself to the image, recognizing the splatters of paint on the black wall first. Two people with paint all over their clothes wrapped their arms around each other in the foreground, kissing like nobody else was around. I recognized Darius immediately, but I was surprised at how little I'd looked like myself. Our playful makeover in the shop had obviously had an effect. I smiled at the memory of Darius's fingers tangling in my hair and his soft, confident kiss.

"This is what I was trying to warn you about," Todd said.

Warn me? His words and this whole show of sneaking into my house to wake me up didn't compute. "About what exactly?"

"Darius. He can't be trusted."

Oh. He didn't think it was me in the photo. I scrolled to the caption and saw he wasn't alone. Whoever had snuck a phone into the carnival and taken the shot had thought the same thing. So had the commenters, who happened to also be the usual offenders.

"Todd, go home."

He swiped his phone off the bed and stood. "I can't believe you. You give me all this crap for talking to another girl, but with Darius—"

"Stop. Just stop."

Todd crossed his arms and shut his mouth.

"I'm going to say this one more time, and we are never having this conversation again. I know that you cheated on me. I saw it with my own eyes. I know it was not *talking* to one girl. You know it, too. The lies pouring from your mouth aren't going to change what I know. Please stop lying about it. It makes any kind of closure for us, our families, and the friendship we've had our entire lives impossible. Stop lying to me. Stop trying to paint a picture of some reality with you as the victim. That reality doesn't exist." I snuggled back against my pillow. "There's more to say about it, but that's enough for now because it's six o'clock in the morning, and I'm tired."

"And what about the picture?"

"It's kind of hot. I'm glad you showed me."

"What?" Todd shook his head and paced the room. "Who are you?"

"Me? Who am I? I'm the girl in the picture."

He rolled his eyes. "Now who's lying?"

"You know. The last thing I should have to do is prove anything to you, but I want to go back to bed. He created a new exhibit for me—paint splattering. I pointed to his phone. We snuck inside before it officially opened and created that." I pointed to the corner of my bedroom where my splattered canvas was up against the wall. "If you look closely, you'll see that exact canvas is in the photo behind us."

"It doesn't even look like you," Todd said, confusion etched across his face.

"That would be because I went to the shop and had fun playing dress up at the beginning of the night, yet another surprise from Darius. And after everything he did for me, people like you continue to drag him through the mud."

Todd opened his mouth, but in a miraculous turn of events, no words came out.

"Go home." I rolled over and pulled the covers up to my neck. "And when it comes to Darius, just don't anymore."

I waited for the soft click of my bedroom door before I

sighed and reached for my phone. If Darius hadn't seen the post, I'd have to be the one to break the news. He'd been right about us being overly optimistic. It had been a matter of time—not much time—before the haters attacked him again.

———

We opted for takeout for lunch to avoid another public appearance. After we finished our sandwiches and cleaned up the kitchen, Darius and I escaped to the basement where he immediately relaxed into the couch and started scrolling on his phone.

"What are you doing?" I asked him.

"I'm looking for places to volunteer."

I snuggled next to him. "Why?"

"I need to go to places, do good things, take pictures, and post them on social media."

"Tell me you're not serious."

"None of this is getting better. In fact, it's getting worse."

"You think it's going to make it better to exploit the poor for your reputation? You think that's going to make social media kinder to you?"

"I have to do something, not just for me but for you, too. Right now, they think I've duped you into this relationship, but when you continue to spend time with me after all of this is out online, then they're going to target you, too. Right now, it's either you bring me up, or I bring you down."

"If you weren't so good at pissing off Todd and getting my parents to stop pressuring me about him, a third option might be appealing."

"Thanks for the compliment."

"You can't just volunteer at a food bank and benefit

from that. You have to have a meaningful relationship with your volunteer work."

He set down his phone. "Keep talking."

"Something you're passionate about. What means something to you?"

"Animals."

"Great! Like zoo animals?"

"Pets," he said with a nod. "I've been thinking about becoming a vet."

"Wow," I said.

He shrugged, and I wondered how someone like him could lack confidence in anything.

"People love their pets," I said, trying to steer us back to the present predicament. "That's great. What about an animal shelter?"

"I see where you're going with this, but it's definitely easier to stack cans at the food bank than to shovel shit at the animal shelter."

"I can see how that would be easier. But, um, not gonna have the desired outcome."

"Your snark is on full display today."

"And is it a beautiful display?"

"A work of art," he joked.

"I do love my art."

"Fine! I'll volunteer at the animal shelter, but you're coming with me."

"What? No. My volunteer work is standing at the museum to make sure no kids touch the paintings."

He shook his head. "Nope. We do it together, and it looks like you've influenced me into being a better person and all that. You've brought me up."

"I did kind of though. I don't have to volunteer by your side for that."

"Yes, you do," he insisted.

"No, I don't. Have you been a part of this conversation?"

"If you're not there, who's going to take pics for my social media?"

"Literally anyone with a phone."

"Diney."

"Don't," I said. Talk about the most annoying nickname ever.

"Diney diners."

Somehow, he'd proven me wrong. "Stop!"

"Diney diners dine dine," Darius said, testing my patience even more.

"Fine!"

He clapped his hands. "I also have a question. Something I've been thinking about from last night. Did you not like the exhibit?"

I pulled his phone out of his hands and held them instead. "I loved it. Why would you think I didn't like it?"

"You seemed so tense. Not sure what to paint. Frustrated even."

"That wasn't about the exhibit."

Darius ran his fingers over the back of my neck, tickling my skin and relaxing me. "What was it about?"

I closed my eyes and relished the peaceful rhythm of his caress. I laid my head on his chest and stayed like that long enough to hear my parents' footsteps stop above me, meaning they'd cleaned up everything in the kitchen and headed to the front porch for iced tea and neighborhood watching.

"D?" Darius nudged.

"I want to be an artist."

"You *are* an artist."

"Not really."

"I'm missing something," he said.

"Artists see the world in unique ways. They create art that helps other people see and feel the world, too."

Darius waited, but I couldn't find any other words to make sense of how I'd been feeling about my art lately.

"You don't think your art makes people feel something."

"It's not my art. That's the thing." I pointed to the boxes of canvases that lined the painting studio section of the basement. "Everything I've painted has been based off a tutorial or video—someone else's vision."

"You're still the one who painted it," Darius argued.

"It's all derivative. If I want to be an artist, I need to look at a canvas like the ones we had last night and see something other people can't see."

"We were painting with squirt guns. That's not exactly high art."

"An artist would still look at a canvas, even with a different style like splatter painting, and see something. All I saw was—nothing, I guess."

"So you want to make a work of art that isn't from a photo or a tutorial but something from your own vision."

"Yes."

Darius pushed the hair back from my face. "You will."

"You don't know that."

"I do."

I tried to smile.

"In the meantime, we have some cages to clean."

I'd rather splatter paint for sure.

SIXTEEN

WITH THE START of the school year taunting us on the August calendar, I spent a lazy Monday morning poolside— my last day before locking myself in the windowless carousel room to paint the exhibit. The sun warmed my skin while I lounged on my favorite float, dipping my toe into the cool water when the rays became too much and when the water spun me to face Todd's bedroom window.

"Haven't seen you out here in a while," Mom said. "You've been busy."

"Is that a passive aggressive comment or an observation?"

My mom untied her coverup and lowered herself into the water. "An observation."

Better than the alternative, but I wasn't one hundred percent sure I believed her.

"Any plans for the day?" she asked.

"Are you asking if I'm seeing Darius?"

"You were a little grumpy while he was away, so as your mother, I'm curious, but can we also have a conversation

without you assuming there is an ulterior motive to everything I'm saying?"

I sighed. "Sorry."

"I get it, Dinah. We love Todd. We always have, and
yes, part of me thought you two would be one of those
couples who had grown up best friends, gotten married, and
lived happily ever after."

"We were never best friends. It was always me caring
more about him than he did about me and him taking advantage of that when we finally went out."

Mom swam around the pool, kicking ever so gently. "Is
that why you broke up?"

"Mom…"

"I know you didn't tell us the whole truth, and maybe
it's too weird, but I'm your mother. Before anything else. I
want you to know that." She spun my float, so I was facing
her and gave me a puppy dog face that intensified every few
seconds until I laughed and rolled my eyes.

"I got it. Thanks, Mom."

She pulled me around the pool by my feet like she had
when I was five years old. "So…do you have anything to
tell your mother who loves you?"

"This feels a little heavy handed."

She just smiled and kept pulling me.

The sound of someone calling, "Hello?" from the back
porch saved me. Kierk appeared on the deck and waved.

"Hey," I called. "Come on down."

"Who's this?" my mom asked.

I introduced my mom to Kierk.

"Mackenzie's boyfriend, right? You're the head of the
carnival," Mom said.

"Not exactly, but I help with a lot of things."

What Kierk didn't say was that his father was the official head of the carnival, which is a piece of information not

many people knew. I wasn't even sure if he knew that I knew.

"I have to admit, I didn't allow Dinah to go at first, but now that I know more about it, well, you've done a good thing."

"Thank you, ma'am."

"Dinah's excited about the carousel project."

Kierk patted the envelope in his hands. "That's why I'm here."

"I'll let you two chat and get some lunch started. Kierk, can I make you a sandwich?"

He politely declined. Twice. Until my mother finally convinced him he wasn't leaving without food in his stomach. I dried off and opened the umbrella for the table next to the pool—both to give us shade and to ensure Todd couldn't spy on us from his bedroom, if he was even home.

"What did you find?"

Kierk grinned. "Everything. Apparently riding the carousel in Darius's family is such a tradition that they have photos of him riding with his grandfather every year of his life." Kierk handed me a stack of photos. "His mom said you can keep these. They're copies."

"She won't tell him?"

"No. She thinks what her son's new girlfriend is doing for him is sweet."

I couldn't decide if I was happy for winning brownie points with Darius's mom or terrified she would learn our relationship was fake and despise me. A worry for another time. I opened the envelope and slid the photographs out onto my hands.

"Oh my gosh."

The first one showed Darius sitting on the black horse he'd told me about. He held tight to the pole, pressing his cheek to it and smiling wide, revealing a mouthful of white baby teeth. He wore a striped polo that matched his grandfather's. His grandfather managed to look even happier than him.

Darius grew up in the photos, which had been in chronological order. In the last one, I guessed him to be about ten years old.

"His grandfather died that year," Kierk said.

"Have you always known each other?"

"Fortunately and unfortunately," he joked, but anyone could see how dedicated he was to his friend and vice versa. "We go way back to kids playing basketball on the playground."

"Like me and Mac, except we weren't playing basketball. We carried around tiny notebooks and pretended to interview everyone for the big story we were working on."

He shook his head. "Sounds like her."

"Once…" I laughed so hard, I could barely continue the story. "We told an elderly woman in her neighborhood that an asteroid had struck a few blocks away and asked if she wanted to comment on how the blast felt."

"No, you didn't."

"We had no idea how awful something like that could turn out. The woman grabbed her chest and had to hold onto the porch railing until she collapsed onto a chair."

Kierk's eyes were like baseballs.

"Just when we thought we'd killed her, she shot upright and asked if we wanted her to play along or not."

Kierk practically fell out of his chair laughing.

"You'd think something like that would slow Mac down," I said.

"No way. I bet she kept right on."

"She always did."

Kierk knew that from experience.

Changing the subject, he pointed to the photos. "So what are you going to do with these? Will they work?"

I looked closer at the horse in the pictures. They'd been taken from different angles each year, giving me a variety of details. "I think I can recreate the horse's design from these. I might miss a few colors here and there, but overall, it should be close."

"Not to be a hater, but do you think he'll recognize the horse?"

"He better!"

I'd have to think of a way to make sure of it. Otherwise, I was setting myself up for disappointment.

———

The quiet carnival during the week suited me more than the overcrowded version on the weekends. Tuesday morning, I slipped into the carousel room with a rolling suitcase of every chemical and tool I'd need to restore my masterpiece to its original glory. Fortunately, the company Carnivalesque had bought it from had already done a lot of the work. After all, I did not have the seven years it took the massive team of conservationists to restore the Coney Island carousel. I had two weeks, tops.

The twelve-horse ride sat still in the space—a blank canvas waiting to be painted. I pulled the sketches from my bag and placed them around the carousel, matching them to the horse I'd selected for that particular design. I planned to keep the last two to myself for a while in case anyone spilled details to Darius or he couldn't help himself and snuck in for a peek. Every horse leading up to the final two would refine my skills.

It could be great. Or an epic fail.

"Good morning!" Em stepped into the room with a cup

of coffee in her manicured hands and a smile on her mask-less face.

"Good morning," I said slowly.

"I figured we could drop the masks since we know each other, and painting the kind of detail we'll have to paint will be nearly impossible without peripheral vision."

I swallowed some acid from my stomach. "We?"

"I'm your helper!"

SEVENTEEN

"DARIUS SAID that the art director would be assigning someone. Someone from the art department."

"Last minute change," Em clarified. "I'm sure you don't mind."

On the contrary, her grin told me she was sure I would mind.

"I've taken several painting classes, and my cousin is an artist in New York. I've assisted her on some projects. I even studied color theory, which the *art director* thought would be helpful for a project like this."

So she was qualified, maybe even more qualified than me.

"Look. I get that I have history with your boyfriend, but that's ancient. I'm excited about this project."

"It didn't feel ancient when we were in line for the Thunderbolt," I blurted.

"Is that why you two made out in front of us on the ride? To make some claim or something?"

I crossed my arms. "I kissed him because he's my boyfriend."

She nodded with that smug grin of hers.

"What about you?" I challenged.

"Oh I assure you I'm way over Darius."

"Because you're with Todd now. Do you even know why the two of us broke up?"

"I know his side of the story."

I scoffed. "Does his side of the story involve him hooking up with another girl in my swimming pool while I watched from the bathroom window?"

The peak in her eyebrow told me it had not.

"You know what?" I said. "Forget it."

"Forget the guys, or forget working together on this project?"

I had two weeks to paint the entire carousel, and whether I liked it or not, Em was the help I had. I rolled my suitcase across the cement floor. "We don't talk about Darius at all. Or Todd. Deal?"

She extended her hand. "Deal."

I shook it and swung the bag onto a table to unload. "Our first step will be to prime it from top to bottom."

"It's already primed."

"Yes, but I don't know how many coats of primer it has or the quality of the primer, so we're priming again. Then we'll paint."

Em rolled up her sleeves and pulled her hair back.

"Darius—" I paused when I realized I'd already broken our deal. "To clarify, we can talk about Darius as he relates to the project but nothing personal."

She offered me an amused nod.

"Darius likes the carousel at Kennywood, so I took a few pics of the horses there for inspiration."

"You went to all that trouble? We could have found pics of random carousel horses online or painted them whatever colors we wanted."

"I did that too," I clarified. "But it's my version of a good time to ride the carousel at Kennywood about twenty times to find the right horses and take pics of them from every angle."

"I would have vomited," she mumbled. "Of course, if Darius was my boyfriend, I'd probably vomit about that, too."

"Em, I see Darius differently than you and every other girl in the Milkshake Mafia. He's different with me."

"Because you deserve respect and we didn't?"

"No. I don't know why." Except I kind of did. Our relationship wasn't real. There were no stakes between us. I couldn't hurt him, so he could be himself around me. And vice versa. "The carousel restoration is important to him, so it's important to me. And if it's not going to be important to you, maybe you shouldn't be here."

"I told you already I want to be here."

"Then show it," I snapped.

"Fine," she said through clenched teeth. "But remember that just because Darius didn't hurt you—yet—doesn't mean he hasn't hurt me and a bunch of other girls."

I took a deep breath and debated whether it was more important to have someone working with me who had skill or someone who didn't despise the person we were working to surprise. My phone buzzed with a message from Darius: *How's it going? You finish yet?*

I rolled my eyes and texted back: *Yes. Em and I are riding it now. Then we're going to paint each other's nails and sing Girl Scout songs together.*

Darius: *Em?*

Me: *She's my helper.*

My phone rang.

"She is not the helper I found for you."

I glanced at Em, who was already studying the sketches

I'd laid out around the carousel. "She's the one who showed up."

Darius made a noise that crossed between a groan and a growl.

"I'm guessing she's the type of person who goes after what she wants," I said.

What or *whom*.

"Do you want me to reassign her?"

"We have a tight deadline. If she can help me meet it, then she can stay."

"I'm sorry about this," Darius said. "If you'd let me help you, we could spend more time together."

Was he turning on his flirtatious side to benefit Em since he knew she was there with me, or did he mean it? Either way, I figured my best approach was to reciprocate.

"If you were here every day, how could I surprise you?"

"I could think of a few ways."

Oh my gosh. My cheeks had to be redder than the paint Em was mixing. Her raised eyebrows told me she probably noticed, too.

"I better get to work."

"Your call. Let me know if you change your mind. I'll be upstairs most of the day cleaning up a space and hanging drywall for a new exhibit."

I didn't know the committee had something new in the works already. "What's the exhibit?"

"No idea," he said. "Meet me for lunch?"

I glanced at Em who was clearly still listening to our conversation but doing her best to pretend otherwise. "Lunch is perfect."

I hung up the phone and sighed, not for Em's benefit but because it sort of came out.

"I mixed up some paints to match the photos. I'll seal them until we can finish the primer."

I studied the three colors she had in the works. The red had an orange hue, and a green blended a bright blue perfectly. "That's pretty good."

"Thanks." Her voice held a note of surprise. "I mixed paints for my cousin."

"You're good at it."

She gave me a sideways glance. I guess I couldn't blame her for being cautious, but I wouldn't withhold an honest compliment for someone who deserved it. It was about being who I wanted to be, not about her.

"Darius left the primer for us," I said, finding the cans under a table where he'd said they'd be. I pried a can open, dipped the wooden stick into it, and mixed while Em collected two brushes from my supply pile. Already, I could see she anticipated the needs of the project without being asked. I'd compliment her on it, but I didn't think she was ready to hear another kind word from me—at least not yet.

Instead, I thanked her for the brush, and we got to work on two horses that were side by side. After a few minutes, she suggested we play music to pass the time. I thought it might also be to fill the awkward silence. Either way, we alternated playlists and worked through ten of the twelve horses before a knock on the door startled me.

"That will be your lunch date," Em said.

I knew she was listening.

"We still have two more horses to prime," I said.

"I'll finish them up."

"You will?" I said, not able to hide my disbelief.

"What are assistants for?"

Darius knocked again.

"I can reschedule with him."

"Bring me back a sandwich, and we'll call it even," Em said. "The primer on the first horses we painted should be dry by now. Are you good with me starting the red-orange on that design?"

"Yes, but…"

"Have you tried that deli on Main Street? So good."

Was this the Twilight Zone?

"Go. Text me when you know where you're heading. By then I'll have this paint washed off my hands and can give you my order."

The hairs on my forearms were standing up from how nice she was being.

"I don't have your number," I said.

She smiled at me as sweetly as I imagined a snake in the grass would smile. "Darius has it."

I forced a fake smile, too. "Great."

Since the carousel hadn't changed any since the last time Darius had seen it and there was no surprise to ruin, I threw open the door and greeted him with a kiss that had him holding onto the doorframe for support. I didn't even look back to see if Em had watched the show.

Game on.

EIGHTEEN

BEFORE WE EVEN LEFT THE carnival, Darius asked, "What did she say to you?"

"I don't know what you mean?"

"You wanna run that kiss through your mind and try that lie again?"

I rolled my eyes. "I can't kiss you?"

"Girl, you can kiss me any time. Like, *any* time. But that was more than a kiss. That was a claim."

"Fine. She reminded me that you have her number."

"I don't have her number," he said with a straight face.

"Seriously?"

He shrugged. "Deleted."

I couldn't stop my massive grin.

"Is someone a little jealous?"

"Not anymore."

Darius laughed hard enough to lean against the wall. "You kill me."

We'd gotten too far from the carousel room to run back and get Em's number, although the look on her face when she found out Darius had deleted it would have been worth the trip. Instead, while he drove to the deli she'd recommended, I searched Em on social—an easy task considering how often she liked and commented on Darius's hashtag—and sent her a DM that I hoped she'd see before we had to order.

Darius parked behind the small building, dodging pedestrians along the way.

"I've never been here before," I said. Not a huge shock considering Mac and I lived in a different suburb of the city.

"You'll be back. I promise that."

The line ended around the side of the building but moved quickly. Darius chatted about his work on the exhibit upstairs from where I had been working on the carousel. I tried to pay attention. Like really tried, but he'd *emphatically* said I could kiss him *any* time.

Like now? What if I wanted to kiss him now? And all the time?

Breaking it down logically, kissing was fun. Scientifically, it did good things to the brain, although I couldn't remember from middle school health class exactly what. Watching Darius scroll through the deli menu on his phone, his eyes squinting in the sun, I wondered if kissing being fun and good for your brain had anything to do with what I was feeling.

"You know what you want?" he asked.

"Chicken salad sandwich on sour dough with lettuce, tomato, oni—" Better hold the onion. "Um, and provolone cheese."

He nodded and tucked his phone into his pocket. "They have this Cajun Reuben I always get."

"When will you finish the exhibit?" I asked.

"The room was pretty wrecked. Beat up floorboards, holes in the walls, the works. Prepping a space for a new exhibit isn't my favorite, but it's paid. Tuition and books aren't cheap."

"No." I sometimes forgot Darius would be heading back to college soon, as a sophomore. Most of the Milkshake Mafia were in college, at least as far as I knew, and they probably wondered what Darius saw in a high school girl. At least I had an early birthday and would be eighteen in a couple of weeks.

We moved forward enough in line to step into the air-conditioned deli. Darius grabbed an iced tea from the cooler and offered me a water.

"Thank you," I said, twisting the cap. I tipped my head back for a sip and caught the attention of a corner table of girls. They tapped each other, whispered, and then gaped at us.

"Do we know them?"

Darius studied the group. "Hard to say. One of the downfalls of wearing masks in the carnival. If history is anything, though, when a girl looks at me like that, she usually knows me."

I cringed. "That's a little harsh."

"You forget the first night we met."

I leaned into Darius and rested my hand on his chest. "Should we be concerned?"

My answer came when we stepped up to the counter to order, and two of the girls joined us, smiles on their pretty faces. Darius did his best to ignore them and ordered sandwiches for us and Em.

"Anything else?"

"Eight chocolate chip cookies," one of the girls said.

"Excuse me?" I asked.

"That'll be all," the other girl said.

"He is not buying you cookies."

"Why not? It's the least he can do. Don't you have to make amends or whatever?"

"It's fine," Darius said, nodding to the cashier. "Eight cookies."

"We'll be waiting at the table. You can deliver them when they're ready, right?"

They giggled their way back to their seats.

"This feels like a mean girls movie," I muttered.

"If I don't buy the cookies, then I'm a jerk, which I'm pretty sure was what they were going for. What's ten bucks to shut them up?"

"I'm pretty sure the cookies are, like…three dollars each."

Darius looked down at his receipt. "Oh."

I looped my arm in his and pulled him to the pickup line, glaring at the girls every chance I got.

"Maybe I was stupid to think having a girlfriend would be enough," Darius whispered.

I wrapped my arms around his waist and leaned into him, so nobody else could hear. "When I told you about Todd, you said that a girl shouldn't have to pretend to have a boyfriend to get a guy to leave her alone. Her word should be enough."

"Yeah," he said.

"Maybe you shouldn't have to fake date a girl to convince people you barely know to stop harassing you online."

The deli worker called our order number. Darius grabbed the bags and headed for the table.

"Hello, ladies," Darius said. None of them replied. I grabbed the cookies from his hand and dropped them on the table.

"What are those?"

Darius's body stiffened. "The cookies you ordered."

"We don't want your bribes. You think you can treat us like crap and then literally buy us off with cookies. We're women, not toddlers."

"Are you women?" I said, leaning over the table. "Or are you whining, little—"

"Dinah, don't!" Darius pulled me back and led me out of the deli. At the last second, I turned around and grabbed the bag of cookies. At least it made Darius break a smile.

In a blur of movement, we ended up back at the car, heat flaring through me.

"They're still watching us." Darius opened the passenger door. "Get in."

We sat in the car, breathing deeply. Imagining their faces prevented me from calming down, so I pushed the images away. When I remembered leaning across the table, I groaned.

"I'm sorry. That must have made it so much worse."

"Are you kidding? That was adorable. Thanks for having my back."

"Even if I threw fuel on the fire?"

"Even if."

I blew out a puff of air. "You okay?"

"I know this is still new, but it feels like it's been forever. I can't even take my girlfriend out for a sandwich without being harassed."

I held his hand. "I'm sorry."

"I shouldn't have dragged you into this."

"You didn't," I said. "You asked me, and I agreed."

He pointed to the building. "Has that ever happened to you before?"

"No."

Darius rubbed the back of his neck and looked out the window before pushing the door open and leaving me alone inside. I made the mistake of scrolling through social to find reels of the incident all over my feed. Already. Now that we were friends, I could see that Em was one of the people who'd liked the video.

A quick search showed she was linked to every girl we'd seen in the deli.

Em had known we'd be in the deli. She'd even suggested it. Did she know her friends would be there, too? Did she encourage them to say something?

By the time Darius had cooled off and lowered himself back into the driver's seat, I had picked up his defused anger and then some.

"Ready to go back?"

I imagined Em alone in the carousel room, watching the clips on her phone, a smug smile on her face.

"More than you know."

NINETEEN

BACK IN THE CAROUSEL ROOM, I threw a sandwich at Em and crossed my arms. "Did you tell your friends to harass Darius?"

She rolled her eyes.

"I asked you a question."

"So what. You think he cares? He's putting on a show for you."

"You're just angry he deleted your number."

She laughed. "You're such a fool. You believe he deleted my number and every other girl's numbers for you? He might not be cheating now because he's being watched everywhere he goes, but make no mistake, he will cheat on you."

"Let me guess. You're hoping it will be with you?"

She scoffed. "I am so done with Darius Moore."

"Right. So done that out of all the exhibits at the carnival, you insist on working with his girlfriend. And then you set him up at a deli and start an argument with me about how done you are."

"Technically, you threw a sandwich at me and started all this."

I threw my hands in the air.

"What happened to not talking about Darius?" Em challenged.

I paced, wringing out my hands. While I'd been gone, Em had finished priming the horses and started the intricate paintwork on the first horse I'd primed that morning.

Our deadline loomed, and the horse looked good.

"No more."

"I can't control every girl in the Pittsburgh area."

"It wasn't just another group of girls. They were your friends. You told us to go to the deli, and you told them we were coming. That's not exactly innocent."

She crossed her arms.

"You've had your fun with Darius. The milkshakes, the embarrassments...It's done now. It's done, or you're done here."

"You can't get rid of me. My d—"

"I get it. Your daddy has money, and you're spoiled because of it. But he's not here." I pointed to the carousel. "If you want to be here like you say you do, and you want the experience of restoring the carousel, like you say you do, prove it by being a decent person."

"You don't know anything about me."

"I know that Darius hurt you. And I'm sorry. He shouldn't have. He knows it, and I know it, but it's over. He and I are together, and you have your choices in front of you, so make them."

She swirled her paintbrush through the red-orange glob. "Fine. No more."

Her response surprised me, but I recovered and continued, "This project is top secret. I know you don't care about that, but I do. If you're going to be here, we're not talking about Darius. Don't even think about him."

"My pleasure."

"And don't talk about this project with anyone."

"I understand the discretion of the carnival."

"Do you?"

"I've been here longer than you. You hooking up with the number two guy in charge doesn't give you the right to boss me around."

"I'm the number one person in charge on this project, so it kind of does. Are you good with those stipulations or not because I'd rather train someone who has no idea what they're doing but is going to be loyal."

"Is that a compliment? Are you saying I know what I'm doing?"

"Your only takeaway from that whole exchange was a selfish one?"

She scowled at me.

"If we're doing this," I said, riding the wave of the intensity that had exploded from me. "This is the way it has to be."

Em wiped the paint off her hands and opened the sandwich. "I'm in."

———

Despite the disaster that had been my lunch break, I couldn't stop smiling all afternoon. I'd stood up for myself. Finally. After months of being afraid to tell my best friend I wanted to quit journalism. After weeks of tiptoeing around my breakup with Todd. I finally let go of everything I was thinking and feeling, and it worked.

Em and I switched back and forth between two horses. We'd paint as much as we could, and while it dried, we'd shift to the other horse. By the end of the day, we each had a horse about halfway finished and a second started. At that rate, we might make the two-week deadline. My alarm on my phone buzzed, reminding me it was time to call it quits and meet Darius for dinner.

"I have to go," I said. "Are we cleaning up, or are you staying longer?"

Em peeked at her watch. "I have about another hour to paint, and then I can clean up."

I returned all of my brushes to the main water pot and sealed my paints, leaving them strategically on the sketches under my horses, so I could start again the next morning, knowing exactly where I'd left off.

"Think we'll finish this in two weeks?" Em asked.

"Hope so. Maybe the art director could spare an extra painter a day or two. I'll make plans to stay late tomorrow night."

"Big plans today?"

I raised an eyebrow at her.

"Got it. Not up for discussion. See you tomorrow." She turned her attention back to painting and sang along to her playlist.

Darius waited for me at his car. He kissed my cheek and opened the door, begging for an update.

"It's going to take us the full two weeks. At least."

He rested his head back against the seat. "Waiting is torture." He started the car. "The good thing is I have something to fill our time until then."

"For two weeks?" I laughed. "What are you up to?"

He guided the car along the backroads of the carnival. "You know how I called the animal shelter and left a message?"

"They called you back?"

"No. So we are showing up."

There were too many things wrong with that sentence, starting with "we."

Darius chatted nonstop about the exhibit he was clearing space for. Most of the talk was about this construction detail or that, and I wondered if his way of dealing with stress was to talk. By the time he pulled up to the animal shelter, a small brick building at a busy intersection lacking curb appeal on an epic scale, I hadn't talked at all.

"I don't know about this," I said when he had parked.

Darius helped me out of the car and locked it behind us. "Too late to back out now."

"I'm not a dog person."

"How's that possible?"

"Don't get me wrong. I don't *not* like dogs, but I'm also not that person that like attacks a dog on the street and has to pet it."

He rested his arm across my shoulders. "You're here to help with my posts. I'll be the one that gets his hands dirty. Cool?"

It had smelled outside, but the inside—I had no words. Darius charmed the shelter director, Josette, who was grateful to have us since they were short on volunteers for the week, and the dogs were eager for exercise. A veteran volunteer named Clara took us—*us,* as in Josette expected me to do more than film Darius—through the process of rotating the animals through outdoor exercise. She did not, however, explain how to survive being in a 20-by-20 concrete room with more than twenty dogs barking at the same time.

"My ears are furious with me."

"And your nostrils aren't?" Darius quipped.

"Oh, they burned to nothing about fifteen minutes ago."

"Probably for the best."

I scowled at him. "Helping with your posts, huh?"

Darius squished his mouth and cheeks into a position that made him resemble some of the cuter dogs around us. And then he panted like a dog, too.

"You are incorrigible."

He licked my cheek.

"Oh my gosh. Stop!"

Darius pulled me into a hug and obnoxiously rocked back and forth until I could barely keep my feet under me.

"Darius!"

"Okay. Okay. I quit."

Clara handed me a leash. "Ready to walk one?"

"Um…"

"They all wear prong collars, so they'll stick with you easily. A couple of loops around the building is all they need."

I glared at Darius, who could barely contain his entertainment.

"I'll get the first one leashed up for you," Darius offered.

Seconds later, a German Shepherd named Batiste climbed up my back, scratched my side, and clawed three red, painful lines down my thigh.

Darius convinced Batiste to sit and ruffled the fur around his neck. "You're a good boy, aren't you, Batiste? Yes, you are."

"I'm starting to wonder if things just go badly when we're together."

"No way," Darius said, in baby-talk mode. "Batiste is gonna be a good boy. Take a scoop of kibble with you. Reward him when he walks next to you or sits. He'll get the hint."

I didn't buy it, but Batiste wagged his tail at the opportunity to prove me wrong. With a crunch of kibble every few steps, he'd trotted his way into an angel. I left him a few extra pieces when I secured him in his crate and headed for the next pup. Three dogs in, my perspective concerning dogs transformed. I wore a smile with my scratches and smears of mud.

Then…Peaches happened.

Peaches was an alliteration lover's dream—perky, playful, and pleasant.

Also, peace out. As in after a leash malfunction—I couldn't explain how if I had to in a court of law—Peaches soared free. Before I realized why nothing tugged at the leash in my hand, she'd pranced around, celebrating her freedom. Before I could call for help, she tore into a never-ending series of circles around me. I'd never seen a dog run so fast. She was passionate and powerful at it.

"What happened?" Darius yelled.

"I don't know. She got loose."

"Obviously." He positioned himself in a low stance, ready to do what—I had no idea. Only an Olympic sprinter had the chance of catching this dog. "I got this."

I wasn't convinced, but I figured I'd humbled myself for this animal shelter mission of his. Made sense that it would be his turn.

Darius had mentioned once that he'd played football—wide receiver to be exact. He'd assured me he'd been deadly in the open field. I could see that in the way he juked and hit full speed through the grass.

Peaches wasn't persuaded.

"You'll never catch her," Clara called. "Make a triangle around her. Slowly close in on her."

We listened, stepping lightly over the ground. I even shook up the kibble in my palm. Peaches considered the food with a tilt of her fluffy head and blew through our triangle like the paltry defense it was.

"She's going for the road," Clara yelled.

Every other human at the shelter poured through the doors. Six adults—us included—climbed the roadside ditch Peaches had soared over like a playful deer. The commotion in the road sent a sports car to a screeching stop. The shelter workers stopped traffic in all directions while Darius called to Peaches.

"Here, Peaches. Who's a good girl?"

Apparently, not Peaches.

"Come, Peaches!" Darius yelled in his deep voice. Peaches perked her head up but decided surrender was not in her best interest.

By then, multiple drivers had exited their cars in the universal commitment to pets. One had an extra leash and joined in the chase. Another tried to lure Peaches with a brand new bone she had in her grocery bag for her own dog.

I slumped over, hands on my knees, sucking wind.

"You okay?" Darius asked.

"Just thinking about how I've never worked this hard for social media."

Darius's eyes widened. "You're brilliant! Film me catching Peaches."

I stood. "After all this, you think you're catching that dog."

He tapped the camera icon on his home screen and handed me the phone. "Someone has to."

And then he was off again, chasing Peaches through the parking lot of a restaurant across the road. He even tried to lure her with fried chicken leftovers from a concerned patron.

"This dog has shut down the entire neighborhood," I said into the camera.

"Peaches! Come here, girl," Darius called, chicken leg in one hand and a dinner roll in the other.

Peaches did not come. She did manage to get close

enough to swipe the dinner roll and take off again, leaving Darius sprawled in the gravel behind her.

"Looks like that hurt," I narrated.

People share a special love for dogs—no changing my mind on that point, especially after watching a horde of drivers and passengers from the cars stopped along the highway, the shelter workers, and people pouring out of the restaurant form a circle, complete with hand holding, around Peaches.

"She won't bite," Josette called. "She likes to play."

I crossed the parking lot to get a better view as the circle shrunk, step by step. Peaches pranced around like the center of attention she was. In a swift move, she tried to escape the circle between two teenage boys who closed the opening between them. She halted and turned in the other direction. Within seconds, the team had closed all of the openings.

Darius stepped into the circle, knelt and called for Peaches. Like an angel who listened every time she heard her name, that dog sauntered right to him and licked his face. Darius leashed her and collapsed against the pavement, Peaches licking him to her heart's content.

It was social media gold.

TWENTY

PEACHES SLEPT it off in her crate while the rest of us stared into the distance, clothes torn and sweaty, faces red from the heat and dirt-ridden from the endeavor.

"That…was a disaster," Clara said.

Josette sighed. "I wish it didn't happen all the time."

"Wait. That happens all the time?" I asked.

"Often enough." She dusted her clothes off and sorted through the paperwork on her desk. "Our board has been trying to raise money for a fence for years, but every time we get close, the roof leaks or the electrical wiring cuts out."

"Or we find black mold," Clara offered. "Or a hurricane strikes the south, and we end up with an influx of rescues."

"It's one thing after another," Josette said. "Sometimes I feel like we're spooning water out of a boat littered with holes."

Darius and I glanced at each other. I wondered if he was also feeling like we'd found our way into a private moment. Eager to lighten the mood, I said, "Well, unless you need a drawing of a dog, I better step back from my volunteer duties."

Josette swiveled in her chair. "You draw?"

"Yeah," I said slowly, curious about her interest. "And paint."

She and Clara grinned.

"Why do I feel like I'm missing something?"

"The board's been looking for an artist willing to donate pet portraits," Clara explained. "Owners will pay just about anything for their pets. If we could give them a drawing or painting of their pet, we might be able to raise enough money to get out of this cycle."

I mentally calculated the little time I had available between restoring the carousel for Darius and pretending to be his girlfriend. And the tiny detail of wanting to enjoy a few pool days my last few weeks of summer. On the other hand, this was an opportunity for my art to hang in countless homes around town. *My* art. With my name in the corner.

I practically choked on my breath. "How would it work?"

"We'd give you a picture of the pet, and then you could work on your own time."

A picture. I wouldn't have to design anything.

"Would it be possible for me to include a business card in the packet? In case the families want portraits of their children or something?" That could help with spending money this year and college expenses the next.

"I don't see why not," Josette said. "Does that mean you're in?"

"It could take me some time. I have a lot going on with the carnival right now."

She grinned. "That's not a problem. If you could finish them by say, Christmas, I'm sure that would work."

Three months for some pet portraits and publicity for each one? "Deal."

Darius rested his hand on the small of my back and

smiled. Clara and Josette chatted about some list they had of pet owners who'd shown interest in portraits at a previous fundraiser.

"If they're still interested," Josette said, "we might be able to raise enough for fencing materials."

"Labor costs is another issue," Clara said.

"I work on construction projects in the carnival," Darius said. "I could see if a couple of the guys could donate the labor to install the fence."

Josette hugged us both. "You two were meant to come to the shelter today. Someone give Peaches an extra treat. Good girl!"

I wasn't sure I'd go that far.

"You know," I said, back in Darius's car and completely exhausted. "Before I started dating you, I spent my summer days by the pool and painting random art projects I'd found online."

"If that's a thank you," he said, starting the ignition. "You're welcome."

"Not a thank you."

Darius laughed. The pain in my joints didn't even let me enjoy the sound.

"Is it me, or did we just turn a one-time volunteer shift into a project that will likely take weeks or months?"

"That's exactly what we did," Darius said. "But did you get the best footage of your life?"

The memory of Peaches snatching the dinner roll from Darius's grasp and leaving him to sprawl across the gravel, a cloud of dust puffing up around him, made me laugh until I couldn't breathe. We were halfway to my house by the time I recovered.

"It was pretty fun. In retrospect," Darius said.

One tiny detail prevented me from celebrating just yet. "The thing is, I'm not sure I can draw or paint pet portraits."

"Sure you can."

I rolled my eyes at his instant encouragement. "I've never drawn a dog. Or a cat."

We stopped at a red light, and he rested his hand on mine. "I've seen your stuff. If you want to do it, you can do it."

Fake boyfriend or not, he definitely supported and encouraged me, something Todd hadn't done in our *real* relationship.

The light turned green, and he shifted his hand back to the wheel and hit the gas. "Besides, I've never built a fence before, and apparently, I'm doing that."

"Good thing—not just for Peaches. That place could use some curb appeal."

Darius gripped the steering wheel even tighter.

"You okay?"

"Seeing those dogs all piled in like that." He shook his head. "It shouldn't be that way."

The overcrowding at the shelter didn't sit well with me either. "Clara said they're over capacity right now, and with hurricane season just getting warmed up, they'll probably have more transplants from the south looking for space."

"And no space to give them," Darius said. "When I thought about being a vet, I imagined dedicated owners bringing in the pets. Yeah, there'd be some dark stuff, but for the most part, my work would be ruffling the fur of a few pets and gently caring for them to keep them healthy."

"You giving up on your dream of building carnival-like rooms for people and making a killing doing it?" I joked.

Darius looked pensive. "Maybe I'll build animal shelters with style or cool pet rooms in houses—something with obstacles and snuggle spots for them. On the side, though. I think I want to go to veterinary school."

The moment felt epic. Darius had decided what he wanted to do with his life, and I got to be there to see it. I reached across the console for his hand. He'd supported my art so much, I wanted to think of a way to support him.

"Maybe we can help them with an adoption drive or something," I suggested, as if we could spend one hour at a place and solve all of their problems for them.

Darius flipped on his turn signal and pulled into a parking lot.

"What are you doing?"

He grabbed my cheeks and kissed me. "You are brilliant, Dinah Zimmerman. Absolutely brilliant."

"Uh. I am. Sure, but what is going on in that head of yours?"

"For a drive to work, we need people who want to adopt a pet."

"Sure."

"Lots of people."

"The more people, better the chances, I guess. Where are you going with this?"

Darius held his hands out as wide as possible in the car. "If only we had a place where thousands of people went every weekend…"

"I don't follow."

"The space we've been clearing out," he said with a bigger smile than I'd ever seen. "We create an exhibit at the carnival for pet adoptions. Mac can write an article about it and send it through our PR channels. People could come in, play with dogs and cats, and then take them home."

Pets running around the carnival? Oh, gosh, not Peaches, please. Would they wear masks? I laughed at the thought of dogs wearing Mardi Gras masks. Beyond that, I had so many questions. "How will it work?"

His smile faltered but didn't fully fade. "I have no idea."

TWENTY-ONE

WHILE DARIUS ATTEMPTED to build an entire exhibit dedicated to the shelter dogs, I spent my days painting carousel horses alongside Em and practicing sketching pet portraits at night until I couldn't keep my eyes open. I searched online videos of other artists creating portraits. Some used watercolor, but that was emphatically *not* in my wheelhouse yet. After employing the guess and test method with different media, I decided to use charcoal on grey-toned paper. The tone of the paper gave the images something extra, and the charcoal proved forgiving.

Mid-week, Clara called me with the first stack of pet photos.

"That didn't take long," I said when I picked them up on the way home from painting the carousel.

"We sent an email out to our newsletter list and already had twenty people sign up."

Twenty. Wow. In two days.

"How many are you accepting?"

"Our goal is fifty—if that works for you," Clara said, her hands folded in prayer.

"I'll work on these and get back to you."

Appreciating the perfect evening weather, I set up my supplies at our poolside table and selected a black lab for my first portrait, thinking it was mostly one color—easy peasy. I sketched, smudged, erased. Over and over. Eventually, the squareness of the snout took shape, I found humor with a spark of white in the dog's eyes, and by the time I blended my final edge, the charcoal dog in front of me resembled the photograph in my hands.

"Wow."

A look at the clock revealed it had taken me two hours to finish the portrait. I counted the stack of photos donors had given along with their one-hundred-dollar check, hoping Clara had made a mistake. She had. There weren't twenty pets. There were twenty-*two*.

My phone buzzed with a flirty text from Darius about meeting him at the carnival. Despite it being eight o'clock, I packed up my supplies and drove to the carnival.

———

I found Darius in the communal carnival office the committee used to brainstorm and plan exhibits. It was one of those locations few people who came to the carnival got to see. Darius didn't hear me come in, so I had the unique pleasure of watching him for a few seconds, studying a computer screen with an adorable look of concentration on his face.

"You summoned me, fake boyfriend?"

He shushed me and looked around.

"Nobody's here," I whispered.

Darius patted the seat next to him. He waited for me to get settled and smiled.

"What's going on?"

"You were working on your pet sketches, and I was working on my pet plans."

I unloaded my bag onto the desk next to him. "And?"

"Since we both have to work, I thought we could do it together."

I pinched his cheeks. "That is the cutest thing."

"Shut up," he said. "Trying to practice being good boyfriend material."

"Perfect boyfriend material."

I sat, and he nudged me with his shoulders. I nudged him back. We giggled.

And then Em walked in, saw us, and crossed her arms. "You two are so cute."

"Hey, Em," Darius said, nonchalantly. "You remember my girlfriend?"

She took a deep breath and smiled. Of course she remembered me. We'd spent every day together painting.

"Make it better," I whispered to him, "not worse."

"Fine," he mumbled.

I nodded at Em and dedicated myself to organizing my art supplies and selected the next pet from the pile. She shuffled around the office, doing who knows what? I didn't watch. I barely looked at her. I definitely didn't notice how tight her jeans were or her toned abs when she reached high and her half-shirt followed. A sideways glance at Darius told me he too had noticed. I kicked him under the table.

"Ow."

"Sorry." I was all sugar and innocence, but when Em wasn't looking, I glared at him.

"What?" he mouthed.

"You're staring," I mouthed back and pointed at Em.

He leaned close. "Sorry. Still learning." He kissed my cheek and tickled me at the same time.

Em side-eyed us. "Does this mean you'll be late for our carousel-painting session tomorrow morning?"

"No," I drew out the word.

"I'll be here early," she said. "Trying to beat the storm. I hate driving in the rain. I'll see you tomorrow."

"See ya."

Em left, and Darius exhaled. "It's hard not to flirt with people."

"Excuse me?"

"I know it's terrible, but that's kind of who I am. Before Sandra—she's the one I told you about."

I remembered. Mac had talked about her, too. She had been the journalist who'd gotten close to Darius to get the scoop on the carnival and then printed all the details behind his back.

"I flirted all the time," Darius went on, "and they flirted back, but I was like this stupid kid or something. No game to see it through. Don't tell anyone I admitted that."

"Our fake relationship is a vault," I said. "What changed with Sandra?"

"My experience."

"Gross."

He rolled his eyes at me. "Not only like that but also that."

"I'm starting to regret that our relationship is a vault. I'd like to forget everything you just said."

"Don't play. You're picturing it right now."

I covered my eyes. "Oh my gosh. Stop!"

"I quit." He peeled my hands back from my face. "For real, maybe it was my confidence or just getting older. Now, flirting usually leads to something."

"That's why I don't flirt."

"You flirt."

"I do not."

He smirked and quirked an eyebrow, making me want to flirt even more. "Stop! This is embarrassing."

"It's not," he challenged.

"Easy for you to say. You're confident and hot."

His smile could not be contained. "You think I'm hot?"

I scowled at him, not willing to play his fishing scam.

He raised his hands in surrender. "Fine. I'm hot. But I don't get it. So are you."

I rolled my eyes and directed my attention back to the pug I'd been sketching.

"C'mon. You're gorgeous, crazy talented, and actually a nice person, which doesn't happen all the time. What's going on in that head of yours?"

What was going on? Why had hearing about him and Sandra sent me into such a self-conscious spiral? How did I even get so critical of myself?

"Probably Todd," I answered aloud. "All things seem to lead back to…that."

"How so?"

It was a good question. I hadn't entirely made sense of it myself, but the way Darius watched me with patience and concern, I wanted to. "Maybe it was all the years of my family insisting that Todd and I were going to get together someday, so me thinking that it was going to happen, too, when I was worthy of someone like him with his popularity and whatever. I needed to be better to earn being his person, you know. And once I finally was his person, he had a lot of other persons."

"That sucks. I'm sorry."

"Why are you sorry?"

"I knew him then. I saw him hanging with different girls. People whispered about him having a girlfriend, but I didn't think anything of it. I should have cared."

I squeezed his arm. "You care now."

"It's my path to reformation. No more random hookups or at least not multiple ones in the same night."

"Whoa. Pace yourself."

His elbow nudged mine. "You think we can add some benefits to our arrangement?"

"We've kissed," I said.

"Maybe…more than that?"

"No."

Darius sucked in a breath. "Wow that answer came fast and didn't even require any consideration."

I shook my head, trying and failing to keep the smirk off my face. The fact he wanted benefits flattered me to my core, but I could barely handle the kissing without confusing feelings for attraction.

"For real, could you have pretended to think about it?"

"I don't pretend," I teased and was rewarded with Darius's laughter.

"You know, as fake girlfriends go, you're a good one."

"Thank you," I said. "Now, let me work on this volunteer project you suckered me into."

"You? I'm over here designing a fence for the shelter and calculating supply costs." He nudged me again. "There are a few other things I'd rather be doing."

"Oh my gosh!" I nudged him back harder, and then we both got to work.

TWENTY-TWO

I HAD enough time to drive home that night, sleep, shower, and drive back to work on the carousel painting with Em before the storm came. I managed to park in the back lot and run to the building before the downpour.

Darius waited for me at the door. He wrapped his arms around me and squeezed.

"Are you okay?" I asked.

"No."

"What's wrong?"

His shoulders shook. Was he crying?

"Darius?"

"I want to see my surprise," he said.

I swatted his shoulder and pushed him away. "I thought something was wrong."

"It is," he insisted.

"I'm going now."

"Please. Just one horse. A hoof?"

I shook my head and started down the empty hallway.

"No kiss goodbye?"

I whispered loudly, "We're not in public."

Although, it was nice that he wanted a kiss. I sauntered the rest of the way to the carousel exhibit with a satisfied smile. I found Em inside mixing paint colors.

"Hello!" I said pleasantly.

"You're in a good mood."

"I am."

I expected some snotty quip about Darius, maybe a comment about how my happiness was bound to end soon enough if Darius had any influence over it. But Em kept mixing the paints.

"You okay?" I asked.

"Sure. Why?"

"No reason."

"I was thinking that if we work hard today, maybe we can knock a day off our schedule," she said, handing me the paint pallet she'd mixed for our next horse.

"Do you have somewhere to be?"

She tossed her pillow under the horse she was working on and got comfortable. "No. I know you're dying to show Darius is all."

I searched the room for hidden cameras.

I found none.

Was Em nice? Was this a game? Did she have a plan? I pondered while she settled in and started painting the under-side of a horse. Her task involved a lot of blending of the paints to show the shift from auburn to brown to white on the underbelly.

"Are you going to keep staring at me and let that paint dry out?"

I set up my paints and brushes.

"We can start with your playlist if you want," she said.

Seriously, where were the cameras? After a few songs played, Em got chatty.

"School starting for you soon?" she asked.

"A couple weeks."

"Same. I move into the dorm two weeks from today. Can't believe summer's over."

"Me either," I said politely.

"Did you go anywhere on vacation?" she asked.

I slowed my brush strokes as if that would give me more mental capacity to figure out what was happening.

"No," I finally answered.

"We haven't traveled since June," she said, disappointment in her voice.

June. As in not even six weeks earlier. Must have been hard only vacationing every two months.

"Where did you go?" I asked.

"Paris."

Of course she did.

"Have you ever been there?"

"Nope."

"You would love it with how much you like art."

I sat up and smacked my head on the underside of my horse. I stood, rubbing the pain away. "What's going on?"

Em maneuvered herself around her horse more impressively than me. "What do you mean? I'm painting this horse's butt."

"No. The chatter. The friendly talk. The travel suggestions."

"You asked me to lay off, and this is my laying off. I'm trying to…be nice."

"Really?"

"Yeah."

"No ulterior motive?"

"Nope."

I squinted at her.

"Promise."

I was too exhausted to be suspicious. Getting along with

Em would make the carousel project so much easier, and maybe it could lead to Darius getting what he wanted, too—a reprieve online.

"Okay," I finally said.

In response, she lay back on her pillow, got back to painting, and continued on with her questioning. After a few minutes, the tension in the conversation faded. Within an hour, we'd both finished our horses, moved on to new ones, and even laughed a few times.

Then we laughed a lot.

If only Darius could see us now.

Maybe it was some kind of omen, but seconds after that thought crossed my mind, everything went black.

As in complete absence of light.

"Did the power go out?" Em whispered as if the darkness commanded it.

I stopped my brush and hoped I hadn't somehow messed up all my work by brushing it against something I'd already painted. "How did the power go out? It's not even storming that bad."

"This happens at my house all the time. It's so frustrating."

"Let me check with Darius. Maybe they heard something from the power company." I reached for my phone and felt the stickiness of wet paint on my fingertips. "Ugh."

"Do you need a light?" Em asked from across the darkness.

"Yes."

She shuffled for a few seconds.

"Are you okay?" I asked.

"Yes," she said.

Thud!

"Or not," she groaned. "I hope the paint bottles were closed."

"This is a disaster."

"If I keep reaching around, I'm going to knock everything down," Em said.

"I could move straight towards the door," I said, thinking aloud. "That path doesn't have any paint."

"Do you remember where you put your phone?" Em asked.

I did not. "You're right. This is a disaster."

A knock at the door made me jump. "Dinah, you okay in there?"

"It's Darius," I whispered, panicked about him seeing the carousel.

"Not like he can see anything now," Em pointed out.

"Just a second," I yelled and crawled toward what I thought was the door. I reached the wall and stood but couldn't find a doorknob. I shuffled to the left. Then to the right. "I have no idea where I am."

Em laughed, and another thud came from her direction. "Another paint bottle down."

We both laughed then.

Epic. Disaster.

The sound of her voice gave me a sense of direction, so I moved along the wall to the right. "Darius?"

"Yeah?"

Definitely the right. "Keep talking."

I moved toward his voice and finally found the doorknob. I opened it only a crack, not wanting to reveal the carousel behind me. Darius flashed the light from his phone up onto his face, giving his edges an eerie glow.

"Creepy."

"Check out the hall," he answered, flashing his light in both directions to reveal an endless nothingness. "What took you so long to get to the door?"

"Kind of hard to find a door in the dark."

"Where's your phone?"

"Good question."

"The power company has us down for three hours. You should probably pack up, unless you think you can work by flashlight."

I didn't want to risk it. When the lights came back on, the colors might not match, or the design could look messy.

"Do you think it could come back sooner? We're gonna fall so far behind."

"Maybe. A couple of us are going down to the parade route to open the garage doors and let some light inside while we wait. Better than driving home in the rain."

"Let me talk to Em," I said.

"Do you want me to wait here for you? It's a little creepy in here."

"No. We have some cleaning up to do first. Oh! Can I borrow your phone a quick second?"

He handed it over, and I closed the door.

"Really dark out here," he yelled.

Em and I laughed.

"I don't blame him," I said. "It is creepy out there."

Darius's flashlight illuminated paint poured out all over the floor.

"They're planning to paint the floor, right?" Em asked.

"If they weren't before, they are now." I found my phone and used the flashlight app to return Darius's to him in the doorway.

He looped his arm around my waist and pulled me to him. "Thank you." He pressed a sweet kiss against my lips. "Just in case she's paying attention."

"Good thinking," I whispered back.

The door clicked shut, and I leaned against it. A roll of paper towels in one hand, Em swiped the globs of paint off the floor and into the trash, leaving smear marks of different colors behind.

"Did you hear we're going to hang out on the parade route?" I asked her, jumping into help with the cleanup.

"Okay. Sure. Um…" Em fidgeted with the paintbrushes. "I'm sorry. I don't know if you want me to come, like you're inviting me, or if it's awkward, and you'd rather I leave and go home."

"You can't drive in the storm," I said.

"That's considerate, but does that also mean you do find it awkward?"

"Today has been fun, and we're trying this whole getting along thing. I won't lie. Being with Darius is new for me, and you have a history with him. Which is why we aren't supposed to talk about Darius."

She nodded. "Sometimes I don't get why you're with him, and other times, I see it. He's different with you."

Maybe because we are only friends playing pretend. "Look, Em. I just want to say that although we're together, it doesn't mean I think the things he did in the past were right."

"But you don't think he's going to do them again? Not to you?"

"I don't, and I like spending time with him. I'm hopeful but realistic."

"I hope it works out for you, too."

"Thanks," I said. "We totally fail at that no talking about Darius thing."

"True. Clean up and leave?"

"Clean up and leave," I agreed.

TWENTY-THREE

TEN MINUTES LATER, we pushed through a door from a dark, creepy hallway that Em said reminded her of a high school hazing challenge to make it through an abandoned hospital in the dark. A breeze from the wide-open garage doors welcomed us. As far as parade route standards go, the crowd was light, but more people hung around than I'd expected. When Em and I were locked in the carousel exhibit, it was easy to forget how many other exhibits and projects were being developed around us. Some of the crew hovered around a barrel fire, keeping their hands warm and laughing over stories we couldn't hear. Others scattered around in clusters, chatting, laughing, and snacking.

"Do you know anyone?" I asked, not seeing Darius.

"Not many," Em said. "Darius commands a certain loyalty, and I upset that when I baptized him in butterscotch banana."

And we were back to Darius.

I found a corner with blankets and cushions spread across the floor. I tossed my bag down and settled in. "I know we mentioned this upstairs, but we're not good at not talking about Darius."

"I noticed that," Em said.

"Why don't you tell me about you?"

"You want to learn about me?"

"It would prevent us from talking about my boyfriend who happens to be your ex, and you have been asking me questions all morning, so it seems fair."

"Good point," Em said, settling onto a cushion of her own. "I'm a daddy's girl, and daddy has a lot of money. I'll forever be the spoiled brat with a rich daddy."

"Sounds limiting."

"You could say that."

"Is that one of the things you love about the carnival? That you can come here and be anything you want to be?"

"It was like that at first, but then when I got involved with the committee, it changed. People know you, or at least think they do, and it becomes the same kind of experience as you have everywhere else. You lose your anonymity, I guess."

"I get it," I said. "But you can always change your mask."

"True. The feeling of nobody knowing you and you being able to do anything you want, go anywhere you want, dance with whoever you want—it's empowering. Some-times I wonder if that's why I want to open a new franchise. I could go to a new city where nobody knows me and have a fresh start."

"But that fresh start includes you being the daughter of the boss, which is something you can never change."

"I know," she slumped against the legs of a folding chair. "Sometimes, I think I could pull an undercover boss situation, like on that TV show or whatever."

"That would be fun," I said, picturing Em attempting to

hide her obvious glamour.

"I just think that we're only defined as one thing, you know?"

"Em, do you hear yourself? I'm not going to say his name again, but there happens to be someone around us who is defined as one thing right now, and it's hard for him."

She covered her face. "Ugh. Makes sense."

"If you could decide how other people see you," I asked, "who would you want them to see?"

She took a deep breath and shrugged. "Someone who is funny, who makes them laugh. Someone who is beautiful in a way that doesn't involve fancy clothes and makeup but beautiful for being a good person. That sounds so cheesy and stupid, but I have a lot of good people around me, and I want to be a good person. I want people to talk about me like I light up the room or make the world better. I don't know. Something."

"I'm sorry," I said.

"For what?"

"For thinking you were just a rich daddy's girl."

"Are you saying you think more of me now?"

"Don't go fishing for compliments," I joked, and Em laughed.

"What do you want people to think about you?" she asked.

Immediately, only one thing came to mind. "I want to be known as an artist who makes people feel something. The problem is right now, I'm just learning so much about art that I don't think—I don't know how to explain it." I took a moment to collect my thoughts while Em waited patiently. "People in the art community would say I haven't found my voice yet. I don't know what inspires me, and I don't know what I want to create to inspire other people. I'm torn between trying to be patient until I can develop that and worrying it'll never come. Should I already have my voice? Would a true artist have that, even if they were new to art?"

Em took a deep breath. "I'm not an artist. I love to draw, and can hold my own, but it's not something I want to do with my life. I won't pretend to have answers for you, but I will say this: you can grow in anything. You can grow in art. You can grow in kindness. You can grow in friendship. I mean, look at us."

"True."

"If you enjoy art, keep at it, and when you're a boring grown up, you can make a decision about whether it's the responsible thing for you to spend your time on, but now, at our age? It's the time to do whatever you want, however you want, with whomever you want."

"That's pretty deep for a rich daddy's girl."

"See? More to me than you thought."

"Guess so."

She pulled my bag of art supplies closer. "Tell me about these portraits."

The pet pictures, charcoal pencils, and grey paper poured out of my bag as I explained the task. Em took a paper and pencil and offered to sketch a Labradoodle. With the stack of pictures still left, I didn't have the option to say no.

We chatted and sketched. Darius's name didn't come up again. Within minutes, we were laughing. Then we'd turn serious and sketch in comfortable silence before one of us told another story that sent the other into fits of laughter again.

Darius might have been somewhere in the crowd, but he still hadn't stopped by to see us yet. Thunder boomed, and I had to erase the line I'd messed up at the sound. Figuring it was as good a time for a break as any, I set aside my sketch and watched the massive rain.

"I love rain."

"I prefer snow," Em said.

I imagined sitting by the fire watching the snow fall outside and moaned, making Em laugh at me.

"I think you were right about us getting to know something about each other outside of Darius and painting," she said. "It feels different now."

I nodded. "Better."

"Hey!" I looked up to see Mac running across the room, Kierk following slowly behind. She fell onto me. "I haven't seen you forever, Miss Busy Pants."

Water dripped from her to me.

"You're all wet."

She rolled off me and settled onto a cushion. "In case you haven't noticed, it's raining. I got stuck on one of the dirt paths and had to run here. Kierk was kind enough to offer me a change of clothes."

"I bet he was," I teased, and my best friend's cheeks reddened.

"Who's this?" Mac pointed to Em, trying to change the subject.

"This is Em. She's working with me on the carousel."

"Ooh! Top secret." Mac said. "Wait, weren't you part of the milkshake mayhem?"

Em groaned. "It's something we're working past."

Mac smiled in Kierk's direction. "We all make mistakes. Kierky, darling?"

Kierk glared at her.

"He doesn't like that nickname," Mac whispered. Em and I bit our lips to prevent laughing.

"Serenade us with your brilliant guitar skills," Mac said, and everyone cheered.

The once-empty space Em and I had sketched in filled quickly with committee members from design, construction, culinary, and more. They pulled up cushions, blankets, benches, and chairs. The rain continued outside the open garage door as everyone settled, and Kierk turned the silver knobs to turn the strings of his acoustic guitar.

Darius sat behind me. I leaned into him, and he whispered in my ear, "What are you doing over here?"

"Sketching the pet portraits,"

He kissed my cheek and nodded toward the sketches. "How many have you finished?"

"Five," I said. "But Em's helping now, so it's going faster."

"Em's helping?" Darius's eyes fell on Em. Her hand moved across her page with purpose. A gust of wind blew through the door, and her blonde hair flew up around her as if she were the focus of a music video.

"She's gorgeous," I whispered.

"I hadn't noticed," Darius said. Instinct told me he was lying.

Kierk strummed the guitar and played a familiar 80s rock song for everyone to sing along, too. While he played, and they sang, the rain fell, and I sketched. A pug. A German Shepherd. A boxer. Each sketch Em or I finished, we slid into a plastic sleeve and moved on to the next one.

After an hour, the rain showed no signs of stopping, so a few of the construction guys braved the storm for a stack of pizzas from a place in town. Kierk and Mac rounded up drinks and cookies. Darius led a group searching out tables and chairs. Just like that, we turned the wet afternoon into a party on the parade route. I met everyone and heard about their exhibits. Thousands of people came to the carnival on the weekends, but they never had the privilege of seeing this —the people behind the mask, working every day to make magic.

Darius brought me a warm chocolate cookie on a napkin.

"How did you warm this up?"

He pointed to the barrel fire. Someone held a pizza peel covered with a layer of chocolate chip cookies over the flames.

I bit into the gooey treat. "Delicious. Thank you."

He tucked his hands into his pockets and took a deep breath.

"Everything okay?"

"What do you think about me talking to Em?"

I stopped, a bite of cookie halfway to my mouth. "Talking to her?"

"Apologizing to her."

"Oh." Like apologize because it was the right thing to do? Or apologize because he wanted to fake breakup with me and go out with her for real?

"You two are friends now, right?"

"I guess so."

"And it's the right thing to do."

"She was *the one*, though, Darius."

"*Was*."

"Do you want her to be the one again?"

Darius rubbed the back of his neck, and my chest twisted into a knot. It didn't matter what he said next. His reaction told me everything I needed to know. The way he was looking across the tables at her slammed an exclamation point on what I'd already figured out for myself.

He could flirt with me, kiss me on the cheek, even talk about how attracted he was to me, but that's where it ended. It didn't matter how the movies or books portrayed fake dating. And really, they wouldn't make movies about fake dating that *didn't* end in happily ever after. Where would the fun be in that?

Fake dating didn't always end with real love. Some of them just ended.

Like mine with Darius would end.

"Sure," I said, swallowing the lump threatening to form in my throat. I'd walked into this situation with my eyes wide open. Darius hadn't lied or misled me. "Talk to her, but remember, no flirting."

"It will be good practice," he said, seemingly in an attempt to lighten the mood.

I gave him a nod, my last effort to convince him I had no apprehensions about him leaving me to talk to the girl who turned out to be nicer than I'd realized, more gorgeous than anyone realized, and the first person he'd wanted to be serious about since breaking up with Sandra.

Darius skillfully inserted himself into the small group Em had been chatting with and whispered something to her. She nodded, and the two walked away together—never far enough that we couldn't see them, but nobody could hear them.

Mac looped her arm in mine. "You okay?"

"Fine. Why?"

"You look disappointed."

"Was hoping to make more progress on the carousel today, but it looks like this rain isn't going anywhere."

"So your heaviness has nothing to do with your boyfriend chatting up his ex in front of you?"

"That's not what he's doing. I know exactly what they're talking about. He talked to me first, and I trust him."

"If you're sure—"

"I am," I interrupted.

And I guess I was, at least about one thing. Everything between Darius and me was—without a doubt—decidedly unreal.

TWENTY-FOUR

WHEN THE PATTERING of rain no longer sounded against the asphalt outside, everyone dispersed to their cars. By the time I left the carnival property, raindrops started falling again. They thumped across my windshield like memories of Em and Darius laughing together. Mac had called out my lies with her raised eyebrows every time I looked at her.

She may not have caught on that I'd been fake dating Darius, but she'd picked out my lie about not caring that he and Em had become friends again easily. I stopped at a red light in time for the rain clouds to pour.

Finally at home a few minutes later, I left the finished sketches in the car and ran into the house, dripping wet by the time I stepped inside.

"Oh, honey!" my mom rushed to me with a towel.

I thanked her and dried myself at the kitchen island, not sure the stool could support me and all the weight I was carrying.

"Dinah! I'm so glad you're home. We have good news." Mom cut a piece of lemon cake and pushed it across the island with a smile.

"You made lemon cake. Excellent."

"That's not the news. A renter backed out at the last minute, so we got a free week at the beach house."

I stopped the fork halfway to my mouth. "Who is 'we'?"

Mom took a deep breath. "You know we always vacation with the Wilkinsons."

"Mom! I cannot go on vacation with Todd." I held my head together with both of my hands because no way was it not going to explode.

"It won't only be them. Your cousins are coming, too."

I turned my phone over in my hands, wondering what my buffer would say about this.

My mom hugged me. "You've always loved the beach house, and with you going to college next year, you'll be packing up to move into the dorm in August."

She wasn't wrong on either point. The beach house was a three-story Victorian in a small New Jersey beach town. From an attic balcony, you could see along the beach in both directions thanks to a town ordinance that prevented the planting of trees along the stretch. A boardwalk separated the beach from the road and the glorious sand where I'd plant an umbrella and sketch the day away, taking the occasional break to cool off in the waves of the Atlantic.

But—Todd. I couldn't. I wouldn't.

And Em would be here working on the carousel alone, taking lunch breaks with Darius. They'd get closer and closer, and when I came back, he'd happily reveal our experiment had been a success, that Em wanted to date him for real. He'd thank me, and that would be the end of us, and the beginning of me dodging Todd all over again.

"I want to bring Darius," I said without thinking the words through in any sort of logical way, which was totally reflected in my mother's expression.

"I didn't realize you two were that serious."

"I'm not sure that we are, Mom, but I don't feel right going on vacation with my ex-boyfriend and not even offering the trip to Darius. The house has plenty of room, right?"

"Well, yes."

"Todd needs to understand that things are over for us."

"I'm not sure it's necessary to invite another boy on vacation to make that statement."

Oh, naive mother.

My mom repositioned my plate, so the cake was in front of me once again. "Deal."

————

The next morning, I got to the carnival early to paint. I should have asked more questions about the vacation. It started Monday. Monday, as in I had three more days to paint before leaving the finishing touches to Em. I set aside my pet sketching goal for the day, knowing that I could pack my supplies to sketch those at the beach. The carousel wouldn't fit in my suitcase.

The power company had restored the electricity overnight. I used a side door key Darius had given me and made my way through the silent halls. Even with the lights on, an empty carnival managed a creepy vibe. In the carousel room, though, I played music and fell into the rhythm of rotating painting a horse's intricate reins and blending shades of brown for his tail. While the front half dried, I painted the back and vice versa.

Em arrived with coffee and donuts at eight. "I thought I was early."

I took a break to indulge in a Pittsburgh cream donut.

"You okay?" Em asked.

"Yeah," I said. "Some stuff on my mind. I want to get as much done as possible today."

She pointed to the horse I'd been working on. "Those reins look intense."

I took another bite of donut. "Pretty much."

We dusted the powder sugar from our hands and fell back into our paintwork until my phone beeped with a 911 message from Darius telling me to meet him in the parade garage.

"I'll be back," I told Em and ran through the carnival, throwing open the exit door closest to the parade garage. Darius jumped at the sound and stared at me. "You're already here?"

"Where did you think I was?"

"Driving. I thought you'd see the message when you pulled in."

"I was working on your surprise."

He pulled me into a hug and kissed me on the cheek, our usual public greeting. "You're the best fake girlfriend."

"Don't I know it. What's this text about? Nothing seems 911 to me."

"I have the best news."

So had my mom the day before, but her best news didn't align with mine.

Darius went on. "The committee approved my exhibit."

"What?" I jumped into his arms. "Shut up!"

He spun me around in too many circles for me to successfully stand upright without holding onto him when he finally set me back down.

"It's all happening. An obstacle course for the pets, a playroom, a how to train your dog session, an adoption center. All of it."

"I'm so proud of you."

"Me? I couldn't have done this without you. And the

construction committee agreed to help with the shelter fence. They said we should consider more volunteer work overall."

"See! That cost analysis worked out."

He shook his head. "I love the carnival, but this is the first time I feel like we're doing something powerful with our resources."

"I'm proud of you."

"Thank you."

"And...I have some news, too. Not nearly as exciting."

He intertwined his fingers with mine, and we headed for the main building.

"I'm going on vacation."

"Oh," he said. The sadness that crept into that single word did all sorts of dangerous things to my heart.

"And the news is that..." Oh my gosh. Breathe. I was so inviting my fake boyfriend to my real vacation. "I wanted to ask if you, well, if...do you want to come?"

He stopped and smiled. "You want me to come on your family vacation?"

It made no sense to blush, but I did anyway.

"Yes," I finally said.

"I'm honored. Are you asking me because you want me to come, or is this strictly business?"

"Do you mean is Todd coming?"

He nodded.

"Yeah. He is." But going wasn't strictly business either.

"So you need your buffer."

"I do."

"When is this vacation happening?"

"That's the thing. We leave Monday."

His face fell.

"What?" I asked.

"I'm sorry, D. The committee wants to take the pet

exhibit live next weekend since it's the last big weekend before everyone heads back to college."

"That soon? That's incredible."

"A planned exhibit isn't ready, so it was the perfect timing. And with hurricane season and everything, the shelter needs this sooner rather than later. I start work on it this weekend. It will be around the clock."

"I'll stay home and help."

"You can't miss your vacation for me."

"I can't go without my buffer."

He draped his shoulder across mine. "I'll have a chat with Wilkes before you go. Trust me. He will be on his best behavior."

"You sure?" As in you sure I should go on vacation with my ex, Todd, while you stay here with your ex, Em? Please say no. Please say no!

"Definitely."

I swallowed hard, but the attempt did nothing to curb the fear creeping up my throat. "Speaking of chats. How did yours go with Em?"

"Good. I can't believe we haven't talked about it already."

I nodded, hoping for more than a one-word answer. I'd been looking more for a play-by-play, or word-by-word commentary.

"I apologized and said I wanted to change, and she pretty much said the same thing."

"That's it?" They'd been talking for way longer than that.

"We talked about you a lot," he said, lowering his gaze like he was embarrassed.

"Talking about me how?"

"Em's impressed with your work on the carousel. I'm dying to see it."

"Yeah. I'm going to work through the weekend to try and get it as close to ready as possible. Em should be able to finish it up next week without me."

He intertwined his fingers with mine. "I promise I will not go in that room until you come back."

We'd reached the door leading to the carousel exhibit. I slid my arms around Darius's neck and hugged him longer than normal hug lengths—by any standards.

"You okay?"

"I don't want to go without you," I whispered, surprised at my own honesty.

Darius responded by hugging me tighter.

TWENTY-FIVE

I STEPPED out of the car and inhaled the deepest breath of oceanside air my lungs would allow. Across the beach road, children ran through the sand, flying kites. A few guys surfed the small waves, and beach volleyball players smacked and swatted the ball, sand sticking to every inch of their bodies.

Mom looped her arm around my shoulders. "It's beautiful, isn't it?"

"Perfect."

Except Darius wasn't there. He was back at the carnival with Em, who'd graciously offered to paint the horses while I was away.

"Why don't you take a walk on the beach?" Dad suggested. "We can unload the food and get the other stuff later."

"I can help."

"No. The weather's perfect," my mom insisted. "It was a long drive in a tight space. Go stretch your legs."

I grabbed one of the beach passes that hung on a hook

inside the front door and tucked it into my crossbody purse. "You guys sure?"

"Positive."

I crossed the beach road and walked the boardwalk, the wind kissing my face, and thought about everyone back home. Mac was in The Muse offices, working on advertising plans and ideas for fall issues. She'd crush that position even more than her predecessor, Lola St. James had, and definitely more than Mac's ex-boyfriend who had been the editor the year before. Kierk would be doing his Kierk things at the carnival. Darius would be rushing around day and night to make the pet exhibit happen. Last I heard, he had a ton of help. Not a shocker considering the help Peaches had riled up in the road. Most of the committee loved dogs or cats or both, too. Anyone with free time volunteered to help with the exhibit.

I pulled out my phone and texted: *How's it coming together?*

Bubbles appeared immediately, making me smile.

Darius: *I'm not doing any work.*

Me: *Why?*

Darius sent a pic of more than twenty people in the small exhibit space, all working on different pieces of the puzzle.

Me: *Are you supervising?*

Darius: *What I do best. You there yet?*

I took a pic of the beach and sent it to him.

Darius: *Nice. I've never been to the ocean.*

Me: *No!*

Darius: *Not once. I would have loved to come with you.*

I would have loved it, too.

Self-consciously—at least I could admit that—I searched Darius's picture for Em's blonde hair and thin physique. Because I couldn't help myself, I texted her to ask for an update. She replied with a pic of the horse she was working on—number nine. We were so close!

Darius: *Have to run. Bring me some sand and a souvenir?*

I promised I would and made my way to our family's first beach tradition spot—The Hot Dog Hut. While I waited for them to prepare and bag the dozen Chicago dogs I'd ordered, I found our beach house in the skyline of homes in the distance. Way up on the third floor, the small white balcony fence stood out against the bright blue siding. The most gorgeous view on the beach could be seen from that very spot. No arguing. No alternatives. That was it. For eight years, I'd visited this beach town and dreamed of a singular, romantic, movie moment—watching the sunrise from that balcony. The beach would be quiet save a few silent photographers.

Above the world, with the endless ocean in front of us, we'd stand on that balcony, him behind me, me leaning back into his chest. He'd loop his arms around my waist, and we'd watch the sky turn from a dark blue to a mix of blue and orange, the sun peeking out from the surface of the water until it pushed all of the darkness away.

For years, the boy in that fantasy had been Todd. The summer before, he'd fought with me the whole trip, ruining every opportunity of a sunrise and anything else romantic. This year, well, this year was this year.

I had a fake boyfriend stuck at home.

The guy behind the hut counter passed me the bag and a pile of napkins. I walked back to the house with the balcony in the center of my view the whole time.

The rooftop sunrise fantasy would have to wait for another year.

———

Back at the house, my parents' car wasn't the only one in the driveway anymore. My aunt and uncle's car was there and so was the Wilkinsons'.

Deep. Breath.

I opened the front door and called out that I was back. By the time I dropped the bag of hot dogs on the counter, my littlest cousin, Gabriella, came thumping down the hallway and jumped into my arms.

"Gabs!" I shouted, swinging her around.

"Diner!"

We laughed and squeezed each other. When I set her down, she climbed to her tip toes for her official greeting.

"You give me hug and kiss. I give you hug and kiss," she said.

I bent down and complied, following the greeting with a couple of little tickles on her belly. She giggled and squeezed my leg.

"Why do we have to drive so far to get here?" she asked.

Here we go. "Because we live far from the beach."

"Why?"

"Because that's where our parents decided they wanted to raise us."

"Why?"

Someone, please rescue me. The good news was someone did. The bad news? It was Todd.

He leaned over the railing from the second floor. "Hey, D."

"Todd," I said with as much patience as I could. "Hello."

"You get Chicago dogs?"

"A dozen," I answered.

"Sweet." He leaned back up the stairs. "Autumn? You hungry?"

Autumn?

Gabs rolled her eyes and scowled. "*She* did not want to play matching."

"Who is she?"

"His *girl*friend." She tilted her adorable four-year-old head to the side. "I thought *you* were his girlfriend."

"Not anymore," I muttered.

Todd brought a girlfriend. To our family vacation!

They walked down the stairs together, holding hands. She wore her bikini—well, I might add— under a see-through coverup. Her hair was short and dark brown, falling to her shoulders in a stylish bob.

"Hi," I waved. "I'm Dinah."

"Autumn." She smiled, but I got the sense she felt more awkward than happy. Couldn't blame her.

I pushed the bag across the island. "Chicago dogs. It's our first day beach tradition."

"Todd told me," Autumn said. "I love Chicago dogs."

Gabriella climbed onto a stool, and I put her plain hot dog on a plate.

"I like ketchup now," she said proudly.

"Ketchup it is." I grabbed it from the fridge and squirted it along her hot dog.

An awkward silence settled over the kitchen like an acrid smell you couldn't locate the source of.

"I'm gonna go unpack." I left the kitchen with my Chicago dog uneaten and my appetite destroyed.

My mom met me at the top of the stairs. "We have a situation."

Maybe I should have stayed on the beach longer.

"What's that, Mom?"

"You're sharing with Gabriella."

"Why not Elyse?"

"Gabriella refused to share with Autumn."

"Why?"

"Something about a matching game, apparently. I don't know. But Elyse is sharing with Autumn, and you're with Gabriella."

I loved Gabriella. I did. A lot, but beach vacations were usually a week-long sleepover with Elyse, Gabriella's way older sister.

"Look on the bright side," Mom whispered. "You're not sharing with Autumn."

Autumn. The girl who got my ex-boyfriend—not a major loss there—my bedroom, and my hot dog. I schlepped my stuff to my assigned bedroom hoping the list of things she took from me ended there.

TWENTY-SIX

ON ONE HAND, I got the hypocrisy. I'd tried to bring a boyfriend, but how ridiculous could Todd be? Guaranteed he'd met Autumn in the last week. I'd asked him where she went to school, and he'd had no idea. He didn't even know where she lived. Something smelled, and it wasn't the seafood boil.

Elyse caught it too. "She's here to make you jealous. Bottom line."

Another Todd Wilkinson ploy. I'd lost count.

"Is it working?" Elyse asked.

"Jealous he has someone here and Darius couldn't make it. That's about it."

Elyse hid behind her massive sunglasses, watching Todd and Autumn swim in the deep end of the pool. Autumn whispered in Todd's ear so close that no water could move between their bodies. Then she stepped out of the pool in her tiny bikini, water dripping from her dark brown hair and over the curves of her body.

"You look so much better in a bikini," Elyse said.

"Liar." I sighed. Why did I even care? I reclined in my lounger and closed my eyes.

My phone buzzed with a text from Em. She'd sent a picture of horse number ten. She was done painting for the day, but the next morning, she'd start fresh on either Darius's favorite horse or mine.

"I shouldn't have come," I muttered, setting my phone back on the table between us.

"Don't let him ruin your vacation."

"It's not only that. I was painting this carousel for the carnival, and I wanted to finish it." I explained about the horses.

"I get it," Elyse said. "You must really like this guy."

I groaned and closed my eyes. The build up of everything between Darius and me, the constant questioning about what each kiss and touch and look meant, if anything at all—it weighed on me so much I would sink if we were in the pool.

"Dinah?" Elyse said in a soft voice. "What's going on?"

I glanced at Todd and Autumn and then pulled my cousin out of her lounger. "Let's get the beach passes."

On the beach, the whole story poured out. How I caught Todd in the pool with some girl, how I met Darius, him asking me to fake date him.

"Wait," Elyse had stopped our walk in the sand on that point. "Did you say *fake* date?"

"Yeah, but that's top secret."

"Obviously." She grinned. "Like in the movies? You two are just pretending?"

"Yeah."

"But he's hot?"

"So hot."

"Then what's the problem?"

"I'm confused. I expected to be, but it's worse than I imagined."

She nodded, so I went on to debate the looks and comments and all of the minute details between us. After about an hour of walking and talking, Elyse shared a couple of crucial takeaways.

"First, you are so over Todd, and I could not be happier because that boy does not deserve you. Even if your feelings for Darius aren't real—which I think you need to still sort through, so I can't help you with that—the reality is hanging with him or flirting with him or whatever got you over your ex."

"What if flirting with *me* reminded Darius of how much he wants to be with his ex?"

"Then nothing you can do will change that," Elyse said. "Learn it while you're young. A guy wants what he wants. Games might change that superficially, but on a deeper level, they won't work."

Like all of Todd's games weren't working on me.

"Maybe him being back home with Em while you're away is a good thing," Elyse suggested. "It could help you both figure things out."

Distance. Right. I'd enjoy the beach, sketch the pets, swim with Gabriella, and let her crush me at matching. I'd play card games with my family and even Autumn. I did *not* want to realize I actually liked Darius only to watch him fall for someone else or not be committed to me. I could do without an unfaithful boyfriend the rest of my life after Todd.

With a deep breath of ocean air, I re-centered my vision.

"You good?" Elyse asked.

"So good," I said, burying my toes beneath the warm sand until they reached the cooler layer below. "Tell me what's been going on with you."

———

That night and the next day, I sketched, swam, walked the beach, and played games. Darius and I texted, but I followed Elyse's advice and tried to give us distance. Em started work on the replica of the horse I'd been riding when Darius and I had first kissed, sending me photo updates along the way.

After a long day of nonstop family time, I fell into bed shortly after my toddler roommate. Gabriella snored lightly while I sketched by nightlight. I finished a Dalmatian portrait and finally falling asleep around ten o'clock.

Hours later, I shot upright when something caused the floor to creak next to my bed. In the moonlight, an outline of a person shifted, and I opened my mouth to scream. Before I could, he fell onto the bed, covering my mouth with his hand.

"It's me, D," Todd said.

My heart thumped with relief and then irritation. I swatted him until he moved off the bed. "What are you doing in my room?"

"I missed you."

"You *missed* me? Your new girlfriend is down the hall."

"So?"

"You are a nightmare," I said.

"No. You're awake."

"A metaphorical nightmare! What? How? I can't even. This is my room! Gabriella is sleeping on the air mattress."

"Come to my room then."

I had to be in an alternate universe.

"C'mon, D. You're out there in your bikini—"

"We are at the beach. And are you a middle school boy with no self-control?"

"You don't have to be mean."

"Mean? Me? You're here with a new girlfriend. I'm with

Darius. Yet, you're trying to climb into my bed in the middle of the night, and I'm the mean one?"

"If things were so serious with you two, why isn't he here?"

I was trying my best to whisper. "None of your business. See that's the thing when someone breaks up with you. Their life is no longer any of your business!"

"Keep it down. Our parents are gonna freak if they find me in here."

"Better be on your way then."

He brushed his fingertips across my cheek. "D, please."

"Don't touch me, Todd."

"I just know if you give me another chance, it will be different."

"I'm not going to warn you again," I said.

"Kiss me one time, and tell me you don't feel anything."

I punched him in the face as hard as I could.

"Shit, Dinah." He groaned, rocking back and forth next to the bed.

"Kindly see yourself out of my room, and don't come back."

"You punched me!"

"Observant. Don't make me scream for our parents and tell them what you snuck in here for."

"I'm going," he said. "I—"

"Say another word, and you'll earn another bruise to match the first. Get. Out."

The floor creaked again on his way out. With the help of the moonlight, I watched his silhouette slip into the hallway and heard the door close behind him.

I kicked the covers off to check on Gabriella, but thankfully, she slept through the encounter. I settled back into the bed and swiped my phone on. Tapping my social media, I scrolled through Darius's posts. His smile was contagious. I pulled the covers over me again and snuggled into my pillow. His photos showed how fast the pet exhibit had progressed. The committee had challenged Darius to be ready in a week, and he was pulling it off. The comments on his posts didn't compare to the comments surrounding him a week earlier. Things like: "This is the best idea ever."

"I've never been to the carnival, but I'm going next weekend for sure."

"Perfect timing. I need a new pup!"

I searched for his hate hashtag and found nobody had posted on it since the cookie incident at the deli. I considered blocking the door with the desk chair but worried Gabriella wouldn't be able to move it to use the bathroom or to sneak out early in the morning while I snoozed. Instead, I scrolled through photos of Darius, letting them soften my emotions like a good meditation.

After a few minutes, my eyelids drooped, and I returned my phone to the charger.

Given my midnight visitor, we obviously hadn't succeeded at expelling Todd from my life, but if Darius kept his focus on the exhibit and kept out of trouble, he might finally reclaim his reputation or even improve it.

Selfishly, I lay in bed in the middle of the night hundreds of miles away from him, wondering what that would mean for me.

TWENTY-SEVEN

EARLY THE NEXT MORNING, I packed some fruit and water and headed to the beach with my sketching supplies. No Todd. No Autumn. And a commitment to refrain from endless scrolling on Darius's page.

I opened my umbrella, secured my beach blanket in the sand, and settled in for a long, long, long drawing session.

The night before had been like riding the Thunderbolt all over again. Todd had had a girlfriend a year ago, and he had one now. I would not be the girl that messed with that, but I didn't know how to tell Autumn the truth either.

I sketched a boxer while I chatted with Mac through my earpiece.

"Oh! I'm covering the pet exhibit at the carnival," she said. "It will be our first feature of the year."

"Sounds great," I said. Darius would appreciate it, and Mac would manage to find kids from our school who were involved for the local angle.

After catching up, we ended our call, and I sketched a shih tzu. After a quick snack, I found I had to use the bathroom. I glanced toward the house but didn't see movement. I texted Elyse.

Me: *Are they around?*

Elyse: *Swimming in the pool. Every time the back door opens, Todd breaks his neck to see who it is. Can't imagine who he's waiting for. Any idea how he got that shiner?*

Crap.

Me: *What did he tell the parents?*

Elyse: *That he walked into a door. Creative.*

A few seconds later, she added: *Come back. Gabriella and I are making cookies and then playing matching.*

I finished the shih tzu, packed my beach belongings, and carted them across the road. I tossed the umbrella and chair in the shed and bypassed the pool by pretending to dig through my bag for my phone. I felt Todd's eyes on me.

"Nicely done." Elyse slid the cookie recipe across the counter.

"Two seconds," I said. "Bathroom break."

"Me too," Gabriella said jumping off the stool and walking crookedly down the hall.

Minutes later, all three of us were back in the kitchen and ready to go. Elyse's phone rang, and she held it against her chest. "It's him."

"Him" referred to her current crush.

"No," I said. "We're baking."

"Two seconds. I have to answer."

I rolled my eyes. "Go."

Gabriella shook her head. "Boys."

"Tell me about it."

Except then my phone rang, and it was Darius.

"Guess I have to make the cookies myself," Gabs said.

"I will help you," I promised and answered the phone.

"Hey, beautiful," he said.

Gabriella waved the recipe, and I pointed to ingredients

in the picture. She pushed the stool around the kitchen collecting them while Darius energetically updated me on the exhibit's progress. I moved around the kitchen, preheating the oven and pulling the cookie trays from the cupboard above the built-in microwave, the sound of his voice like a settling white noise.

Until he asked, "What's up with you?"

I made the mistake of looking out the kitchen window and seeing Todd and Autumn splashing around the pool. "Nothing much."

"I ramble for five minutes, and you give me 'Nothing much'?"

"I'm making cookies with Gabriella. We're going to play a game."

"Is it raining or something?"

"No," I said. "It's beautiful outside."

"But you're not on the beach or in the pool?"

"Not currently, no."

Gabriella crossed her arms and tapped her toes.

I pulled the phone away from my face and whispered, "One sec. Promise."

"You don't sound okay," Darius said. "Is it Todd?"

I took a deep breath, not sure how much I wanted to say.

"So it is Todd."

But this was Darius. We told each other everything. We had each other's backs. The words tumbled out.

"Todd? The guy who brought a new girl on vacation to make me jealous?"

"Is it working?"

I grabbed the butter and eggs from the fridge. "Please don't bore me with your stupid questions."

"For real."

"No, and I think it's pissing him off even more," I said, helping Gabriella measure ingredients while I talked. "He flirts with her during the day in front of everyone and then..." I turned away from Gabriella and whispered, "Sneaks into my room at night."

The line went quiet.

"Darius? Are you there?"

"He snuck into your room?"

"Yes, but I made him leave." More silence. "Are you okay?"

His deep sigh told me he wasn't. We dumped the first few ingredients into the standing mixer and turned it on. It filled the silence between us.

"There's an art studio in town that has an open painting night tomorrow," I said after a few seconds, trying to change the subject. "I'm going there to blow off steam."

Darius was still quiet.

"How's everything else at the carnival?"

He took a few beats to muster the words, but he finally spoke. "Good. Everyone's focused on the pet exhibit. I've never seen anything like it. We have more people working on this exhibit than any other we've ever had."

"And social media is being kinder to you."

"I haven't had time to check."

"I did last night," I said. "When I couldn't sleep."

"Because of Todd?"

"No more of him. I want to hear more about the exhibit. I'm sorry I'll miss it."

"Me too. Look, I have to run."

I couldn't hide the desperation in my voice. "Already?"

"Sorry."

"Sure," I swallowed. "No problem. I should..." Continue making cookies with my preschool-aged cousin and dip them in ice cream while watching a cheesy rom-com.

"See ya," Darius said and hung up before I could reply.

I stared at the home screen on my phone and replayed the conversation in my mind. He was *not* happy with Todd. But had I done something? I debated it for the hour or so until the cookies were blended, trayed, baked and cooled, but no violation sparked in my mind.

I turned my phone over in my hands while Gabriella smeared a warm cookie over her joyous little face and Elyse swooned over her latest boy. We played matching. Gabriella crushed both Elyse and me. Actually, we played multiple games, and she won every time. When my pride couldn't take another loss, I bribed her with a snack of chocolate animal crackers to quit playing.

"I'm going to walk the beach," Elyse said. "Want to come?"

"Pool! Pool! Pool!" Gabriella shouted.

"I'll stay with her," I said.

Elyse nodded toward the pool. "You sure?"

"I can't hide in the house the whole vacation, and since they've made their official residential address the pool, I don't have much of a choice."

"Good luck," Elyse said on her way out the door.

I might need much more than luck in my life.

Gabs tossed a lion in her mouth and showed me its insides while she asked, "Why do I have to swim with a grownup?"

"To be safe," I told her, eating a hippo.

"Why?"

"It's important to be safe."

"Why?"

"So you don't get hurt," I answered more slowly, wondering if I'd need another bribe to get out of this series of questioning, too.

"Why?"

"Because people love you and don't want to see you hurt."

"Why?"

Definitely needed a bribe. "You ready to go swimming?"

With wide eyes, she scooped up her pile of animal crackers and threw them in the air. "Yes!"

When the crumbs settled, we cleaned up and changed into swimsuits.

"I love your swimsuit," Gabriella said of my sparkling blue bikini, but I thought hers won the prize with tiny rainbows, unicorns, and balls of sunshine. I squeezed her little hand in mine and loaded up on towels and toys. I lined them along the corner opposite of Todd and Autumn, refusing to even look their way.

In the pool, it didn't take long to learn the string of bribes would have to continue through requests to hold her up while she floated, get her a snack, throw her in the air, play Barbies, get her a drink—after two hours, I needed a nap.

The four-year-old did not.

The pool area filled in with my family and Todd's, so I passed off Gabriella-watching duties to them and snuggled on a chaise in the shade. A breeze chilled my wet skin. I turned my beach towel into a blanket and snoozed until someone decided to blast the speakers above the pool.

Despite the loud music, chatter, and even Todd's presence which filled the space to smothering proportions, my mind wandered so far away that it all faded. Darius's first exhibit—one that he'd designed himself—would open in three days. Maybe I could convince my parents to let me leave early, but how would I get home? They'd never let me drive five hours by myself.

They'd suggest Todd come with me. Hard pass.

I scrolled through Darius's posts of him with the dogs. He'd make an incredible vet someday. I laughed out loud at a picture of a German Shepard named Bruno licking Darius's cheek. Darius had closed his eyes and scrunched his face together in mock disgust. The next photo showed him laughing. Every photo broadcasted authenticity. After the exhibit opened and Mac wrote an article about it, puppies and kittens from all over the region would certainly find homes.

I landed on a photo carousel of Darius and me, each picture showing a different angle. Him kissing my cheek. Me pretending to poke him in the eye. Him watching me smell a flower. I stopped on that one. The softness in his eyes and the curve of his lips twisted my insides.

My intuition screamed the appreciation on his face was every ounce as authentic when he looked at me as his emotion had been in the shelter photos. I tapped my screen until I found his name. My finger hovered over it for a second before I shook away my apprehensions and called him.

The phone rang. And rang. He'd answer. So our conversation had been a little weird earlier. *Ring.* Our relationship wasn't complicated. We were friends pretending to be more. *Ring.* I tipped the phone away from my ear and listened. For every ring in my ear, I heard another ring coming from the house.

"Dinah," my mom called from the back porch. "You have a visitor."

Darius had to duck under the frame to make his way out the sliding glass door. He wore swim trunks, a white t-shirt, and a bashful smile. He held up his ringing phone. "You called?"

TWENTY-EIGHT

SOMEHOW, I'd moved from the chaise to the back porch. "What are you...? How did you...?"

Darius bent forward and slipped his arms around my waist. I closed my eyes and fell into him.

"I can't believe you're here."

"Everyone," my mom announced. "Meet Dinah's *friend,* Darius."

They launched into a chorus of, "Hi, Darius!"

"Maybe you want to take Darius on a walk down the beach before dinner," Mom suggested.

I squeezed his hand.

"Sounds perfect," he said. "Thanks, Mrs. Zimmerman."

We didn't move. I stood on the deck staring up at him, wondering if I'd fallen back asleep in the shade and dreamed him here.

He laughed and kissed my cheek.

"You're here?"

"I'm here."

"Dinah?" Mom said, handing me two beach passes. I slipped them around my wrist and tugged at Darius' arm.

We left through the back gate and crossed the beach road to the boardwalk access, laughing every few seconds.

"I'm sorry. I'm so…"

"Surprised?"

"Yeah! Is this why you had to get off the phone so fast?"

"My mom was heading to work. I wanted to tell her I was going for a drive."

"A very long drive."

He lifted my hand to his lips and kissed it. "Sounded like you need me."

I leaned my head onto his shoulder. "Darius, it is shocking how much I needed you."

My mind was all set to tell him about my afternoon of worrying that I'd done something to hurt or upset him, but I realized what I'd said to my fake boyfriend—that I'd *needed* him. With him standing next to me at the beach, having met my entire family, his fingers intertwined with mine, my stomach performed a tumbling routine.

Darius's lips curved into a smile the moment we stepped on the sand. Like a toddler, consumed by the ocean, he walked straight ahead.

"I almost forgot," I said. "You've never been to the ocean."

We found an open space and stood arm-in-arm. The wind greeted us, and the water rushed toward us only to wave goodbye, again and again.

"The sound…" He closed his eyes and took a deep breath. "I've heard it in movies and online, but hearing it and feeling the wind and the heat of the sun, I get why people love the beach."

I rested my head on his shoulder and closed my eyes, too. Experiencing the beach with him for the first time was like taking little Gabriella on new adventures —magical.

Darius kissed the top of my head, and we started walking again.

"Thank you for inviting me," he said.

"Are you kidding? Thank you for coming!"

He glanced sideways at me a couple of times, a smirk forming at the corner of his lips. Finally, I nudged his hip.

"What?"

He laughed and shook his head.

"There's something. Tell me."

"You're in a bikini."

Oh. I'd forgotten that.

"I haven't seen you in a bikini before. It's, um, hard to look away."

My cheeks warmed even more than they did when the sun was at its height. "That's both sweet and disturbing."

"I mean it as a compliment." Darius laughed. "Come here." He leaned against the boardwalk railing, the Atlantic Ocean rushing to the shore behind him, and pulled me to him. I wrapped my arms around his neck, and he locked his in the curve of my lower back.

"Is it okay that I'm here?"

I nodded, afraid to say anything.

"When you told me about Todd, I got…angry. And jealous. He was here with you, and I wasn't. And I know this isn't real, but the fact he would do that and disrespect you…"

Everything he said made sense, but I couldn't move past him saying this wasn't real. I mean, I knew that. Obviously. But hadn't all the movies told us it gets real at some point? If you let it go on long enough?

If you worked alongside someone and laughed with them.

If you mixed the undeniably real physical moments with the emotional pretending.

If you went on vacation together.

He dipped his head low and looked at me above his sunglasses. "I missed you."

A breeze sucked the oxygen from my lungs. Darius had missed me. After only two days apart?

"If my reaction when you showed up at my beach house didn't show you I missed you, then…" I laughed and shook my head. "Wait! How can you be here? Your exhibit!"

"Kierk's overseeing finishing touches. I have to be back Friday."

Two nights and one day. That's all the time I'd have with Darius at the beach. And then I'd beg my mom to let me go home with him, so I wouldn't miss his exhibit. Maybe that could be my surprise to him. *And* I'd be home in enough time to paint the final horse on the carousel.

Got to love when a plan comes together. I held tight to Darius's arm as we walked, and I pointed out all the notable beach haunts.

"No!" I said. "I should have brought my purse. You have to eat a Chicago dog on your first beach day. It's a rule."

"I have money. Lead the way."

We ordered two Chicago dogs and bottles of water at The Hot Dog Hut—it would be inhospitable to let him eat alone.

"You can't tell anyone," I whispered while we waited for the food. "My mom wouldn't want us to ruin our dinner."

"I'll eat dinner, too. No problem."

I sighed and shook my head. "You're here."

"I'm here."

I gazed into his eyes long enough for my body to tingle. With an awkward laugh, I looked away.

"You're doing it again," Darius whispered.

"Doing what?"

"Biting your lip."

"Oh." I hadn't noticed. I mustered the courage to look into his eyes again.

"We are in public," he said.

I looked around. "Seems pretty public."

The universe chose that exact moment to send a gust of wind through the boardwalk, whipping my hair around my face in post-pool time tangles. I tried to flick the offending locks back into place, but they only tangled more.

So much for a romantic moment.

I stepped back from Darius and turned into the wind, letting nature right its wrong. After a few seconds of swinging and swaying, I could see again.

"Attractive," I said sarcastically. "I know."

Darius held my wrist and gently pulled me to him. His tingle-inducing fingertips brushed my cheek to tuck the last wild strand of hair behind my ears and whispered, "You're always attractive."

His soft lips enveloped my bottom lip. And then the top. His gentle kiss both satisfied me and left me wanting more —totally fitting for the anomaly that was Darius Moore.

Footsteps came to a stop so close to us that the person they'd belonged to cast a shadow over me. "Darius, what's up, man?"

Todd.

Darius rested his forehead against mine. "The problem with our whole 'public' rule is that there are other people in public."

As in, we should have been kissing in private?

Todd introduced Darius to Autumn. They nodded at each other, but I didn't miss how her eyes worked their way across his shoulders and down his torso.

"Your mom asked us to find you for dinner," Todd said.

I checked Darius's watch. "Dinner won't be for another hour. I'm sure we're good."

"Suit yourself," he said, pulling Autumn further down the beach, clearly not concerned about dinner.

"Do we need to get back?" Darius asked.

"My mom would never send him for me. He's playing his usual games."

The worker at the Hut called my name, and we retrieved our traditional, first-day-at-the-beach meal.

"Do you think he has any other games planned for us?" Darius asked.

Sadly, I had no doubt.

TWENTY-NINE

ELYSE PULLED Darius into a game of matching with Gabriella the second we got back to the house. "It's a rite of passage," she said. "And if you don't play, she won't like you."

"Can't have that." Darius rubbed his hands together. "Let's do this."

"Don't get excited," I said. "You're not going to win."

He huffed. "She's four."

Elyse and I laughed knowingly. Ten minutes later, Gabriella's stack of matches destroyed Darius'.

"That was humbling," he said after Gabs ran off to play with her toys. "What's up for tonight?"

"Dinner and beach bonfire," I said.

"How are your sketches coming?"

"I drew a couple of cats yesterday."

He cozied up in the pile of pillows and blankets on the couch. "Want to draw some now?"

"You want me to leave you to rest? I can show you to your room."

"Nah," he said. "I like watching you draw. You get this serious face, and your eyebrow does this cute curve thing."

"Cute curve thing?" I asked, amused.

"Please?"

I shook my head and laughed, but minutes later, we sat on opposite ends of the couch with me sketching a German Shepard and him alternating between watching me and nodding off.

———

Darius captivated everyone at dinner with stories of volunteering at the shelter. Mr. Wilkinson nearly choked when we told the story of Peaches' grand escape, complete with video evidence.

The more everyone adored my new boyfriend, the more my ex-boyfriend huffed and puffed. Before he blew the house down, we packed up for the beach bonfire. On the beach, the parents joined a circle of neighbors, Gabriella played with their children in the sand, and my generation sat around the fire, waiting for the metaphorical flames shooting from Todd to consume us.

Didn't take long.

"What hotel you staying at tonight, Darius?" Todd asked.

Darius rested his hand on my knee. "I was planning on bunking with you."

Todd sucked in a breath.

"What's the problem? You don't want me to know about your late night walks?"

Todd threw a glare in my direction. "I don't know what you're talking about."

Autumn was too immersed in something on her phone to follow the conversation. Too bad.

"The way I see it," Darius went on. "If I'm in your room and you leave to sneak into someone else's room, I'll know about it. I might even sleep in front of the door."

Todd snickered. "You've come a long way, D. Running to your big, bad college boy to protect you."

Darius' body stiffened.

"I got this," I muttered. "Let's be clear. I didn't need my boyfriend to kick your ass out of the room. I did that myself, and you have the bruise to prove it. My *boyfriend* has enough respect for women that he doesn't take it well when some jerk is sneaking into a girl's bedroom uninvited in the middle of the night."

At some point, I'd stood and pointed my finger in Todd's face and attracted the attention of the rest of the beach. Darius tugged at my side gently. Registering his subtle cue to regain my composure, especially in front of my parents, I sat but this time closer to him and with my arm looped in his.

"When I think of Darius Moore, respect for women is one of the first things that comes to mind," Todd said.

"Watch it," I warned.

"No, let's get it out in the open. Maybe I should show your parents the posts online about their daughter's perfect, new boyfriend. See how romantic everyone thinks it is that he drove all this way then?"

"Todd, shut up."

Todd glanced at our parents. I didn't need to see the concern on their faces to know it was there.

"That's what you want? Everything out in the open? *Everything*?"

"Your threats are getting old, D."

"So are your games." I stood and dusted the sand from my clothes. "I'm done with them. Stay away from me."

I packed my bag and stomped through the sand—not the

easiest task in the world. My feet slid on each step, making achieving the kind of attitude and intensity I had intended impossible.

I had no choice. I had to convince my mom to let me leave with Darius.

"Dinah, wait up!"

I stopped and swiveled. Darius had been moving so quickly, he nearly plowed through me. When he made contact, he wrapped his arms around me and broke my fall, landing on me in the process.

He laughed and rolled over in the sand. "Sorry about that."

Side by side, we watched the night sky, clear and bright with stars. I reached across the cool, soft granules until I found his hand and slipped my fingers into his.

"You okay?" he asked.

"Honestly?"

"Always."

"Yes. Because you're here. When you suggested this whole fake dating thing, I thought it was a stupid plan. That I didn't need it, but now, it's so good not to feel alone."

He squeezed my hand. "I get it. When the whole spinning wheel-egg extravaganza happened, you being there, it changed everything."

"I'm glad I was there."

"Me too."

"Still, you didn't have to come all this way," I said.

"I wanted to."

I closed my eyes and let those words hang in the breeze. Darius wanted to be with me. I wouldn't taint the statement with clarifications about why or for how long.

"Sometimes," Darius whispered, "I can't even imagine how this ends."

The breeze could capture that sentiment and take it as far away as it wanted.

"Ending our fake relationship…" he clarified.

I propped myself up on my elbow. "Are you saying you think it's time for us to…you know…?"

"No. Do you?"

I shook my head. He rolled onto his side, too. The move brought our faces and bodies even closer. My skin tingled at the proximity more than usual. I chalked it up to Darius mentioning the end of us. Theoretically, I knew a breakup would come. Most real relationships ended, so what chance did the fake ones have?

"Will you meet me tomorrow morning?" I asked, eager to take advantage of all the tingles I possibly could until we decided to say goodbye. "To watch the sunrise?"

"What time is that?"

"About five-forty-five."

Darius whistled.

"I know, but it's worth it."

"Okay," he said.

I finally had a date to watch the sunrise.

THIRTY

I WOKE UP TOO EARLY, digging through every outfit I'd brought to the beach. No piece of clothing could do justice to the fantasy I'd built in my mind for more than half of my life. *It's not real, Dinah.*

I wondered if anyone else's internal voice ruined the crucial moments of their lives.

I settled on a pair of jean shorts and a simple tank top—in case my inner voice was, in fact, correct, and the moment wouldn't be real. Didn't want to send Darius mixed messages, or in this case, the accurate messages.

I closed my door quietly and practically bumped into Darius in the hallway. His eyes widened as if the moment was a complete surprise.

"You ready for the sunrise?"

He stepped back. "Oh. Right. I forgot."

"You normally get up this early?" I teased.

He looked back at the door to his and Todd's bedroom. "No. I, uh." Darius took a deep breath and smiled.

"Are you okay?"

"Perfect. Let me grab my hoodie, and we'll go."

I leaned against the wall outside the door. Darius reappeared within seconds and took my hand. We tiptoed up the stairs to the loft window and climbed through. The sun still hid behind the horizon. We had time.

The morning chill cooled my bare legs, and I shivered. Without a word, Darius pulled his hoodie over his head and slipped it over mine.

"You don't have to," I said.

"I'm not that cold."

"Thanks."

He looked away and rubbed the back of his neck. I'd spent enough time with him to know something was up.

"Did something happen?"

After a few seconds, he answered. "Nothing you have to worry about."

"What are fake girlfriends for?" As soon as I asked the question, I realized my worst fear: I hated that I'd had to add the word "fake" to that sentence.

"For watching sunrises."

I checked the horizon, but still no sun. "Good answer."

"You do this a lot at the beach?"

I closed my eyes and took a breath. The moment I'd met Darius, I'd felt that dangerous attraction. Being his fake girlfriend offered me the opportunity to get to know him as a friend. I couldn't guess where we'd be in a month or even a week, but I'd known the second he showed up at the beach that I'd wanted to be here with him—in this moment.

But Em had been insistent, Darius was going to cheat on me. He was going to hurt me. What if our perfection relied on the fakeness of our relationship?

"You okay?"

I exhaled, my decision made. "We always come to this house. Every year. As a kid, I remember Elyse bringing me out here to watch the sunrise. We'd watch these cutesy romance movies the night before—age appropriate of course —with these epic first kiss scenes at the end."

"Sounds cute."

"It was. One summer, my cousin brought her boyfriend, and I caught them up here, watching the sun rise. She was leaning back against his chest, his arms wrapped around her. When the sun passed the horizon and was fully awake for the day, he kissed her. I remember being this kid, thinking how epic it had been. Like my cousin was in her own movie."

I looped my arm in his and rested my head on his shoulder before continuing. "I guess, ever since that day, I wanted my own sunrise movie moment."

Darius stilled when the sun finally appeared. It teased in the distance, warming the horizon with its orange hues, sparking the promise for more to come. My heart raced as if its sole task was to pump the sun right up from the surface of the water.

"I've never watched a sunrise over the ocean before," Darius whispered.

I didn't dare look at him. I'd offered up one of the deepest desires of my heart. I'd admitted I'd wanted that moment with him. Not to mention two crucial details. We were alone. If anything happened between us, it could—or maybe even *would* without question—mean something.

"What do you think?" I asked, clarifying, "Of the sunrise?"

The sun broke free, its bright yellow appearing as a sliver at first, but then rounding out. Darius moved behind me, pressing my back to his chest and wrapping his arms around me. The ball of energy in the distance didn't have anything on the fire in my heart.

The sky brightened with my hopes. Darius pressed his lips against my cheek and then my neck, pulling a wistful gasp from my throat. "Can I be the guy from your fantasy?"

"You already are," I whispered.

He kissed my ear. "What else should I know?"

I'd always imagined the moment being so hot that my boyfriend couldn't take my eyes off of me to watch the sunrise. I told Darius that, and he chuckled.

"Done. I can close my eyes and picture you in that biki-ni." He smiled against my cheek.

I reached my arm back and around his neck. He responded with a trail of kisses along my cheek.

"Darius?"

"Yeah?"

"We're not in public."

He spun and lifted me, wrapping my legs around his waist. "Thank God for that."

The world around us brightened, shining light on the two of us, intertwined on the balcony, my back pressed against the house, and Darius's lips moving against mine in ways they'd never had before.

He slowed the kiss with a few final toe-tingling, lingering pecks and rested his forehead against mine. "I hope I met your expectations."

"Exceeded," I muttered. "Definitely exceeded."

"Dinah?" my Mom called softly from the loft. "Are you up there, honey? It's time to start breakfast."

Darius quietly lowered me to my feet. I smoothed my hair where his hands had been tangled seconds before and poked my head in the window. "Darius and I are watching the sunrise. Be right in."

"Oh, good. Have fun, sweetie."

I bit my lip and glanced sideways at Darius.

"I had fun," he said deadpan.

I covered my face.

"Isn't it early for breakfast?" Darius asked.

"It's tradition that we go to this aquarium during every visit. My aunt insists on arriving the second it opens to avoid the crowd. Today's the day, which means an earlier morning."

Darius pulled me into a hug and kissed my forehead. "One last look at the sunrise?"

The rays reflected off the rushing water. Clumps of the earliest beach-goers formed on the beach, propping up their umbrellas, tents, and chairs, all relishing the promise of a new day.

I couldn't blame them.

"Thank you," Darius whispered. "My first sunrise *exceeded* my expectations."

I swatted his shoulder.

"I'll never forget it," he added.

"Oh my gosh. You are so embarrassing."

"I quit. Let's go make some breakfast."

As if I could concentrate on the benign task of making a fruit salad after this. I couldn't think of anything that could successfully distract me from running the rooftop moments through my head all day long.

THIRTY-ONE

WITH ALL THE families in the house, breakfast had become an epic collaboration over the years. My mom made the best French toast sticks, so that was her domain. Elyse delivered on cinnamon rolls, and Mrs. Wilkinson had mastered the meats—bacon, sausage patties, and ham. I handled the fruit. As long as my fingers were steady with the knife, it was hard to mess up.

Darius helped by plucking red grapes from their stems and peeling a handful of clementines. Every few seconds, we'd make eye contact and laugh, or look away with impossible-to-hide smirks on our faces.

At one inopportune moment, Todd caught my eye and glared.

"Don't," I warned.

He shook his head and pushed the front door open with a thud.

"He's been especially weird this morning," I mumbled.

"Has he?"

Something in Darius's tone had me setting the knife

down on the cutting board to study him. "Did something happen with you and Todd?"

He put his head back and sighed.

"Darius?"

"I promised not to lie to you."

"So don't."

He whispered, "Not here."

I followed him out the front door to the small yard, my mind racing through the possibilities of what Todd could have done to Darius. A direct attack approach wasn't usually his style, especially when he was outmatched.

Darius paced and took a few deep breaths.

"I'm freaking out," I said. "What happened?"

"Autumn sort of climbed into my bed this morning."

"Excuse me?"

"That's why I was awake in the hall."

"Wait. Back up. She slept in your bed?"

"She didn't sleep there. I mean, I guess she did, but only until I woke up and found her there and then *I* left."

I sat on the front step and put my head in my hands.

"Nothing happened, Dinah. I swear."

His words were an echo, one I'd buried deep in the back of my memories with the hope I'd never hear them again. Nobody, not even Mac, believed I should trust Darius. Even Kierk challenged why I'd give him a chance given everything. Em had insisted he'd cheat on me, that he'd hurt me.

My phone buzzed. Todd sent me a link to an online post I was pretty sure I didn't want to look at. I let the phone fall through my fingers and crash against the sidewalk.

"What is it?" Darius asked.

"Todd."

He retrieved the phone, tapped the screen, and swore under his breath. "I'm going to kill him."

"It's the two of you," I whispered. "Isn't it?"

"Dinah, I swear…"

Todd rushed through the creaky front door. "Dinah, I'm so glad I found you."

I stood and held a hand up to him. "Stop!"

"Me? I'm a victim in this, too. Your boyfriend slept with my girlfriend."

Darius dove for Todd, but he jumped over the porch railing and out of his reach.

"What's in the video?" I asked quietly.

"You don't want to see it," Todd said.

"Then you shouldn't have sent it to me. Darius?"

He handed me the phone, and I pressed play. Todd's girlfriend playfully climbed under the blanket, and the blanket started to move. A lot. Along with some noises. I muted the sound.

And wished I could "mute" my eyes.

"You can't even see me in the video," Darius protested.

"Convenient planning on your part," Todd countered.

"Where's your girlfriend? Maybe she can clear up who was under the blanket with her."

"No need," Todd said. "Keep watching."

Sure enough, the video cut to a still blanket. Autumn rolled over, pulling some of the blanket with her and revealing a sleeping Darius.

I closed my eyes.

"Dinah, you know me better than this," Darius protested.

I did. I knew him as the guy who couldn't deal with emotions, and when he thought he could feel something for a girl, the only approach was to wreck the budding relationship to avoid getting hurt.

"Is this because things changed between us?" I whispered.

"What? No."

"Changed how?" Todd asked.

"None of your business," I said at the same time, Darius growled, "Man, shut up."

"Make me."

It was like we were in middle school again.

Todd lunged at Darius, the two of them hitting the ground with a thump and taking a flower pot with them. It cracked as it hit the cement. Darius and Todd kicked flowers and soil as they scrambled around each other. Scuffling from the house alerted me that this was no longer a private conversation.

"Stop it," I said. "Both of you."

But they didn't stop. Todd tackled Darius, raised himself up, and punched Darius in the cheek as hard as he could.

"Todd!"

Darius rolled him and landed his own punch.

My mom gasped from the bottom of the stairs, and both my dad and Todd's dad dove into the mix, demanding the guys break it up. They scrambled to their feet, clothes rumpled, blood dripping from their lips.

"Dinah?" my mom said. "What is this?"

"I need a minute."

I ran down the sidewalk in my bare feet, getting as far from the house as I could. I crossed the beach road, the video of Darius under the covers with another girl torturing my memories. I traveled the boardwalk until the clues flooding my mind were as infinite as the grains of sand around me.

Darius looked at me when I talked to him. Not his phone or other girls. He'd driven to the beach to be with me because I needed him. He'd kissed me on the roof...oh how he'd kissed me. Even before things had become real with him, he gave me the attention that Todd never had. Todd, who couldn't get off his phone and couldn't dismiss a pretty girl within a mile when I was sitting right in front of him.

I played the video again and caught a detail I'd missed before. In the, um, more action-packed part of the video, a shadow—very slight, but still there—fell on the wall. Some light source was coming from that direction, maybe a few rays of sun from the window. In the video of Darius sleeping, the shadow shifted in the other direction. The light wasn't natural.

I'd been with Darius on the beach when the sun had set the night before.

That one detail changed everything.

————

My mom, Todd, and Darius waited for me in the front yard. The guys hung back while my mom crossed the beach road and hugged me.

"Sweetie," she said.

"Hey, Mom. Sorry for all this."

"Don't you apologize for two boys that couldn't help themselves. This is on them. You want to talk about it?"

I shook my head. "I know what I have to do."

She held my hand while we crossed the road.

Darius was the first one to speak. "Can we talk privately?"

"No," I said.

"Dinah, please. You think I'd drive five hours to come to the beach, to be with you, and hook up with another girl. While you were sleeping in the same house?" His expression seemed to add that after the moment we'd had on the roof, could I believe there wasn't something real, something worth protecting, between us?

No. I didn't think that for a second.

"She has it on video, so you can stop lying now," Todd said.

"Stop talking," I said.

Darius's face fell. I lifted the tip of his chin, pulling him up to face me. And kissed his cheek.

"What...?"

Months earlier, I might have lost my temper with Todd, but I didn't have anything left for him.

I slid my hand into Darius's and turned to face a stupidly surprised Todd. "I know you did this."

"Me? You can blame me for a lot, but it's not my fault that my girlfriend and your boyfriend slept together."

"Todd!" my mother gasped.

"It's true," Todd argued.

"Enough," I said. "Todd, we're done. We are not getting back together. Have some class and get over it."

"Agreed," Autumn said from the doorway, a duffle over her shoulder, and her travel suitcase wheeling behind her. "Look, you're a good time, but you are toxic."

Todd's eyes widened, and he shook his head.

"Sorry. Even a beach vacation isn't worth this." She wheeled her suitcase across the sidewalk to me and handed over her phone, which showed a series of texts between her and Todd. "He told me if I pretended to be his girlfriend to make you jealous, I could enjoy a free beach vacation. Climbing into bed with your hot boyfriend was a bonus, I guess."

"Autumn!" Todd warned.

"Todd, is this true?" my mother challenged.

"Of course it is," I said. "Todd filmed *himself* with Autumn, cut the video, and then filmed a sleeping Darius next to Autumn hours later."

"Told you she'd figure it out," Autumn told Todd.

Darius squeezed my hand, and I felt every ounce of his gratitude. He'd promised to never lie to me. He'd earned my trust.

"Darius didn't do anything wrong, Mom. And he didn't deserve this. He's leaving, and I'm going with him."

"What!"

"I'll stay at Mac's, but I'm done with this twisted vacation. If you want to be friends with the Wilkinsons that's fine. Be friends with his parents. I'm no longer friends with him."

"Dinah," Todd protested.

"What? Give me one reason I should still consider you a friend." I crossed my arms and waited.

But I didn't have the time I'd need for him to find an answer apparently. I kissed my mom on the cheek and headed upstairs to pack.

THIRTY-TWO

DARIUS and I avoided the Todd saga most of the ride home. My mom had cleaned up the cut on his face and begged us to stay, but I couldn't be in the house with Todd Wilkinson for another minute. My mom had insisted he delete the video which was one saving grace since it hadn't picked up momentum in the twenty minutes it had been online.

"I'm sorry your beach vacation was cut short," I said.

"I've never had such a short but memorable vacation," he joked.

"At least this way I'll get to be with you for your exhibit opening."

If I had still been with Todd and had tried to show up where he didn't expect me, he would have made an excuse to keep me from going. My change of plans would have meant he'd have to change plans with whatever girl he was currently sneaking around with.

Darius didn't try to dissuade me from going. He grinned and reached across the console for my hand.

"Thank you for believing me."

"I trust you," I said.

He scoffed.

"You've earned it."

He took a deep breath. "Thank you. I'm sorry that I hit him."

"Are you kidding me? I wish I would have hit him."

"It was your family's vacation, the rental house...I shouldn't have done it."

"That flower pot was ancient," I said, eager to look on the bright side.

"You're being cool about this, but let's be real. What got me into this situation was being impulsive."

"With women," I said. "Not with jerks like Todd. He's been asking for it. What he did was borderline illegal. Actually, I think it might be entirely illegal. He's done nothing but cause you trouble. Sometimes the only way to stand up to somebody is to stand up to them."

"That's deep."

"You're teasing me."

Darius laughed and relaxed against the driver's side door. "I hope I don't have to stand up to someone like that again then."

"That's fair, but about being impulsive," I said, thinking about our morning kiss on the balcony. "I don't think your impulsive decision to drive to the beach was bad."

Darius licked his lips and raised an eyebrow at me. I adjusted the air conditioning vents, and we both laughed.

"You always put it out there, you know? Keep it real." Darius said with a nod. "It's one of the things I like about you. I never have to guess what you're thinking."

Except when it came to the number one rule of this whole fake relationship.

I muttered, "Thanks."

Darius gave me a sideways glance, and I swear he telepathically sent me a very-specific, so-important, must-know-the-answer question: Was what happened on the roof real?

I didn't answer it. I didn't tell him what I was thinking. I didn't put it out there. I didn't keep it real. He liked that I did all of those things, but in the passenger seat of his car, leaning as far away from him as I could, shoulder smashed against the window, I lied to him and to myself.

"Does it strike you as a little ironic that your ex-boyfriend found a fake date to your family vacation because you had a fake boyfriend?"

I suppressed my mess of fears and emotions and said, "Such an amateur."

"That's what I'm saying."

"He couldn't make fake dating work for a weekend, and here we are three weeks strong."

"We deserve an award," he joked, but his words cut me a little too close. Every day I had the privilege of pretending with Darius had felt like a prize in itself. If someone had asked me that morning, I would have said Darius and I were on the path to transitioning from this fake reality to something very real, but even after today's events, here we were alone. Darius was still calling our relationship fake.

Maybe I'd been wrong about what had happened on the roof. Or maybe the events of the day had scared Darius away from the feelings of our sunrise, movie moment. Or maybe they were real to both of us, and since I'd built a reputation with Darius of speaking the truth, he had no choice but to believe I didn't feel the same way since I didn't say so.

I closed my eyes and rested my forehead against the window, imagining Darius lifting me off the ground and pressing his body into mine. The softness of his kiss and the rawness of the moment, unexpected chaos contradicted by the reliability of the sun rising behind us. My chest hurt from how badly I wanted to open my mouth and tell Darius what I felt. But if he didn't feel the same way, then I'd lose him. We'd have no choice but to end our fake relationship.

All of my options led to one reality: my prized days with Darius were numbered. Like the persistent waves of the Atlantic, reality rushed closer and closer every second.

———

We drove straight to the carnival for Darius to deal with something that had come up with his exhibit, which gave me the chance to check in on Em's progress. I knocked on the door, but she'd left it unlocked. I let myself inside and gasped.

"Hey!" Em yelled from under a horse. "Nobody can be in here."

"It's me, Em."

She smacked her head on the horse as she shimmied out from underneath. "That's a surprise."

"Tell me about it," I said.

In the couple of days I'd been gone, my assistant had transformed the room by painting all but the last horse and installing twinkle lights along the baseboards and inside crown molding attached the walls a few inches below the ceiling giving the effect of the light shining upward.

"Have you even taken a break since I left?"

"Do you like it? My dad helped me install the lights. I wanted it to be a surprise."

"It makes the room, Em. Seriously. It's great."

A smile spread across her face, which was still remarkably beautiful despite the swipes of different-colored paint all over it. "Thank you."

"And the horses. You even did the touch-ups."

"Can you tell the difference?"

"The outlines and highlights are perfect. Have you been working day and night?"

She shrugged. "I know you wanted it done as soon as possible for Darius."

"That's sweet. Thanks."

"Is, um, everything okay with you two?"

I stilled. "Why would you ask that?"

"No reason," she said, fiddling with paintbrushes.

"Em?"

She shrugged.

"You saw the video, didn't you?"

She exhaled. "Sorry."

Guess that destroys my theory that not many people had seen it.

"I didn't share it though. Or like it."

"Thanks." I patted her shoulder. "Definite improvement."

"We'll skip over how condescending that is," she joked before turning serious again. "So, are you okay?"

"We promised not to talk about Darius, but if you have to know, the video was faked. It wasn't Darius. It was Todd under the blanket. I blew up on him. He accused Darius. Darius punched Todd."

"Wait. Darius was at the beach with you?"

I couldn't stop the smile from spreading across my face. "He drove down to surprise me. He was sharing a room with Todd, and after he fell asleep, Todd filmed his fake girlfriend climbing into bed with Darius."

Em shook her head and held up her hands to stop me. "Fake girlfriend?"

"Let's say you missed a lot, but none of it was Darius cheating on me."

"Honestly, Dinah. I'm glad to hear it. Forget all those

things I said before. I can see how much he likes you, and getting to know you like I do now, I see why."

"Wow." I sucked in a breath.

She rolled her eyes. "I know. I'm going to ruin my rep as a mean girl if I keep talking like this. I better get back to work."

I draped an apron over my neck and tied it behind me. "Want any help?"

THIRTY-THREE

I SLEPT at Mac's but might as well have spent my nights in the residential suite of the carnival. While Em and her dad installed faux hardwood flooring around the carousel, I painted the final horse—my horse. Or maybe *our* horse made more sense.

It took me from sun-up to sun-down to perfect the design, at which point I could barely stand upright. Muscles I didn't even know I had cramped.

The carousel exhibit wouldn't officially open for a few weeks, but Kierk had agreed to host a soft opening for the committee members Sunday night. Darius had no idea. All of his focus was on the Friday opening of the Adopt a Pet exhibit.

I'd made my decision: at the carousel opening, I'd honor our rule and tell him my feelings for him were as real as the blood, sweat, and tears that had gone into the project.

My head spun like the carousel itself just thinking about the moment.

"You okay?" Em asked as I crookedly cleaned up my paints.

"Sore but finished."

She tread lightly over the new floor and studied my work. "It's stunning. I can see why you wanted to paint this last one yourself."

Visually, maybe, but she had no idea of the horse's significance. Only Darius would see that. Hopefully.

"Are you going to Adopt-a-Pet tonight?"

"Everyone is," Em said. "I'm kind of impressed with all Darius's work. I heard there will be something like a hundred animals."

That sounded like a lot, but Darius was the go big or go home type, so it was certainly possible. I know that he'd worked with multiple shelters, not just the one that housed the infamous Peaches.

Em and I cleaned up and headed for Darius's exhibit, and big was definitely the word to describe it. He had mini play parks set up around the room. Carnival goers could sneak in and play with as many pets as they wanted, all night long. They could leash them and take them through a side door to the lawn behind the carnival. I'd never seen a new exhibit so crowded. People especially fought over the puppies and kittens.

One kitten wouldn't leave Darius, so he supervised with her on his shoulder, her tiny claws digging into his button-down shirt.

"Can I find you a towel or something to put under her?" I asked him, swooping the kitten away.

He pulled his shirt free from her claws and rubbed his shoulder. "I tried that. She pushes it away and digs her claws right back in. I think I found someone who is a perfect match for her. Come with me."

We squeezed through the crowd to a play park where two girls who looked a lot alike waited.

"You two were looking for a kitten, right?"

They squealed and lifted her from my arms. "She's perfect."

Darius chatted health details with them.

"Can we take her to the parking lot to meet our mom?"

"Sure," Darius said. "Let me grab a carrier."

"I'll get it," I said.

"Thanks, babe," he said and kissed my cheek.

I shuffled through boxes in the storage room and found one of the cat carriers. When I came back to the exhibit, it felt even more crowded, although I wasn't sure how that could be possible. Across the room, Darius talked to the girls with the kitten, but he wasn't alone anymore. Em stood next to him.

Very close.

She rested her hand on the small of his back and leaned even closer to talk to him.

When I was close enough, I slid between them. "Here's the carrier."

"Thank you," the girls said.

"I'm going to walk them out," Darius said. "I'll see you in a few minutes."

I didn't see him again, though, until the end of the night when the crowds had faded, and the Carnivalesque team cheered and toasted the exhibit's success. I hung back, giving Darius the spotlight. It didn't take me long to realize my mistake.

Em stepped forward to congratulate him, but her hug was more than friendly. Just like how she stood close to him earlier in the night was more than friendly.

Kierk found me in the crowd, and I forced a smile.

The celebration continued, but all I could think about was how tightly Em had hugged Darius. It could have been nothing.

Or it could be everything.

The Adopt-a-Pet exhibit led to the adoptions of fifteen pets on the first night. Saturday night, I helped process applications in the parking lot. Teens who had been interested in a particular pet brought their parents back Saturday to meet the lucky dog or cat and finalize any paperwork. By the end of our very busy shift Saturday night, Darius's brainchild had found homes for forty-three pets, and he had plans to rotate the pets in the exhibit until Christmas to keep finding homes.

I'd watched Em and Darius closely all night. They chatted occasionally but nothing more than that. I started to believe what I thought I saw Friday night had been nothing after all.

When the lights had all been turned on, and the masked carnival-goers had left, I found Darius in one of his favorite spots—the roof under the lights and the stars.

I jumped into his arms. "Congratulations! Forty-three pets! Josette said she's never seen anything like that."

"She told me they have space for hurricane transplants now."

"All the shelters will," I said. "What you're doing is seriously amazing."

He lowered his head. "I don't know."

"Are you okay?"

"Trying to be."

"Did someone say something on social?"

"Not yet," he said with a sigh.

I rested my head on his shoulder. Even after all his work on the exhibit, he worried about whether social media would be kind to him. The last thing I wanted to do was leave him like that, but I also had to get a good night's sleep and get back to the carnival right after church the next morning to touchup any paint and finalize details for the soft opening, which Darius still had no idea was happening.

Everything had to be perfect for the moment I admitted to him that what had happened between us was real.

Darius faced me and took my hands. "I have something to tell you."

I squeezed his hands and held my breath. Was he going to steal my thunder and admit that he had feelings for me? I guess it didn't matter how it came out as long as it did. Then we could stop pretending.

"Em…kissed me."

I replayed the words in my head until they finally computed.

"Dinah?"

"Oh."

He wasn't telling me he had feelings for me. He was telling me goodbye.

"She said she's seen everything I've been doing with the shelters and the exhibit and how I've been with you, and I've changed."

"You have changed."

"Yeah."

Except for the part where he kissed someone behind another girl's back. Behind *my* back.

I dropped his hands and sat on a bench.

"I didn't kiss her back, D," he said, following me to the seat. "I told her that you and I are together."

My tongue stuck in the void that was my mouth.

"Dinah, say something, please."

"Do you want to be with Em?"

"No. I mean I used to. I don't know."

"It's okay if you do. The purpose of this whole thing was to make you more attractive to girls who wanted a boyfriend not a hookup. You've always said she was girlfriend material." And she had been the one he'd liked from the beginning. *Really* liked, not fake liked.

"She is, but it's not the only reason we did this. We also did this for me to be your buffer and for me to look out for you around Todd. I still want to do that for you. I want you to be able to explore your art and not be imposed on by him."

"Ever since the beach, I haven't heard anything from him. My parents aren't spending time with his anymore either. For a while. Maybe I don't need a buffer anymore." What I didn't say was that didn't mean I didn't need Darius.

Darius took a deep breath. "I should be with Em then?"

"If you want to."

Darius bit his lip and nodded. "If I want to."

I forced a smile and prayed the tears that threatened the corners of my eyes didn't escape. "We did it. Em was one of your biggest critics. We convinced her you're boyfriend material."

"I'm boyfriend material because of you," Darius whispered.

If I'd turned Darius into boyfriend material and he hadn't chosen to be *my* boyfriend, what did that say about me? I didn't trust myself to speak.

"So that's it then?" Darius asked. "We succeeded?"

"We did."

We did a lot of other things, too. Like supporting each other to reach for experiences we wouldn't have considered apart. Holding each other in the early morning of an east-coast sunrise. Kissing like our souls had committed more than we'd ever admit.

"My parents came home from the beach. They're at home waiting for me."

"Oh. Okay."

I gave Darius a hug and a quick kiss on the cheek.

"I can't believe I'm saying this, but promise me we're going to be friends. Everything we were to each other, except some of the benefit stuff of course. We'll still be those things?"

My voice failed me.

"D?"

I nodded and managed a whispered, "Of course."

THIRTY-FOUR

SUNDAY AFTER BRUNCH, I trudged to the carnival, hair in a bun, clothing pre-stained with errant paint splatters and splotches. I'd spent the night and the better part of the morning toggling between anger at myself for not telling Darius how I'd felt sooner and relief that I hadn't embarrassed myself by admitting I'd cared about him. Especially when he'd had eyes for someone else the entire time.

Light glowed from under the carousel exhibit doorway. The thought struck me that Darius had snuck in, and I'd missed his reaction. I threw open the door to find Em already hard at work.

"Oh," I said.

She stopped painting and faced me, biting her lip. She knew I knew.

"Morning," I said.

"Morning," she replied, more quietly and slowly than I'd spoken.

I closed the door behind me and mentally scolded myself for thinking Darius would have snuck in. He'd promised me he wouldn't. He'd never broken a promise to me.

I busied myself mixing the perfect color to finish touchups on what I had thought of as *our* horse. I'd wanted the tail to blend black and brown, exactly how the Kenny-wood horse had looked, but I hadn't quite nailed the look on my first pass. I pulled the photo up on my phone and zoomed in, matching the strokes and swiping in lighter-colored paint to catch the light. While the paint on the black stallion dried, I inspected the other twelve horses. A few required a touchup here or there. I mixed the paints and dabbed the colors. Em and I didn't speak. She brushed bright red paint onto an intricately patterned horse bridle.

Despite the sadness warring with my emotions, I admired my work. The black stallion matched Darius's photo perfectly. I was only sorry he couldn't ride the horse with his grandfather by his side. I retrieved a picture frame from my bag, hoping Darius would see it as the next best thing. I weaved through the horses to the center of the carousel. Across from Darius's horse, I wiped the metal of the center pole with rubbing alcohol and pressed an adhesive hook to it. Once it was secure, I slipped the loop on the back of the frame over the hook. Careful it didn't fall, I held it in place until I could be sure the hook would support it.

After a few seconds, I took a deep breath and stepped back. A photo of a young Darius, smiling that confident, beautiful smile of his, looked back at me. His grandfather, Harvey, draped an arm around his shoulders, grinning as wildly as his grandson.

"Is that Darius?" Em asked.

She stood close. Too close. "Yes."

Em looked back at the horse I'd been perfecting. "You painted this horse to match the one in the photo?"

"Yes."

"For Darius?"

"Obviously," I said, irritated with her questions. "Are you finished? I'd like to clean up and get ready for the opening."

She didn't answer. Instead, she stared at me.

"What is it?"

"That's incredible."

"I painted it after the picture. Not an artistic masterpiece."

"That's not what I meant," she said.

I wasn't sure I could talk about Darius without tears pouring down my cheeks. But Em didn't wait for an answer. She lowered her head into her hands.

"I'm a terrible person."

I stilled, curious at the turn the conversation had somehow taken and also not wanting to agree with her. At least out loud.

"I thought the carousel was just a surprise, but it goes deeper than that."

The fact she didn't know Darius like I did but still managed to win him made my body flush with heat. "Darius loves carousels. He found this one at an estate sale for some carnival company or something, and he wanted it restored because it reminded him of his grandfather. They always rode the carousel together."

"Which is why he hasn't come in here once?"

"I made him promise he would wait to see it until I finished."

Em was on the other side of the carousel, pacing now. "I thought you were all caught up in your art and that's all that mattered to you."

"You thought wrong."

"I even wondered if you two were faking this whole thing to get all the social media buzz to die down."

My throat felt suddenly constricted.

"But none of that was true. You were honoring every detail of a memory of his that I didn't even know about." She pointed to the photo. "You were planning just about the sweetest thing I've ever seen in my life, and…"

I crossed my arms, finally getting a sense of where we were going with this. "And?"

"And I kissed your boyfriend."

The words dangled in the air between us, neither of us breathing deeply enough to blow them away.

"Darius told me."

She closed her eyes. "I shouldn't have done that. I'm so sorry."

I wanted to say it was okay, but it wasn't. That night at the carousel opening, I'd planned to tell him I was falling for him. That this fake dating thing had turned so real, at least for me. And who knows what he would have said.

Or, I guess we all know. He'd have left the conversation by fake breaking up with me and instead planning for us to be friends and for him to date Em—likely his plan all along. Being in the same room with her was like horse hooves thumping over my body. Looking her in the eyes that Darius would be gazing into within hours—that was a pain worse than a trampling death.

"You should go get ready for the opening," I said, turning away from her gorgeous face.

"Dinah, I…"

"You've apologized."

"It doesn't seem like enough. I helped people drag Darius through the internet mud because he'd been unfaithful, and then I went and kissed him knowing he had a girlfriend."

When she put it like that, I agreed, the apology wasn't

enough. But none of that mattered. Darius wanted to be with her, not me.

The admission tore something open in my chest.

"Can you please just go?"

I turned my back on her, busying myself with cleaning up the colors we'd mixed and dunking every brush into a can of water. By the time I finished, Em had left. Finally alone, I closed my eyes, letting the heaviness of the past couple of days settle over me and the tears that came with that weight fall over my cheeks. I locked the door behind her, so I could allow myself a proper cry, one complete with shoulder-shaking, breath-catching, throat-gurgling sobs.

When all my tears had left me, I sat on the black stallion, begging God that my good cry had purged every emotion I'd had for Darius.

One painful glance at his childhood photo hanging next to me told me my prayer had not been answered—at least not yet.

THIRTY-FIVE

KIERK GAVE me access to the residential suite to shower and get dressed. His somber mood told me Darius had—at the least—told him our relationship had ended. Maybe he'd told him we were faking the whole time. I was only sure he'd told him something.

Showered and dressed, I checked my phone messages to see a missed call from the animal shelter. I called back, and Clara answered.

"Hi, Clara. It's Dinah. I missed your call."

"Thanks for calling back. I was calling because we loved the first round of pet sketches, and we were wondering if you might be interested in another art project?"

"What kind of project?" I asked.

"A mural."

I stared at the phone. "A mural?"

"It's part of our plan to freshen up the property and the shelter's image. Would you be able to come by sometime tomorrow to discuss it?"

With my carousel project done, I had some free time— not much with school starting soon but some. Not to mention I wouldn't be spending time with Darius or at the carnival, and I had said I wanted to paint a mural someday.

"I'll be there," I told her.

Someone knocked on the door of the bedroom where I was getting ready. Clara and I arranged a time and hung up.

I answered the knock to find Darius, dressed up, masked, and looking so good my chest ached.

"Can I come in?" he whispered.

"Sure."

He closed the door behind him and ran his hands together. "I'm little-kid excited about this."

"I'm glad."

"I'm sorry I didn't know before," he said. "We should have held off our fake breakup until after the carousel opening. Now I won't even be able to celebrate with you."

"Em kissed you, though," I reminded him. "We didn't have much of a choice."

He nodded slightly, but I got the sense he wanted to say something else. He stayed quiet though.

"Besides, that's what surprises are—surprises."

He nodded. "Anyways, I wanted to thank you and tell you that when I see the carousel, I'm going to be thinking of you and thanking you and everything else."

I tucked my hands behind my back. "Okay."

"Okay."

"I'll see you down there, then." He grabbed the doorknob but didn't turn it. After a few seconds, he turned back around. "D?"

"Yeah?"

He looked at me and then away again. He wet his lips but didn't speak.

"What is it?"

"I…" He took a breath and lowered his head. "Thank you."

Relief and disappointment shot through me. "You're welcome."

He waved and was gone.

Mac met me outside the door that led to the carousel exhibit where a line of committee members had formed.

She looped her arm in mine. "You ready?"

"My first carnival exhibit," I said and took a deep breath. "Ready."

She and I snuck inside where Em was checking that the lights around the carousel were secure. The music played softly; a mechanical adjustment considering we were in a smaller space.

Mac gasped at the sight of the sparkling room and the horses galloping their perpetual circle. "It's exquisite, Dinah. Wow."

"Hey," Em said.

Mac side-eyed me and ignored her.

"Hi," I said, wishing we could celebrate this together—wishing I could celebrate it with Darius. Instead, the two of them would celebrate, and I'd hide in the corner with my best friend. Some things never changed, I guess.

"The photographer took high resolution shots for you to use in your art portfolio," Mac said.

"Thank you."

"Two minutes until official opening," Em said.

"Can we stop the ride?" I called out to the carnival worker who would be operating it and stepped closer as it slowed to make sure Darius's horse lined up perfectly with the photo of him and his grandfather. I stepped onto the plat-form and admired the artistry of the horse.

"Wow, D," Mac said from behind me. "Is that Harvey?"

I nodded.

She studied the horse and the photo and shook her head. "He doesn't deserve you."

"Your loyalty is epic."

She blew me a kiss.

The door opened, and the VIPs trickled in. They gasped and cheered at the sight of the carousel. Em joined them. I didn't blame her. She'd worked hard on the project. She should be proud.

And she'd gotten the guy—my guy.

"I think I'm going to go," I whispered to my best friend.

"You can't go. You've worked so hard for this."

"What!" Darius stopped in the doorway, the last VIP to enter. He held his hands up and cheered. "This is incredible."

Everyone clapped again. He stepped forward and ran his hands along the horses, studying the paint work. Because of the angle of the carousel, I wasn't sure he'd seen me yet. Em watched him, too, but at least she didn't flaunt their relationship in front of me. I stood frozen until he worked his way around the carousel far enough to see me and Mac standing next to his horse. He offered me the most authentic, natural smile.

"This is…" He shook his head. "More than anything I expected. The paint designs are so intricate. I love the masks on them. And the lights around the room."

"Em installed the lights."

Darius sobered. "Oh. They're nice."

He stepped closer. Seeing the horse next to me for the first time, he did a double take. He held his fist up to his mouth.

"You okay?" I asked.

"It's perfect, D."

"I'm glad you like it."

He swiped a tear off his cheek. "Like it? It's…it's everything."

Mac stepped closer to me.

"Can we get this thing moving?" someone called, and everyone shouted in agreement.

I backed away from Darius's horse. "You have to be the first one to ride it."

He rested his hands on the saddle. "Will you ride next to me?"

Had I not envisioned that for the last two weeks? I'd imagined myself on the horse modeled after our "first kiss" horse at Kennywood. He probably wouldn't even remember what it had looked like.

But too much had changed for us to ride together now.

"I'm going to give the VIPs the first go," I said, stepping off the platform.

Darius lowered his gaze and climbed onto the horse. Other committee members shuffled around the carousel, claiming their spots. Em had the decency to stay back too. From opposite ends of the room, we watched everyone board. Darius glanced at me again, but I looked away. He followed my lead and did the same, but his gaze took him to the photo hanging at the center of the carousel. His body shifted the second he saw it. He stared until everyone else had settled onto their horses, and the ride operator rang the bell.

"We can go now if you want," Mac said.

"Okay," I said quietly.

As the carousel started to move, Darius caught my eye again, but I didn't trust myself to look at him for any longer than a flash of a second.

THIRTY-SIX

I PARKED my car in the animal shelter parking lot. Peaches was the first to greet me, tugging an unsuspecting walker behind her.

"She's a wild one," I said with a laugh while I ruffled Peaches' fur and the walker caught her breath.

"They warned me she likes to break free."

"She does," I confirmed. "Happened to me once, and traffic shut down in all directions."

The girl, no more than sixteen, laughed. "I'm usually good with dogs, so wish me luck."

"Have fun," I said, surprised to feel as though I was missing out. Maybe I could come back and volunteer on my own. When it didn't hurt so much to think of being at the shelter at the same time as Darius. I searched the lot for his car, both relieved and disappointed it wasn't there.

I pulled the box of the final pet portraits from my trunk and knocked on the office door. Josette waved me inside and cleared space on a chair for the box.

"We've been waiting for these." She snuck a look at the few on top and gasped. "They're perfect."

"Thank you. I had a friend help me with some of them." I nearly choked on the word "friend," but I guess at the time we'd painted them, it had been true. Maybe in a way, I didn't want to admit that it still was.

Josette settled into her office chair with a pile of sketches and looked through each one, giving the pages the utmost deference.

"Remarkable," she said.

"I took photos of some for my portfolio. I was thinking of making a website and offering pet portraits for a fee."

"You should. These are...wow."

Her emphasis had me smiling wider than I had in days. "Thank you."

"Clara told me you wanted to discuss our other project. It doesn't pay much although we were able to secure a small grant."

"The mural?"

"Yes. You might have noticed our building is lacking in curb appeal."

"I hadn't," I lied.

She raised an eyebrow at me. "Well, we applied for a grant to spruce things up a bit, including painting a mural of some of our favorite pets on the side of the building."

The map murals from carnival flashed in my mind. Maybe Darius—no, Kierk could connect me to the muralist for some tips and tricks.

"Is that something you'd be interested in?" Josette asked.

Yes. *Yes.* Say yes!

"Yes," I said, ignoring the fact I was *not* qualified to paint a mural. But I'd never sketched a pet portrait a month ago or painted carousel horses, and I'd reached expert status with both fairly quickly.

"Excellent." She slid a photo of the wall with handwritten dimensions on it across her desk. "And here's the grant amount." She wrote one thousand dollars on a post-it.

A thousand dollars?

"Is this my payment or the amount for supplies?"

"Your payment. We will cover supplies with other funds from the grant."

Yowza. Talk about all those pro bono pet sketches paying off.

"I know you'll be going back to school soon," Josette said. "We can get started on the project right away if you're free."

"Do you have a design plan?"

She shook her head. "You have free rein on that. Of course, we'd like to have the pets featured. Peaches because she's a local celebrity after going viral with that video you posted, but the design can be your vision."

She said it as if that were a good thing. None of the artwork I'd ever created had been from my vision. They were replicas of online videos, other paintings, or photos. But one thousand dollars could help me get started with other art projects. I could buy any supplies I needed and even take extra workshops at the museum or classes at the community college.

On the other hand, Josette wasn't only paying me for painting ability. She expected me to design an impactful work of art. Something that mattered. Something that thousands of people would drive by daily and see.

Something I wasn't sure I could manage.

"I'll work on something and get back to you," I promised.

———

I left Josette's office and bumped into Darius. "Hey," I said.

Darius glanced at the office door behind me. "Hey."

"I was dropping off the pet portraits."

"You finished already?"

I nodded. "Em helped me a lot."

His body stilled at the mention of Em. I bit my lip, unsure what to say, or if there was anything to say.

"Listen," Darius started. "About the carousel opening—"

Josette opened her office door, interrupting us. "Dinah, are you staying to walk with Darius today?"

I swallowed hard. "No. Um, I have to start prepping for the mural."

"Mural?" Darius asked.

"I'm painting a mural on the building."

His eyes widened like the puppies' did when they saw a treat. "That's incredible."

In an ideal world, I'd share my apprehension with him. He'd console me, give an epic pep talk. Maybe even a hug and a kiss, and my artistic spirit would find its motivation.

I'd have to find my motivation alone.

"Thank you both," Josette said. "You're the best boyfriend-girlfriend duo we've had here by far."

I lowered my gaze, terrified at the storm of emotions that could rain down on me if I met Darius's eyes.

"Thanks for everything, Josette," I managed, "but I should go."

"See you soon for the mural."

I didn't look back until I was at my car, far enough away that I couldn't read Darius's expression.

And he couldn't read mine.

———

How did people survive before online how-to videos? Seriously. I watched hours of videos, grateful for the distraction from thinking about Darius and Em riding the carousel side-by-side.

And other stuff.

Courtesy of online videos, I chose the best paint and listed all of the materials I'd need for the project—except the list included amounts of paint, not colors since I still had no idea what I would be painting.

I could handle the paints and brushes, but to reach the upper parts of the cement wall, I'd need scaffolding.

"Kierk has a ton of that stuff at the carnival," Mac told me when she came over one afternoon to, as she said, check on my progress. We both knew she'd come to check on me.

I grabbed some lemons to squeeze us the perfect late summer poolside drink. "Mind asking him if I can borrow it?"

"You don't want to go to the carnival and ask him yourself?"

"You know I don't."

She pretended to focus on washing the lemons, but after a few seconds, she erupted, "D, fight for him."

"He chose her. I'm not chasing someone who doesn't want me. Ever again."

"Todd and Darius are totally different people."

"Wow," I teased. "You've changed your tune."

"You two were happy together. I've been around Kierk a long time. I've seen Darius with one girl after another, but he never seemed authentic to me. It always felt like an act. With you, he was authentic."

Talk about irony.

"Maybe he'll be authentic with her, too," I said, squeezing the last of the lemons over the pitcher.

She rolled her eyes.

"I can't even be angry at him."

"Why not?" she said. "I'm angry."

I sighed, wondering if it was time to break the rules.

"What aren't you telling me?"

I dumped sugar into the lemon water and stirred. "Darius and I weren't really together. It was all for show."

She squinted at me. "What do you mean?"

"It was fake. Our relationship. To get girls to back off him and see that he was datable. And to keep Todd away from me. A mutually beneficial arrangement."

My best friend pressed her fingertips against her temples and held them there.

"Are you okay?"

"I'm just running through every memory of the two of you...and totally not buying it."

"It's true. We liked each other, or let me say it like this: we liked spending time together. We admitted that we were attracted to each other, and there were a few hot moments, but none of it was legitimate. Him going out with Em isn't anything against me."

Mac offered me a sad smile. "Then why are you acting like it is?"

I groaned at the fact her personal lie detector rivaled the equipment at Langley. "We had this rule. If it turned real for either of us, then we had to say so. Right away. It turned real for me a while ago, but I didn't believe it. Or was too afraid to do anything about it. By the time I'd gathered the courage, he told me Em had kissed him. He looked happy, and I couldn't mess that up for him."

"Oh, D." Mac snuggled next to me on my chaise.

"Thanks for being here," I whispered.

"Always."

"Good because I have a favor to ask."

"More than the scaffolding?"

"That's a favor from Kierk."

"What do you need from me?"

"Help painting a mural."

"You're the artist," she said. "Not me."

Since I'd crossed out every design idea in my sketch-book with a massive "X," I wasn't sure I agreed.

THIRTY-SEVEN

MY PARENTS WERE the most adorably excited people when I told them about my mural project. They asked to see my sketches. I told them the design was a surprise.

So much for not lying to my parents.

My mom didn't think twice. She clapped her hands and bounced on her toes. My dad dug tools out of the garage that might help. Ladders, brushes, and even a sprayer.

"This will save you so much time when you spray the primer," he said.

"Thanks," I smiled, guilt rising for how I'd seen my parents as the Wilkinson's best friends. For months, I'd hidden the truth about my failed relationship with Todd from my mom, thinking she'd side with him.

She hadn't spoken to him since the beach. Our family dinners had taken a break too. My home was mine and theirs, not the Wilkinsons'.

"I have a few more days I can take off work," Dad said the morning I was set to prime the side of the shelter building. "Need any help?"

"Seriously?"

"Are you kidding? Spending the day with my daughter instead of working? It's like a dream." He kissed my cheek.

"That'd be great, Dad."

He ran upstairs to change from his work clothes and we were off, his truck fully loaded with all the supplies we needed. Josette had had someone pressure wash the concrete a few days earlier.

Luckily, we'd had nothing but sunshine since.

We sealed off a frame about one foot from each edge of the square facade I would paint.

"This is the fun part," Dad said, handing me the sprayer. He taught me how to work it and suggested I start at the top. I climbed the ladder as high as I could. It took me three tries to even let go of the ladder rung long enough to reach for the sprayer.

The ground looked so far away. If I fell, I wasn't sure what would make more of a mess—me or the paint.

"You can do this, honey," Dad coaxed.

I finally took the nozzle, and he held the paint bucket for me. I sprayed as widely as I could, repositioned the ladder, psyched myself up to climb it, and sprayed again, until the top portion of the wall had gone from a rough-looking gray to a bright white.

"It looks so clean," I said.

Dad stood back, hands on hips, and smiled at the building like it was an old friend. "I love painting."

I handed him the sprayer.

"No, honey. This is your project."

"I'm going to do tons of painting. Don't worry about that. How about I call in a lunch order to be delivered while you paint, and then we can have lunch together to celebrate the start of the project?"

He took the nozzle from me and scooped up the bucket to position himself on the left part of the wall. "Done."

An hour later, a bright white square shined down on us as we sat at the picnic table and ate club sandwiches and potato chips. Dad asked all the right questions about my mural design, but I didn't have many answers. I'd sketched a few of the pets, giving Peaches top billing, but the design still lacked a certain something.

The slamming of a car door in the parking lot behind us made me jump.

"Uh oh." Dad used a napkin to wipe mayonnaise from his cheek.

"What?" I turned on the bench to see Darius walking across the parking lot toward us.

"I'm going to go, um, get a refill on my Gatorade."

"Mr. Zimmerman," Darius said, shaking my dad's hand. "How are you, sir?"

"Fine. Fine." He nodded and without further explanation, left.

"Hey," I said.

"Hey." Darius pointed to the wall. "The square is a good start. Looks good."

"All the online videos say to prime the surface, so the colors pop."

He laughed. "You could figure anything out."

Emphatically not true, especially given the fact he stood ten feet away looking good enough that I wanted him much closer than that.

"How's the carnival?"

"Good. You coming by this weekend?"

I pointed to the wall. "I'll be working on the mural."

"Oh. Well, when are you free? I wouldn't think of opening the carousel exhibit without you."

"Set a date, and I'll do my best to be there."

He licked his lips and looked away. "I thought we promised not to lie to each other."

I lowered my gaze to my paint-splattered tennis shoes.

"We said we were going to stay friends."

"We are friends," I said.

He nodded. "Right."

"Maybe I'll see you here. When are you volunteering next?"

"Today's my last day with the fall semester starting."

Darius would be back at school, and so would I. He'd see Em regularly, and I'd have to pass Todd in the halls multiple times a day.

"How's Adopt-a-Pet going?" I asked, wanting to think of anything other than being back to school and separated from Darius.

"With the hurricane brewing off the coast of Florida, we're hoping for lots of adoptions this week. Josette and the other shelter directors are expecting transplants."

I pointed to the side of the building. "I have to work fast before the rains from the hurricane work their way up here."

"Need any help?"

Tons. So much. But that would mean spending time with Darius every day. My heart was not excited about that possibility.

"I'm good."

"Good luck. I'm gonna head inside. I guess I'll see you around."

"You were going to tell me when the carousel exhibit is opening."

"Right," he said. "I will."

"See ya," I said.

He walked away with a wave. Seconds later, my dad's arm was around my shoulder.

"You okay, sweetie?"

I took a deep breath. "Good. Thanks, Dad."

I hadn't wanted things to be so awkward with Darius,

yet here we were. He was right about the weather. I checked my phone, and if we were lucky, we'd have five days before the hurricane made landfall along the Gulf Coast and then worked its way north dropping days of heavy rain on us. A flash of the carnival crew hanging out in the factory while the rain pelted outside hit me. This rainstorm wouldn't be like that one.

I wouldn't be with Darius.

"How long do you think before the primer dries, Dad?"

"A couple of hours."

I threw my bag on the picnic table and dug through to find my sketchbook. My favorite artwork told a story, so that's what I would do. I sketched mini scenes: Peaches dodging cars, Josette and Clara driving vans in the rain to rescue displaced pets, volunteers walking dogs around the building—volunteers like Darius. My hand hovered over an empty space on the paper but not for long. I'd drawn his likeness so many times. A few swipes of my pencil tip, and he took shape. I sketched Bruno next to Darius, licking his face. I didn't even have to reference the photo Darius had posted on social media. I saw every detail in my head.

I studied the sketch, touching up lines and edges. Satisfied, I laid down my pencil and stretched my fingers. As if coming out of a tunnel where I couldn't see anything around me, I realized my dad had been on the phone talking work chatter a few benches away. Darius's car had left the lot at some point.

"How'd it go?" Dad said, tucking his phone into his pocket and walking toward me.

"Good. It all sort of came out."

He looked over my shoulder and nodded. "I love it. It tells a story."

"Thanks, Dad."

"Darius left about twenty minutes ago. He waved, but

you didn't see him." He sat down next to me. "Do you want to talk about it?"

"Not much to say. He likes someone else."

My dad laughed.

"What's so funny?"

"You kids." He shook his head. "That boy does not like someone else. Why do you think I let him stick around?"

"I don't know."

"Every time he looked at you, anyone could see he was all about you. I'm not one to promote fighting, but he sure stuck up for you against Todd. The way I see it, Todd must have done something pretty terrible for you to have reacted like you did when you broke up."

"He did," I admitted.

"And he showed his true colors at the beach."

"Yep."

"I got the sense that it was hard for you being there with Todd, and that's why Darius showed up, despite the fact he had something pretty important going on at home."

My parents were clearly more observant than I'd ever given them credit for.

"It's not my decision, honey. It's yours, but make sure you're making it for you and not because of what you think someone else might want."

A fair point, but I'd promised myself not to chase someone who didn't want to be chased or at least chased by me.

"I'll think about it, Dad. In the meantime, I need to show this sketch to Josette and get Kierk and Mac over here. We have a lot of painting to do before the rain comes in a few days."

Dad rubbed his hands together. "Let's do it."

"You're staying to paint?"

"Sure. I'll make a few calls and move a few things around."

I hugged him tighter than I remember ever hugging my dad. "Thank you."

"Always, sweetie."

THIRTY-EIGHT

WHEN MAC AND KIERK ARRIVED, she hugged me and squealed. "I can't wait to do this."

Kierk's tone was more demure. He climbed out of the truck and gave me a nod.

"Hey," I said and then whispered to Mac, "Is he weird about being here?"

"I kind of told him the truth about the whole fake dating thing. He'd suspected because of something weird you said at Kennywood."

"I gave him a hint. Darius never wanted to lie to him, but I didn't want to obligate you both to lie for us."

She put her hands on her hips. "Well, we would have. Don't underestimate my dedication to my friends, okay?"

I laughed. "I'll keep that in mind for my future fake relationships."

Kierk and my dad got to work on building the scaffolding. I finalized the design based on Josette's feedback, and Mac set up her phone on a tripod to take a time-lapse video of the work.

"Good idea," I told her.

"Obviously," she joked. "What else do you need?"

"A projector. When the sun goes down, we'll project the design onto the building, charcoal the lines, and then start painting tomorrow." My heart fluttered. "Oh my gosh. What am I doing?"

Mac looked confused. "I thought we were getting a projector."

I fanned myself. "I have no idea what I'm doing. I watched a few YouTube videos. That hardly makes me qualified. What if I mess up the whole building?"

"Then you paint over it and start again," she said.

"You sound like my mother. Like everything's so easy."

"Dinah, breathe. This is what you wanted. You're painting a mural. You have an awesome design that you made yourself. *You.* You are an artist. You are."

I nodded, still breathing deeply.

"Say it," Mac demanded. "I am an artist."

"I am an artist."

"Good. This is my design."

"This is my design," I repeated.

"It's going to be epic."

I closed my eyes and let the words settle over me. "It's going to be epic."

"I am an artist," she said more quietly.

"I am an artist."

We both breathed in the silence.

"You can do this," she whispered.

I could do this.

Kierk and my dad positioned the scaffolding while Mac ran to the journalism lab at school to borrow a projector and I finalized my digital sketch. An hour later, everything was in place except me.

"You have to climb the scaffolding," Mac said with a grin.

Of course she would find that entertaining.

"Maybe we should paint the mural on the bottom half of the wall," I said, only partially serious.

Kierk locked the wheels and nudged the scaffolding back and forth. It rocked. A lot. Mac's eyes went wide.

I tossed my backpack of snacks, water, and charcoal pencils over my shoulder and reached for the ladder. And held the first rung. For, like, a while.

"Oh no," Mac muttered.

"I'm fine. It's gonna be fine."

"We could always start with the lower half," she said.

I pulled myself up to the second rung. And smiled. "See? Easy."

"Yep," Mac said, not the least bit convinced.

I imagined Darius' face when he would finally see the finished mural and pulled myself up to the next rung. And the next. Until I inched my body weight over the board. Everything shook as Mac hustled up the ladder.

I pressed my stomach against the board and squeezed the sides. "Mac!"

She poked her head over the top of the ladder. "Yeah?"

"Are you trying to knock me off this thing?"

"Not at all. I do want to go on record saying that for years, you've refused to climb with me because of your fear of heights."

"And?"

"Darius is an idiot."

"What's that now?" Kierk asked.

Mac crossed her arms. "Nothing. Just boys being stupid boys. Not knowing what's good for them."

Kierk opened his arms wide. "Should I take offense at this?"

"Yes," Mac said. "Considering it took you months to

come to your senses. Let's hope your bestie doesn't make the same mistake."

"Guys don't say bestie," Kierk quipped.

"Because that's the takeaway."

"Okay," I interrupted. "Let's get things started. Kierk, can you set up the projector, please?"

A few seconds later, he called, "Projector's ready."

"D, you don't have to do this," Mac whispered. "I can do the outline if you need me to."

I studied the crisp, white wall. Painting the brick had already spruced up the building, but the mural would do so much more. Nobody could drive along that busy intersection without seeing the images of new pet owners and their four-legged pals. Nobody could mistake the building for something other than what it was.

I pulled the printout of my design from the backpack and smoothed it over the scaffolding. "Here's a look at the whole design if you need to check on a detail. The projector will only give us one fourth of the whole image."

"It's gonna be epic," Mac said.

"My first design," I whispered. "Everything else I've ever drawn or painted referenced something else. A photo or video. A project with instructions from another artist. This is mine, Mac."

"I don't think anyone in the history of the world has ever been more proud of their best friend."

I took a deep breath and crept up to my knees.

"Ready?"

I nodded.

"Hit the light," Mac called to Kierk, and the projector came to life. Even faded, the design shining on the side of the building couldn't be described in any other word than the one my best friend had used—epic.

———————

Mac and I charcoaled the design outline for hours. Kierk and Dad helped with the scaffolding and the projector. They even gave us a break when our shoulders burned.

"I know I said that was epic," Mac said. "But it was epically exhausting."

"We'll have a couple of hours of sleep before coming back at sun-up to start painting."

"You need some helpers."

"The only person I know who can paint is Em."

"Not her," Mac said. "We'll help. Won't we, Kierk?"

"I can paint big chunks of space," Kierk offered. "No tight corners. No texture or mixed colors. Simple basics."

I laughed. "I'll take it."

We set a time to meet the next morning, slept for a few hours, and were back at it. Kierk protected our work area from prying eyes by hanging drop cloths on the side of the scaffolding. The cloths also gave us shade, necessary in the August sun. I supervised with a paint-by-number approach. Using the design as a guide, I dabbed paint red paint, for instance, in all of the outlined spaces that would be red. Then, I passed off the red paint to Kierk, and he filled in the details. Mac took on the blue, and my dad painted green.

Josette and Clara even painted a bit. By the end of the day, more of the wall was covered than I'd expected. We sat down to a pizza party on the benches just as the sun was setting.

"How much time do we have until the rain comes?" Kierk asked.

"Looks like about three days," I said. "It's moving faster than expected."

"Will we have enough time?" Mac asked.

"I hope so. Otherwise, we'll have to take the scaffolding down."

"We can help tomorrow," Kierk said, glancing at Mac.

"Sure," she said.

"Me too," Dad said. "This is more fun than work, and I'll rope your mom in too."

"I can ask some of the volunteers if they want to help," Clara suggested. "If we keep up the paint-by-numbers technique, I'm sure a few of them would be up for it."

I took a deep breath and thanked everyone. "If we can finish all of the background colors tomorrow, then I can start layering in texture. After that, I could maybe use some help with outlining, but that's it. We might just make it."

Everyone clapped, but while they smiled, a niggling sadness settled over me. When the mural was finished, so would my last connection to Darius.

After that, it would officially be goodbye.

THIRTY-NINE

TODD WAS LEANING against my car when I walked out my front door the next morning. I stared at him from the porch. We hadn't spoken since the beach.

"What is it, Todd?"

"Just want to see how you're doing."

"No you don't."

"Fine. I heard about you and Darius," Todd said, tucking his hands into his pockets.

I wanted to shout at him that he seriously had no shame, but he hadn't exactly crossed the line. "Yeah."

"Does that mean there's a chance for us?"

I'd spoken too soon. Todd didn't even know there was a line.

"Todd? Get in the car. I want to show you something."

While I drove, he glanced at me occasionally. He even opened his mouth to speak a few times but thought better of it and eventually resigned himself to looking out the window. I parked in the lot next to the shelter.

"Let me guess," he said. "This is the animal shelter that inspired Darius's exhibit?"

"It is." I climbed out of the car and waved Todd toward the side of the building that had drop cloths draped from it. Careful not to pull them loose, I slid them to the side and stepped behind them. "Get your flashlight on your phone."

Todd's face registered curiosity, but he didn't question my request. When both of our phones lit the space, Darius' oversized face stared back at us from the center of the design.

"Is that…?"

"Darius," I said. "I painted it."

He stopped at stared at me. "You did not do this."

"I did. Technically, I designed it, and a few friends helped me paint, but I'll be touching up everything for the finished look."

He stepped as far back as he could, gently nudging the cloth aside to take in as much of the design as he could. "Dinah, I couldn't mean it more when I say this is incredible."

"Thank you."

I gave him time to study the details. When he finished, he bowed his head.

"Todd?"

He swiped tears off his cheeks and looked away. "I messed everything up. I was stupid." He pointed to the wall. "You did this for him."

"In a way, but I did it for me, too. I've always wanted to paint something like this."

"But he inspired you."

I studied Darius' huge, smiling face and realized Todd had been right.

"When we were together—I know you won't believe this—but I was so much more into you than you were me."

I laughed.

"It's true," Todd protested. "I knew it. So I pulled away,

little by little, thinking it would be enough to draw you in closer. The first time I talked to another girl, it was to make you jealous, but you didn't get jealous. Even after you knew I cheated, you didn't react."

"And that's what you wanted? A reaction?"

"I wanted you to want me."

"I did," I said.

He pointed to the mural. "Not like this. You had a crush on me forever, and I guess the reality wasn't as good as the fantasy."

"That sounds so brutal."

"I always knew you were too good for me. Probably why I took so long to ask you out. I'm sorry for all the shitty things I did after, too."

"Thanks for saying that, but can I also suggest you change the behavior and not just apologize for it?"

He laughed. "Sure. As long as you can get me out of here, so I don't have to look at the literal mural you painted of your new boyfriend."

We slipped through the cloths again, leaving the stale air and Darius behind.

"Final word on the subject—Darius is an idiot," Todd said.

"Thanks."

"You have to stay here to paint, don't you?"

"Yeah," I said.

"Mind if I stay for a while and help?"

I pressed my hands to my cheeks.

"I get it, D. Finally. I get it. We're over. But I'd like to find a way to be friends."

After nearly two decades of friendship, even given everything he'd done, that didn't feel like too much to ask. "Okay."

He grinned like the little boy I remembered from playing games in the backyard or building sandcastles at the beach.

"But you have to promise me you won't tell anyone details about the mural," I said. "There's going to be a big reveal, and it has to be a surprise."

He offered me a friendly smile. "I promise."

———

By midday, my team had colored in my mural, leaving me to add the artistic touches of texture and depth. They transitioned from active painters to support staff, taking turns to feed me, replace paints, and even occasionally crack my back. I fell into bed two nights in a row so sore and exhausted I could barely lift my phone.

But I did to send a very important message.

Me: *Hey, Darius.*

Bubbles. Oh, painful bubbles.

Darius: *Hey. Glad to hear from you.*

Me: *Can you meet me at the shelter tomorrow?*

Darius: *What time?*

Me: Noon.

Darius: *Yes.*

I exhaled and collapsed into the softness of my pillows. The plan was set.

FORTY

"WHAT ARE you going to say to him?" Mac asked when I told her I'd invited Darius to the small mural reveal ceremony.

Josette had invited some of the top shelter donors, and my family and friends would be there, along with the hundreds of people who drove by in the time it took us to drop the cloth, cheer, and celebrate with faux champagne.

"I don't have a speech planned or anything," I said. "I just want him to be here."

"Right."

"He was part of the inspiration."

She helped twist the top half of my hair into a clip that made me look more sophisticated than I deserved.

"I haven't even seen him with Em in the carnival, D. How do you know they're together?"

"Em has stopped trashing him online. So has everyone else. Since she was likely behind that to begin with, what else would have made her stop?"

"Maybe everyone sees he's actually a good guy."

Even if it was him that had silenced his online haters, there was still one detail that couldn't be overlooked. "He told me they were going to be together."

"*Going* to be. What if something happened?"

"What if you get my hopes up for something that's never going to happen?" I took a deep breath and sprayed hairspray over my curls. "Today is about saying goodbye to Darius."

"Then why do you look so good?" my best friend challenged.

"Because he has to at least know what he's missing."

We both laughed until my parents knocked on my bedroom door and piled us into the car for my second big artistic reveal of the summer. Of the month, even.

August was going to be a tough act to follow.

———

Josette and I did not agree on the meaning of the word small. Hordes of people packed the parking lot which she'd roped off to make space for tables and a spread of food. We parked around the block and navigated the cracked sidewalk with care given our heels. Clara rushed to me, tugging me in this direction or that, introducing me to volunteers and donors.

"We can't wait to see the mural," one of their major donors said. "I've always said this building needed sprucing up. Now we're getting a mural and a new fence all at once."

"And a garden club in town is interested in planting dog friendly landscaping for us in the spring," Clara said.

The donor clapped her hands together in excitement, and we continued with our meet and greet.

In the middle of the crowd, my heart rate increased

suddenly. I knew Darius had to be close by. Josette waved me over to the mural wall. She had volunteers on the roof ready to drop the cloths that had been covering the artwork.

"Thank you all for coming," Josette called, and the crowd quieted. "A couple of weeks ago, this young woman, Dinah Zimmerman, and her boyfriend, Darius Moore..."

We really needed to update her on our situation.

"...Peaches loves nothing more than a new walker. She showed her best moves, and before we knew it, she was free and roaming the highway. The adventure of capturing her was recorded and shared online. The results were bigger than any of us could have expected.

"We received calls from people who wanted to volunteer. Darius made plans to fence in the property. The video of Peaches' great escape went viral and led to an influx in monetary donations for our shelter and others. Dinah donated her time to sketch pet portraits. Many of you have those portraits hanging in your homes."

The thought made my chest swell. I scanned the crowd, wondering who she'd meant, and several people were nodding and clapping. Behind them, Darius stood next to my parents, smiling and cheering too.

If I thought my chest had expanded before seeing him, I was wrong. My body wanted to be next to him. He'd been a better buffer than I could have ever expected. Life without him...phew, deep breath.

"Dinah, would you like to say anything?"

"Oh..."

"It's okay," she whispered. "You don't have to."

"No. I would." I smiled at the crowd. "Thank you all for being here. Josette, Clara, and the other volunteers dedicate so much to this shelter. It's inspiring, what they do. I want to thank them for the opportunity to paint this mural and recognize my team who helped me put it together before the storms arrive this week." I named everyone who had helped, even Todd. Then, Josette declared it time for the big reveal.

We joined the crowd, and everyone counted down from ten. When we screamed, "One!" the volunteers on the roof dropped the cloths, and the mural shone in the bright sun. I gasped at seeing the whole image for the first time. It was bolder than I realized. The colors popped. The texture worked, although I might want to touchup a few brush strokes here and there. All of my hours of sketching Darius had paid off. His likeness was perfect.

Cars driving by honked. The crowd studied the stories I'd told in my design. They laughed at Bruno licking Darius's face. They applauded Josette and Clara for their work, now immortalized in the painting. In a blur of congratulations and compliments, I spun through the parking lot until someone unexpectedly steadied me.

"Hey." Todd rested his hands on my shoulders. "Seeing it in the sunlight like this, the mural is amazing. Professional. Incredible. I can't believe you did that, and at the same time, of course you did that."

"Thanks," I said and hugged him.

We held on to each other longer than was normal for a friendly hug, but given everything that had happened between us, I had the sense we'd both needed it.

"Look. I've been thinking about what we talked about..." He pointed to the mural. "The last time we were here. This may not be the place or time. Not sure if there is enough time in the world for me to make things right again. I know that the stuff I did to you...I tried to figure out why. Sometimes that's the crazy thing about life. You do things you know are stupid, but you don't understand why. At least for me. I'm totally rambling now." He sighed and folded his hands behind his back. "The point I'm trying to make is I think that for so many years, you thought I was some prize to be won, and you worked so hard to win me, and the whole time, I remember thinking that someday she's going to realize I'm no prize. Somehow, deep down, I felt like if you had to keep trying to earn me, then you wouldn't realize I wasn't worth earning."

I hadn't expected such a deep revelation from him, especially after we'd already sort of made up. "Wow."

"Like I said, maybe too much to be said right now."

Someone cleared their throat behind us. I moved, thinking I was in the way, but it was Darius.

"Hey," we all said and stood in a triangle of awkwardness.

Finally, Todd extended his hand. "I'm sorry about what I did at the beach, man."

Darius glanced at me, and I nodded. He shook Todd's hand, and Todd bent to hug me goodbye. "He's an idiot," he whispered. "I know that from personal experience."

"Todd," I scolded.

"Seriously," he said, still whispering. "If he screws something up with you, he's an idiot."

He left us alone, and we did our "hey" thing again.

"You and Todd?" he said. "Really?"

"No," I laughed. "He apologized. He's trying to be nice or whatever."

"Another ploy to get you back?"

"I don't think so." And I was surprised to find I believed it.

"I'm glad to hear it because he doesn't deserve you, but that's not why I'm here, so let's just start over."

"Okay," I said.

Darius took a deep breath and wore that wide smile of his, the one I'd sketched so many times. "Congratulations." He stepped close to hug me and then thought better of it, sort of backing up and asking me with his raised eyebrows if a hug was okay. I nodded. He swooped in, but I was also moving toward him. We bumped off each other before trying to recover with one of those side hugs that included a friendly pat on the back.

Epic. Fail.

"That mural is everything," he said.

"Thank you."

"Your own design?"

"First Dinah Zimmerman original."

"I'm so honored to be a small part of it."

"A small part?"

He laughed. I looked away before I had to watch him lick his lips in that way that crumbled my knees.

"Are you staying on to volunteer after the fence is built?" I asked.

"Not sure. It looks like Em is opening that franchise after all. I might have to travel a bit to help the team."

I had to will myself to breathe normally at his mention of Em. "What about school?"

"I'm going to try to stick to weekends and breaks," he said. "But it's a big opportunity, so…"

Darius and Em jetsetting across the country, working alongside each other every day, falling farther and harder for each other. My throat swelled. "I should find my parents."

"Oh. Uh, real quick. Can you come to the carnival for the public carousel opening this weekend?"

I'd told Mac tonight would be my goodbye to Darius. Seeing him, knowing this would be it, brought with it a numbing relief. But to agree to see him again?

"I don't know," I said. "I have to do some school shopping. I've been working on art projects nonstop."

"I get that, but thirty minutes is all I ask. I'll get you a

VIP parking badge. You can pull right up to the building, see the carousel, and then bounce."

"If it means that much to you," I finally said.

"It does. I'll text you the details. See you there."

He'd see me *and* Em. I'd need a lot more numbing not to feel the pain from that.

FORTY-ONE

IT TURNED out I didn't need a VIP parking pass for the carousel opening. The hurricane remnants had hit us hard. The dirt roads around the carnival property had become mud. The sky poured swimming-pool-sized buckets of water, nonstop. Since people were hunkering down at home, I parked in the wide-open first row of spots and hid under my umbrella while I ran to the staff entrance.

I shook as much water off as I could and stepped inside the quiet carnival.

It felt more like a Wednesday afternoon than a Saturday night. I secured my mask and headed for the carousel exhibit, so familiar with the path that I was sure I could find my way in the dark. Darius waited for me in the hallway. He looked good in jeans and a black, Carnivalesque tee that hugged his body in beautiful ways and a matching black mask.

"Thanks for coming," he said.

"Where is everyone?"

"They'll be here soon. The storm slowed some people

down." He took a deep breath. "Can I talk to you first? For a second? It's about Em."

So I'd gone from his fake girlfriend/friend with benefits to the girl he talked to about other girls. I'd gotten friend zoned so hard.

"She's great," he said. "The kind of girl I'd go after hard. Beautiful. Smart. Whole package."

I nodded, pretending to be interested rather than what I was actually doing—debating how much more painful it might be to dig my eyes out with a spoon.

"Please don't hate me for this," he went on. "But after everything, I don't think I'm that into her."

What now?

"We hung out a bit. Tried, or whatever." His voice trailed off.

"What happened?" I asked, hoping, begging, pleading the answer had something to do with me.

"We talked so much about me changing, and that's the thing. I did change. So much that I don't feel the same way anymore."

"I'm sorry," I said, meaning it more than I expected to. "But if it's not Em, it'll be someone else," I assured him and the part of myself that needed to hear it. "You're on the side of a building. The face of pet care. That mural is going to bring you a lot of clients when you're a vet, by the way. I deserve a commission or something."

He grinned. "I'm sure we can work something out."

I checked the time on my phone. The opening had been scheduled for five minutes ago, but the hallway was still empty.

"Dinah?"

"Yes?" I turned back to him.

He'd opened the door to the exhibit. The room was dim

except for the twinkle lights, but there were also candles everywhere.

"Wow."

The carousel music played softly.

He closed the door behind us. "I have a confession to make."

I urged my mouth to say something, but my brain wasn't working fast enough. The candles and us being alone sparked so much hope inside me, but the doubt that I'd allowed to dominate my thinking since Darius and I first met prevented me from believing this moment could be anywhere near romantic.

"The carousel is ruined for me," he said.

"That's not possible."

"Every time I come in here, all I see is that you're not here."

My breath caught.

"I asked you to ride the carousel with me before, and you said no. So I'm a little nervous about asking again."

"I thought that you—you and Em…" At the soft open-ing, I'd thought they were together but keeping their distance to be kind to me. But what if they hadn't been together? What if I'd messed up our chances when I'd refused to ride with him?

"I'm sorry if I hurt you." He tilted his head toward the carousel. "Come on?"

With a sigh, I climbed onto the horse modeled after our first kiss horse, and he sat on the one adapted from his child-hood memories.

"How are we going to start the carousel?" I asked. "Nobody's here."

He held up a remote control and grinned.

"Fancy."

He pressed a button, and the horses rocked into motion.

I side-eyed Darius, and when he was looking back at me, we both laughed and looked away. A thud drew my attention back to him. He wasn't sitting on the horse anymore.

He was standing next to me. "Thank you for the tribute to my grandfather. You went to a lot of effort."

"Kierk was the one who got me the photos."

"Don't do that."

"What?"

"That self-deprecating thing you do. You did all of this," he gestured to the carousel that was still spinning around us. Kind of fitting in that I'd always felt like the world was spinning with us at the center every time we were together. "And the mural. You didn't have to include me on that."

"Are you kidding? You did so much for the shelter. The fence and the exhibit." I shook my head. "After a few weeks of that, all the animal shelters in Pittsburgh will be empty."

"I wanted you to tell me not to be with Em," he said, pulling the conversation back to us. "That the sunrise on the roof was more than a fantasy."

"It was," I whispered.

"Why didn't you tell me?"

"I wanted you to be happy, and you'd been telling me for weeks about how Em was the one who could do that." I guess I'd been wrong. "Chalk it up to that self-deprecating thing."

"And now?" he asked.

I tucked my knee close to my chest and kicked my leg over the edge of the horse, so I was riding in a very uncomfortable side saddle. "Do you like this horse?"

"Are you asking me if I recognize it?"

"Maybe," I said.

He nudged me off the horse and into his arms.

Darius ran his hand through my hair, and I listened to the sound of his heart beating. Normal at first. Then faster.

And faster. He brushed a strand of my hair back, his finger-tips grazing my skin. "We had our first kiss on a horse that looked exactly like this one. But we're not in public now."

"Thank God for that," I said, repeating the line he'd said to me on the roof at the beach.

He rewarded me with that delicious grin and an even more delicious kiss. If I'd thought the sunrise kiss had been like a scene from a movie, kissing Darius when I'd expected to say goodbye, in the middle of a spinning carousel, with twinkle lights and candles all around was our epic movie moment. Couldn't be topped.

But it could be repeated over and over.

He tipped his forehead against mine. "I missed you."

"Is this real?" I whispered. "Or fake?"

"I'm afraid to answer that question," he said. "Which pretty much answers it."

"I thought you said a girl like me couldn't fall for a guy like you."

"Imagine my luck."

Outside the carnival, thunder boomed. The lights cut to darkness, and the carousel slowed to a stop. The candlelight bounced off the walls and the shiny paint of the horses.

"I keep getting luckier and luckier," Darius said with a chuckle.

So did I.

ACKNOWLEDGMENTS

I've always wanted to write a fake dating story! They've been my favorite to read for years. Thank you to everyone who helped me bring this story to the page.

Thank you Kylee Danko for sharing your art and shelter work expertise. You were the perfect person to help with this story. Thanks to my readers who took the time to give feedback on this very tight schedule: Kathleen Heidecker, Shanah Salter, and Abigail Scheg. To Valerie Gray, thank you for reading this story for authenticity. The insights and guidance from each of you have been incredibly valuable.

My respect and gratitude to the team at Wise Wolf Books. Working with you has been a privilege and pleasure. Thank you for believing in my stories and bringing them to readers Readers, thank you for spending your time with my stories. I hope you enjoy the world within these pages.

To my family, especially my children, thank you for your encouragement and excitement on this journey. Watching you grow into your true selves is the greatest joy of my life. All my love…

A LOOK AT: GRIDIRON GIRL
IRON VALLEY BOOK ONE

Fun friendships, high school romance, and intense competition are at the heart of book one in Tamara Girardi's swoon-worthy, young-adult contemporary series.

Julia Medina, dubbed Jules by her closest friends, wants to be the new, starting quarterback of Iron Valley High School's football team, and no one is going to stand in her way. That is—until her boyfriend, Owen Malone, steps up to the challenge. Wanting to maintain her relationship with her boyfriend, Jules is torn. But while Owen is in her heart, football is in her blood.

Once the idea takes root to quit her championship volleyball team and join the leagues of Iron Valley's toughest teenage boys, there's no stopping Jules from pursuing her dream. In her mind, expectations that the position will go to a male player have gone on long enough, and, even as her decision creates controversy among the booster parents, school coaches, family members, and team members themselves, Jules holds strong in her beliefs.

Which is good—because when parents hear that Jules plans to participate in overnight pre-season camp with a staff of male coaches and eighty high school boys, her tryout is threatened more than ever before. Yet, nobody can deny Jules' skills. As the youngest sister of three former high school quarterbacks, Jules knows the game. She knows what it takes to outsmart opponents, and she's not about to let anyone count her out for being a girl.

But as the competition intensifies, Jules must choose what she wants more—to embrace girl power and lead her team on the field, or be a girlfriend on the sidelines.

Gridiron Girl will inspire you to follow your vision, instead of those dictated by others. Perfect for fans of *Better than Perfect* by Simone Elkeles and *On the Fence* by Kasie West.

AVAILABLE NOW

ABOUT THE AUTHOR

Tamara Girardi writes books for children and teens. Her debut young adult novel, *Gridiron Girl*, tells the story of Julia Medina who quits the volleyball team to compete against her boyfriend for the starting quarterback position. Three additional sports novels in the Iron Valley Vikings series followed in 2022. *Above the Fold* is the first book in Tamara's second series, all about teens exploring their dreams and their true selves through exhibits at a popular, mardi-gras-esque hotspot called Carnivalesque. Also an academic, Tamara is a college English professor. She lives in a suburb of Pittsburgh, Pennsylvania with her husband and four adorably rambunctious children.